Warning: This book contains s adult language and may be considered offensive readers. This book is for sale to adults ONLY, as defined by the laws of the country in which you made your purchase. Please store your files wisely, where they cannot be accessed by under-aged readers.

Keep an eye on her website at http://www.jeannestjames.com/ or sign up for her newsletter to learn about her upcoming releases: http://www.jeannestjames.com/newslettersignup

This one is dedicated to Ann Gibbs who has been Ryder's super fan from the beginning. (I MAY forgive her being a Dallas fan). And I apologize to her patient husband for her obsession with another man, even if Ryder IS a book boyfriend...

A Special Thanks:

To Alexandra Swab for assisting me with Ryder's blurb when I was buried with writing, read-throughs, and edits of two books at the same time. Your help was invaluable!

Ryder's Playlist

SONGS MENTIONED IN THIS BOOK

Friends in Low Places – Garth Brooks
Sunrise - Rascal Flatts
Warrior – Demi Lovato
All of Me - John Legend
Huntin', Fishin' And Lovin' Every Day – Luke Bryan

Chapter One

OUT OF ALL THE places his ass could be, this county was not a place he wanted it to be. While he was sure some parts of West Virginia were just fucking lovely, this area was known for hillbillies, white supremacists and rednecks who thought bullets were more important than teeth.

If that wasn't bad enough, it was infested with members of the motherfucking outlaw MC, the Deadly Demons.

How he got pulled into this detail, he'll never know. No, fuck him, he knew. He drew the short straw this time. Just like he drew the short straw last time. And every other time when it came to this particular "job."

Ryder jerked the wheel of his '78 International Scout into a dark, rutted dirt driveway surrounded by high weeds. After a few seconds, his headlights bounced off an old farmhouse that was lit up from the inside.

At least the shit hole had electricity.

He pulled his Scout up to a line of Harleys parked across the uncut grass and sat staring at the run-down hovel for a few seconds as he braced himself for what was to come. Letting a searing curse rip, he shut off his beloved vehicle, yanked the keys from the ignition, and shoved open the driver's side door. After climbing his tense body out, he jammed his keys deep into his jeans' pocket, locked the door, and slammed it shut.

The weight of his Glock .45 in its holster hidden under his jacket, along with his tactical knife hanging on his hip, at least gave him a little reassurance since he was walking alone into this den of vipers. Worse, he wasn't even sneaking in, he was strolling right through the fucking front door.

He stalked to the rickety porch steps, then carefully picked his way up the rotting boards. Ignoring the handful of drunk Demons hanging out on the slanted front porch drinking beer and smoking dope, he pushed his way past them through the wide-open door of the house amid shouts of:

"Who the fuck are you?"

"Who's that motherfucker?"

"What the fuck?"

If he cared, he'd be asking them the same questions. But, yeah, he didn't give a fuck who those wasted, washed-out, beer-bellied bikers were.

Once he stepped inside, he paused to inventory his surroundings and get his bearings.

To say this house was bad was an understatement. It wasn't only a complete fucking shit hole, it smelled like one, too.

A tweaked-out, half-naked chick sat on the filthy floor of the hallway, the wall barely holding her ass upright. He nudged her with his boot to get her attention, since she was totally spaced. She might have been pretty once, but her bloodshot eyes, long stringy, unwashed hair and hollowed out cheekbones did nothing for her now.

"Lookin' for a woman," he grumbled.

She managed to straighten herself up some more, raking her glazed eyes down his body and running her fingers through her hair, as if that would improve the rat's nest on her head. "Found her."

Yeah, no. He'd prefer eternal celibacy than to stick his dick in anything like her. He lifted his hand to about mid-chest. "'Bout yay-high, long dark blonde hair, pretty blue eyes. Ain't all bones like you, though. Got some meat on her." Did she ever, the bitch had it all in the right places, too. "A bit of a stupid fuck." Because that was the goddamn truth.

She had been making way too many stupid decisions lately, and tonight was another one in a long list of them.

"Slash's slit?"

Slash.

His jaw got tight. That wasn't the first time he heard that name. But it was sure as shit going to be the last.

"Where's he at?"

She lifted a finger that had one spot of black nail polish left in the center—the rest looked like it had been picked or chewed off—and pointed to the ceiling. "Probably up in his room. Said I couldn't join 'em when they walked past."

Thank fuck for that.

Ryder lifted his chin in thanks and pushed past her, even though she reached out to grab his leg and gave a disappointed, "Hey, I could be your woman tonight."

"Next time," he threw over his shoulder, as his balls shriveled up into his body to hide.

At the end of the hall full of peeling wallpaper and water stains, he bounded up the stairs. Hitting the top landing, he tilted his head and listened carefully. It was difficult to hear shit, since what sounded like a stereo blasted somewhere outside, as well as another stereo blasted inside but with a different song. Even so, he held his breath, stilled every muscle, and listened anyway.

Above the din, a female giggle came from two doors

down. One that was closed with light spilling out from underneath it.

In a couple of long strides, he was in front of it. With a lift of his boot, he kicked the door with all the power he could muster, causing it to splinter and crash against the wall as it swung hard.

His eyes landed on the mattress that sat in the middle of the floor. Looked like Slash was a busy boy.

A naked man with shitty tattoos and long black hair sat up in surprise and the two women in bed with him didn't even notice the interruption.

No, they didn't. They were still going at it with each other, one on top of the other, kissing, fingering each other's pussies and pinching each other's nipples.

What. The. Fuck.

The one he was searching for was on the bottom, her normally pretty blue eyes closed, moans and groans coming from her as the fingers being plunged into her cunt sped up.

Jesus fuck. Normally, this shit would get him rock hard. Right now, he wanted to fucking puke.

"Who the fuck are you?"

"A figment of your imagination. Just pretend I'm not here." Taking two steps into the room, he wrapped his arm around the waist of the redhead, yanked her from the woman on the bottom, and tossed her onto Slash.

The biker grunted, and the redhead squealed as she landed on him.

Before the blonde-haired one could react, he had her up and thrown over his shoulder. He didn't give a shit if she was naked or not.

He didn't even care if she just got robbed of a fucking orgasm. She wasn't lying in that bed or staying in that house one more second.

"Hey!" came the very intoxicated, very loud complaint.

"Shut the fuck up," he growled. Making sure he had a

good grip on her, he turned on his heels and strode toward the door.

"Hey! Where... where... you takin' me?"

He tightened his jaw so he wouldn't snap the fuck out on her and headed down the dark hallway.

"My clothes!"

He didn't give a shit about her clothes. She should have thought about them before she took them off.

"Hey! Can't do this!"

The fuck he couldn't.

He was only following orders. He certainly wasn't there because he wanted to be.

Fuck no.

And this was the last fucking time he was doing one of these details for Diesel. The very last fucking time.

―――

As soon as he could find a safe place to pull over, he did so. He checked the rearview mirror one more time to make sure none of those Demons were following them. Though, that wasn't much of a worry, since apparently Kelsea was Slash's "slit" and no MC he knew of took care of their women like the Dirty Angels.

He was also sure the Deadly Demons wouldn't give their right nut for Kelsea.

Which was once again why he had a naked woman passed out in his passenger seat. He wanted to pull her out and take a fire hose to her to clean off all the filth from that house, Slash and whoever that other skank was who was fingering her and shoving a tongue down her throat. That shit had turned his stomach.

Not because he didn't like a little girl-on-girl action, what heterosexual man didn't? He just hadn't wanted to witness it with the pain-in-the-ass sitting next to him.

Princess Pain-in-the-Ass was currently pressed against the passenger side window, her long hair covering her face, and the only thing holding her upright was the seatbelt, which was cutting in between her naked tits. Luckily, he'd had the aftermarket three-point seatbelt installed when Jag Jamison restored his Scout, otherwise she'd be lying in a pile on the floorboard.

His nostrils flared with annoyance. "You awake?"

He didn't miss the slight movement. She was fucking awake.

"No," came the slurred answer.

A muscle popped in his jaw as he shoved his shifter into neutral and set the e-brake. They were on a quiet, dark back road somewhere between West Virginia and Kentucky. Since they had about a four-hour drive to their destination, her remaining naked the whole way just wasn't going to work for him.

So, he needed to do something about that little problem. Plus, he wasn't sure if Slash's DNA was leaking all over his seat.

If so, that shit would put him over the edge.

While his boss sent him to "save" his cousin, if she was taking Slash's dick without a condom, Diesel might have to save Kelsea from Ryder. And worse, he'd have to burn his passenger seat, which would be a sin since he'd paid a pretty penny to have it reupholstered.

With a curse, he pulled the keys from the ignition. Shame he didn't trust her not to take off with his vehicle and leave him stranded on the side of the road by a lonely stretch of woods. He shoved open his door and slammed it shut once more after unfolding his ass from his Scout.

He hated taking his anger out on his baby, but he either did that or on the woman he wanted to strangle. Though calling Kelsea a "woman" was a stretch, since she'd been acting like a petulant child for the past year or so.

He knew why, but right now he didn't give a shit. It was getting old and she was pushing away the people who loved her.

He dug around in the back of his truck until he found his survival kit and located aspirin and a silver emergency blanket. He also grabbed a large bottle of water from the supply he kept in the back.

Once he had everything he needed, he went around to the passenger side door, yanked it open and unhooked her seatbelt, letting her tumble out of the truck onto the grass of the pull-off.

"Hey!" she yelped as she landed in a naked heap.

He tossed the blanket at her. "Wrap this around you and make sure you keep it so your cunt isn't in direct contact with my seat."

She slowly rolled herself over and *sort of* sat up. "Why you worried about that old thing?"

That old thing?

"That old thing is worth a lot more than you right now, darlin'. No fuckin' joke. Wrap that blanket around you before a tick bites your snatch and get your ass back in my truck. Or I'll leave you here for a coyote's breakfast."

He wasn't sure if it was the threat of a tick or a coyote that got her moving, but she finally did.

When she struggled to get the thin mylar blanket around her, he lost his patience and helped her, doing his best not to touch her. He was done touching her. It was bad enough when he had to carry her naked ass out of that hell hole and toss her into his truck.

Until she showered in Lysol or bleach, he wasn't taking any further risks. He wasn't getting hazard pay for this job.

In fact, his ass might get fired with what he had planned. Once they got to the cabin, he'd call Diesel and tell him the details. Until then, he was putting a few hundred miles between him and D's massive fists.

"Get in the truck," he muttered once she got to her feet.

Watching her wobble back and forth a couple of times made him realize she wouldn't be able to get her ass in his truck under her own power.

Fuck.

Holding his breath so he didn't have to inhale her stink, he bent at the knees and picked her up before planting her now covered ass back in the passenger seat. He latched the seatbelt back around her, then tossed the bottle of water in her lap and held out his hand with three aspirins.

"Take these, drink that and shut the fuck up for the next few hours."

Before she could respond, he slammed the door shut and jogged around the front of his Scout and climbed back in.

He waited until she downed the aspirins and chugged a good amount of water before turning the key and coaxing his baby into first gear.

Within five minutes, her head was back resting against the passenger side window and she was asleep.

With a sigh, he found a country station and turned that shit up until he could no longer hear her godawful snoring. He might as well be in an underground den with a hibernating Grizzly as loud as she was.

For fuck's sake, he wished he was back dodging IEDs and taking out suicide bombers in Afghanistan instead of dealing with Kelsea Dougherty.

Fuck my life.

Chapter Two

Kelsea winced and gasped as the corner of her forehead bounced off something hard once again.

Damn, that was going to leave a mark.

Forcing her eyes open, she winced again when the light hit them. She realized she was leaning against a window and it had to be in a car since she could see pavement flying by.

She lifted a hand to the back of her stiff neck, and she was having a hard time lifting her head. She must have been in this position for a long time.

She tipped her eyes down to assess her person. Why was she wearing a silver tarp-like thingy? And naked underneath that?

And in a vehicle?

And, more importantly, who the hell was singing Garth Brooks? She hated country music.

Whoever it was, was making her head throb even harder. *Friends in Low Places* was blaring out of the vehicle's speakers and the deep voice singing along was...

Honestly, not bad. For an amateur.

If you liked country.

Which she didn't.

She pushed through the pain and forced herself to sit upright, biting back a groan when she twisted to see who the singer was.

When she did, the groan slipped out of her anyway.

Fuck!

Fuck! Fuck! Fuck!

She turned down the radio volume until all she could hear was Ryder's deep voice filling the interior of the Scout. He ignored her and kept singing.

"Again?" she asked. She should be embarrassed for being in this situation again, but she wasn't.

Her question stopped his crooning. His chest lifted as he took a deep inhale and without looking at her, said, "Shouldn't I be the one askin' that?"

She steeled herself against the warmth that rushed through her every time she heard his slight southern accent.

She pulled the edges of the silver space blanket, or whatever it was, tighter around her. "Where are my clothes? Why didn't you grab them?"

"You care about your missin' clothes? For fuck's sake, how about your dignity? That's missin', too. You should be more worried about that."

Once again, she did something stupid, forcing her cousin to send one of his crew out to find her.

She'd been on a roll lately. But no matter how many times Ryder had dragged her out of a mess, she just kept stepping right back into the next one.

She closed her eyes, willing the thumping of her brain to stop, but when he hit a pothole and cursed, she opened them.

She swore it was the middle of the night the last time she was conscious. Now it wasn't. The early morning sun made her squint as she paid attention to the passing landscape.

"Where are we? This doesn't look like Pennsylvania."

"How the fuck would you know the difference between PA and any other fuckin' state? Trees and mountains are everywhere."

"I'd know."

Did he just snort?

Whatever.

"How soon 'til we get home?"

When he didn't answer, she turned to study his profile. His jaw was tight, and his fingers had a death grip on the steering wheel.

"It only takes about an hour for us to get from the Demons' church to Shadow Valley. We've been in the car for more than an hour and this isn't Shadow Valley."

He kept his eye on the road and ignored her.

"Ryder. Where are we? Where are you taking me?" She was trying not to panic and tried to keep it out of her voice, but she wasn't being successful. "You better not be taking me anywhere I don't want to go."

"Like where? Work? Home to your family? Back to your mother's? Where don't you wanna go?"

"Rehab."

His head jerked, but he still didn't look at her.

"Please don't take me to rehab," she whispered, gripping the edges of the blanket tighter.

"You don't need rehab. You need fuckin' common sense. The little you had is now non-existent. It's a damn shame, darlin', you're destroyin' your life. And it was a good one."

It was a good one.

That was debatable.

For some, growing up in a motorcycle club was a good life. For others, like her, not so much.

Especially when her mother lied to her her whole life. And it wasn't a little lie, it was a big one. One she still wished she didn't know about. She wished she could go back and unlearn the truth.

When she opened her mouth, he lifted a hand to stop her. "Not now. We're not talkin' about this shit now. Not when I'm drivin'. 'Cause this shit just pisses me off and I'm tryin' to get us there in one piece."

"There where?" A sign caught her eye as he sped by it. "Did that say Kentucky?" She glanced around the vehicle, searching the floor, the seat, the dashboard, the backseat, the center console. "Where's my phone?"

"Probably with your clothes."

"I need my phone. I need to talk to Diesel."

"That's not happenin' any time soon."

Her jaw dropped. "You can't keep me from him. He's your boss."

"And he's your cousin who's really pissed off right now. Not smart to call him, Kelsea."

"I don't care. I'm not going to Kentucky."

"Too late."

"Ryder," she shouted, but winced when her headache intensified. "What's in Kentucky? Why are we in Kentucky?"

"We're here to do a little searchin'."

"Searching for what?"

"Your soul. Your dignity. Your common sense. Pick one. That shit I saw back there in that room, in that bed... Me havin' to come find your ass *again* to get you out of a jam..." He finally turned his head to look at her.

And suddenly she wished he hadn't.

His green eyes bore into her, maybe searching for her soul that he claimed was missing. "All that shit is over, darlin'. It ends now."

KELSEA STARED at the structure Ryder pulled up to. He put

his Scout in first gear, set the emergency brake and shut off the truck.

"What is this place?" she whispered.

"This is your second chance, darlin'. 'Cause if this doesn't work, then I'm throwin' my hands up and I'll make sure D does, too. He's as pissed off as I am. No, more so. Everyone told him that you needed to bottom the fuck out. And what I saw? That was rock bottom. I have no idea what drugs you did or how much booze you drank, but that's no excuse for bein' a slutty skank."

Kelsea cringed at his words.

"I'd fuck Tequila before I'd fuck you."

Damn. He hit her with a one-two punch. Tequila was the sluttiest of the sweet butts that hung around the Dirty Angels' clubhouse. That club whore would put out to any of the brothers with just a crook of a finger.

Well, fuck him and his perfect ass. Like he'd always been a saint. Right. Diesel's Shadows were all former special forces military men who'd done things that were probably not legal. Not only during their years of service, but also while working for In the Shadows Security.

She shook off the sting of his words and turned to face him. "What is this place?"

He faced her. "What does it look like?"

She glanced out of the windshield again. It was a cabin in the woods on a mountain. Not just any cabin. A nice one that appeared rustic but probably had all the modern conveniences of home. Or at least she hoped so.

Because she had a feeling this was their final destination.

"Is this yours?"

He pushed open the door and got out, answering, "Yup," before slamming the driver's door shut.

She blinked and let what was happening sink in. And once it hit the pit of her gut, it all exploded back up like a geyser.

"Fuck!" she screamed into the empty interior of the Scout. "Fuck you, Ryder! Fuck you! Fuck my cousin, too! Fuck all of you! My mother. My goddamn father. Everyone! Fuck you all!"

The passenger door flew open and he stood there, hands on his hips. "Think I couldn't hear that?"

"I don't care."

"You might."

"Doubt it."

"Get the fuck out of the truck."

"You can't hold me captive here. D will kill you."

"I was told to handle it. He's got too much shit on his plate right now with his baby girls and everything else, so I'm handlin' it. And, darlin', I'm tellin' you now, this is the last fuckin' time I'm handlin' it. I'm gonna make sure of that."

"Don't call me *darlin'*."

"Okay, darlin'." And then the fucker winked at her. He stepped back from the Scout. "Get out of the truck."

"If I don't?"

He shrugged and slammed the door shut again. She watched in surprise as he turned on his heels, went to the back of his Scout, snagged a large duffel bag, slammed *that* door and headed up the steps to the front deck of the cabin. He dug keys out of his pocket, unlocked the cabin's front door, threw his duffel inside, followed it, and slammed that door shut, too.

Kelsea finally took a breath. She let it out slowly.

She had no phone.

She had no clothes.

She had no idea where the hell she was besides at a cabin on the side of a mountain in Bumfuck, Kentucky.

She doubted there were neighbors.

She glanced around. All she could see were trees and

another building behind the cabin. A large structure with double doors like were found on a barn.

That was it.

She dropped her head back and screamed "Fuck!" once more.

Ryder glanced at his watch as he heard the front door open slowly.

For two whole motherfucking hours she sat out in his Scout. Naked, wrapped in a mylar blanket and stubborn as fuck.

He shook his head.

He wasn't looking forward to this. But he also was serious when he said this was the last time he was getting her ass out of a jam.

Last night was also the last time he was retrieving her like a lost fucking puppy.

And that was the first and last time he was going to see her naked on some stained mattress on a floor in some shit hole with another bitch's fingers shoved up her snatch and tongue down her throat.

He ground his teeth. It would be a long time before that vision was wiped from his memory.

At least he hadn't walked in while Slash's unwrapped dick was in her. Then there might have been bloodshed.

He took a couple deep breaths to lower his blood pressure but as the door closed quietly behind him, he gave up on that.

He might regret this idea. He might regret every fucking minute being alone in this cabin with her. However, he'd set his plan in motion and he wasn't a quitter. He was sticking to it, even if it killed him.

By stroke. Heart attack. Or she slit his throat with his own tactical knife in his sleep.

This might be his last job as a Shadow. But, damn it, he was going to give it his all.

The rustle of the emergency blanket had him glancing over his shoulder where she still stood by the front door. Hell, the only door in the cabin.

The place wasn't anything fancy and had an open floor plan with the kitchen leading into the living area and a bed tucked into one of the far corners. He'd built a tiny addition on the back years ago, so he'd have an indoor bathroom instead of an outhouse, and for some much-needed storage. But other than that, the cabin was basic.

A wood stove and a propane tank provided heat in the winter. There wasn't A/C for hot summer days, though being tucked in the shade of the surrounding trees helped keep the cabin cool. And as long as the wind wasn't blowing too hard, it had electricity.

He stopped stirring the chili on the stove when he saw her red, puffy eyes. They weren't like that earlier, so he knew it wasn't from her drug and alcohol-induced hangover.

"You been cryin'?"

"No."

He shook his head and turned down the gas burner so the chili he threw together could simmer.

Now all he needed was some really good cornbread to go along with their dinner later. He might have a boxed mix in one of the cabinets. He'd have to look, but right now he had something more pressing to deal with.

He turned to face her, letting his gaze rake down her dirty, tear-stained face, over her matted hair, and her attempt to cover up her nakedness with the blanket. Even covered in something so shapeless, she couldn't hide her curves.

He sucked at his teeth. "Think I'm stupid?"

Her pretty blue eyes, now red-rimmed, lifted and met his. "No."

"Then why the fuck would you lie when I asked you a question?"

"If it's so fucking obvious, then why would you ask it?"

He struggled to keep himself where he was, to keep himself from taking long strides over to her and shaking the shit out of her.

Someone needed to knock the common sense back into her head. Since no one else had been successful, it was now on his shoulders.

Her sister, Brooke, had tried. Brooke's ol' man, Dex, had tried. Hell, even Diesel had had one too many conversations with the woman who stood before him currently looking defeated.

"Every time you lie to me, there will be consequences."

Her chin lifted and her stubbornness returned. "I'm not a child."

"Then stop actin' like one. When you act like an adult, I'll treat you like one. Deal?"

She glared at him. *Jesus*, he wanted to drag her over his lap and spank her until she found a new attitude. But right now, he still didn't want to touch her.

He pointed toward the back of the cabin. "Go shower. Once you wash that stank and skank off you, come back out here with a better attitude. Make sure that shitty one goes down the drain. Make sure you scrub that motherfucker Slash off you, too. Hope you always used a wrap with him, darlin'."

"That's none of your fucking—"

"Right," he cut her off. "Don't need the details. Go shower."

"I have nothing to wear."

"I'll find somethin' you can wear for now."

She continued to stand there, staring at him. *What the fuck.*

"Shower. Now. Before I drag you into the bathroom by your hair. There's a bar of pumice soap by the sink. Use that to scrub yourself inside and out."

"That's not even funny."

"You hear me laughin'?"

"Whatever," she grumbled.

He had to set his jaw and take a step back so he wouldn't reach out to set her straight.

He watched her shuffle toward the bathroom with the emergency blanket dragging on the floor behind her since it was too big.

When the bathroom door finally slammed shut, he stepped up to the kitchen sink, planted his hands on the edge and stared out of the window that overlooked the dirt lane cutting through the woods.

He needed to go check the outbuilding to make sure there wasn't any damage since he hadn't been here in months. He also needed to check the propane tank level to make sure they had enough to last them, since it was used for not only hot water but the stove.

By the time he got done doing that, she should be out of the shower and he'd be ready to tell her what her life would be like for the next week or so. Or however long it took for her to pull her head out of her ass.

She wouldn't like it. She may even have a tantrum. But he didn't give a fuck.

He hated pulling her ass out of questionable situations time after time.

He. Was. Done.

He tilted his head and listened to make sure the shower was running before pushing away from the sink and heading out the front door.

When he came back fifteen minutes later, he expected to

see her moping around the cabin in one of his T-shirts or something.

She wasn't.

In fact, the bathroom door was still closed and the shower still running.

Jesus fuckin' Christ. He should've given her a damn time limit on the shower. This wasn't a spa. He had a small well and limited propane, for fuck's sake.

He rushed over to the door and knocked on it.

After a second without an answer, he pressed his ear to the door and knocked again.

No answer. *Son of a bitch.*

"Kelsea, only got so much hot water and you're gonna empty my propane tank." *And I'd like to shower at some point myself.* "If you don't shut that shower off, I'm comin' in and shuttin' it down whether you're done or not. This ain't some lady spa."

He gave her until he finished counting to ten in his head, then turned the knob. He knew it wouldn't be locked because he never installed one on the door. It was never needed.

He flung open the door and saw the shower curtain was wide open, the water running and no Kelsea.

At least not in the shower.

No, she had wedged herself into the tight spot between the toilet and sink. Her head was down, and she was curled into herself.

Had she fallen asleep?

What the fuck!

He rushed over, shut the water off and turned to look at her.

She was naked, and still dirty. Now that the shower was quiet, he could hear it. She was softly crying with her arms wrapped around her knees, her face hidden in her arms and covered by her long dark blonde hair.

If that didn't break his fucking heart, nothing would.

He squatted down and scrubbed a hand down his face before reaching out and pulling back some of her hair. She had her face buried against her knees so he couldn't see it.

"Kelsea," he said softly. "You need to get in the shower. You'll feel better afterward."

"I'm tired," came out on a muffled sob.

"Yeah, darlin', I know you are."

"I'm really fucking tired."

"I get it. I've been there." He'd been there. Too many times he'd wanted to curl up in a ball in a corner and forget all the ugly shit that was going on in the world. But, even so, he had to pick himself back up, dust his ass off and face whatever it was head-on. He couldn't hide because that shit was never going anywhere. It would wait until he was ready to deal with it. Like it or not.

He dropped his ass to the floor, unlaced his boots, jerked them and his socks off, before standing again to peel off his T-shirt, jeans and boxers.

Once he was as naked as she was, he leaned into the shower, turned the water back on, tested the temp and while it was only lukewarm, he was thankful it wasn't ice cold. He'd bathed too many times in his life with freezing cold water, be it from a faucet or a natural source. It sucked.

He turned back to her, wondering how he was going to haul her ass out of that tight spot she was in.

"Darlin', can you stand?" He held out his hand to her, even though her head was still buried.

When she didn't respond, he leaned down, hooked her under the arms and dragged her up. She was dead weight, almost as if she lost the will to live, or even to function.

Yep, he'd been there, too.

He had no idea what was going on in her fucked-up mind right now, but he could understand how some issues could be bad enough to cripple somebody.

He'd seen it frequently.

He'd heard about fellow veterans eating their own guns because they couldn't take whatever was fucking with their head.

Something besides simply wanting to be brat was fucking with this woman's head.

Pulling her against his front, he shuffled her forward and into the shower stall and tensed when the spray hit them. While it was somewhat warm, it wasn't that fucking warm.

Water ran in rivulets over their heads, and down their bodies. He waited until they were both wet before grabbing the small bottle of generic shampoo he kept in the shower and, with one arm hooked around her to hold her up, attempted to not only open the bottle but squeeze some out.

"A little help would be nice, darlin'."

She didn't respond, all her weight rested against him like she was a rag doll.

Somehow, he did it. He washed her hair and his, used the bar of soap to clean every spot he could reach, including areas he'd never washed on a woman before and got them both rinsed off quickly. He shut the water down as soon as he could, then shuffled her back out, snagged the nearest towel and wrapped her up in it after drying her off as best as he could. He didn't even bother to try to dry himself, he just picked her up in his arms and carried her out of the bathroom, across the cabin and tucked her under the sheets in his bed.

When he moved her damp hair out of her face, her eyes were half open, staring sightlessly at the wall.

"Sleep, darlin'. When you wake up, I'll get you fed and then we need to set some rules."

He perched on the edge of the mattress for a few moments, taking in the dark circles under her eyes, and the way she curled up in a ball after he pulled the covers over her.

"Fuck," he whispered. This wasn't what he expected at all.

He had no fucking clue how to deal with her at this point.

But no matter what, he had a call to make.

And he could already hear Diesel bellowing from four hundred plus miles away.

Chapter Three

His back was fucking killing him. Last night after eating two bowls of chili by himself, he had grabbed a sleeping bag and slept on the couch. Problem was, he might have been better off sleeping on the floor than on that old piece of shit.

Kelsea had slept all night and he figured it best not to wake her. She was exhausted. Mentally. Physically. He wasn't sure if the shower and sleep would help, but he sure as hell hoped so.

And when she finally woke up, he hoped it would be with a better outlook. But he wasn't putting money on that one.

Leaning back against the counter, he was enjoying his second cup of coffee when he heard the bathroom door close and a minute or two later, the toilet flush and the water running in the sink.

He must have been too tied up in his own thoughts to have noticed her slipping out of bed and into the bathroom.

He was lifting his steaming mug to his lips when the bathroom door opened and...

Jesus fuck.

Every muscle in his body went tight as she strolled toward him like she was taking a relaxing walk in the woods. Only, she was completely naked.

He kept his expression blank as she came closer and closer, a gleam in her eyes. She was definitely feeling better since she seemed to be up to her old tricks of being a brat.

His breath caught as she brushed against him since his ass was planted next to the coffeemaker. Grabbing the empty mug he'd set out for her, she filled it and, ignoring him, took her first sip and wrinkled her nose.

She probably didn't drink it black normally, but if she wanted sugar and creamer, too fucking bad. It wasn't like he'd had a spare moment for a grocery run. Bottom line, if she wanted to drink his coffee, she'd have to drink it the way the good Lord intended. Black. Which was the direction his mood was headed, especially when she asked, "What's for breakfast?" like she wasn't standing buck fucking naked in his kitchen.

"Not havin' breakfast until you put on some clothes."

She pursed her lips, turned and leaned her naked ass against the counter right beside him. The fuck if she didn't. "Why? Does me being comfortable in my own skin bother you?"

The last thing she was, was comfortable in her own skin. Last night proved it. Once again, she was lying to him. He'd already warned her once that lying had consequences.

"No, if that was true. But pubes in my breakfast do."

She ran a hand down her stomach until she cupped her bare mound. "If you haven't noticed, there are no worries about that."

Unfortunately, he did notice, not only last night when he scrubbed her there, but he couldn't ignore it now that her fingers were caressing it, drawing his attention. Last night when he was taking care of her, he'd shut down all thoughts of her being a living, breathing woman. To him, she'd been someone he had to deal with like any other mission. Do what you had to do and get it over with.

This morning, he was having a difficult time forgetting that she was a woman in her late twenties, with curves and an attitude that wouldn't quit.

"Darlin', you know who doesn't have pubes? Little girls. You know who wanders into a room totally fuckin' naked because she's being a smart ass and also because she's not gettin' what she wants? A little girl."

"In case you've forgotten, I don't have any clothes."

"Hard to forget when you're standin' there buck naked, sippin' on my coffee. But I got a drawer full of T-shirts and I'm sure that ass of yours will fit in a pair of my boxers. Go put them on." That ass would definitely fill his boxers, there was nothing small about it.

He finally took a sip of his coffee.

It wasn't strong enough.

Not nearly strong enough.

If he still drank whiskey, a half bottle in his coffee might be strong enough for him to deal with her. But even then, he wondered.

He inhaled deeply, shook his head, and took another sip of his coffee. As soon as she moved away from him, he turned around, put his mug on the counter and adjusted himself since his "job" wasn't the only thing awake.

Fuck.

He turned his head to watch her stroll back over to the corner of the cabin that held his bed and his dressers. His gaze fell on the sway of her hips and that sweet, plump ass of hers.

The one Slash had tapped. Who knew how many times.

He ground his teeth.

They needed groceries.

She needed clothes.

He needed to go to town before he did something stupid.

———

K‍ELSEA SAT ON HIS BED, bored to tears. He'd gone to "town." Wherever the hell that was.

But if there was a town close by, and if she could find her way to it, that meant she could call someone to come rescue her from the boonies. Because all of this just wasn't going to work out for her.

No. Not after hearing his so-called "rules" this morning.

She answered to no one. Not her mother, not her half-sister, not even her cousin, Diesel.

Especially not Ryder.

She'd be interested in hearing what Diesel had to say about Ryder bringing her here. Knowing her hot-tempered cousin, he wouldn't be thrilled with one of his men kidnapping her and bringing her to Kentucky, of all places.

This morning, as they sat at the small wood table which was situated between what would be the kitchen and living room, eating cornbread with no butter and leftover chili—who the hell ate chili for breakfast? Rednecks, that was who—and sucking down black coffee, he told her his "rules."

One... Life as she knew it was over. That's exactly what he said. Word for word.

Two... Things were going to change. And they weren't leaving that cabin until they did.

Right. That's what he said. That's what she heard.

And three... "No drinking. No smoking. No drugs while in my cabin."

Why was she so misunderstood? "I'm not an alcoholic or an addict, Ryder."

"Know it. But you're headed down that path. And anyway... My place. My rules."

"I didn't agree to any of this," she said, yesterday's panic starting to bubble up again. How can someone just get away with kidnapping another person against their will? It was illegal and he could go to jail. She just needed a phone to dial 911. Or Diesel.

Though, knowing Diesel, he might just grunt and hang up on her.

Ryder continued to shovel spoonfuls of chili into his rule-making mouth. Her attention became caught on his lips as they opened and closed. Full spoon going in, empty spoon coming out. When he'd take a bite of his cornbread, he'd smile as he chewed it. Like the cornbread was as good as sex.

It wasn't. To be honest, she thought it was a bit dry without butter. And to wash it down, she had to use that bitter, black coffee. Who didn't like a bit of cream and sugar in their coffee? Savages, that was who.

But the savage who had sat across from her had mesmerizing lips. And it didn't help that he hadn't shaved this morning, so light brown scruff covered his cheeks and chin. He was also wearing a baseball cap low enough so she couldn't see his eyes clearly.

She already knew they were green. Which were usually narrowed with annoyance on her, since he was right... He'd "rescued" her out of situations too many times before. Even when she hadn't wanted to be rescued. Like the other night. She'd been having a perfectly good time when...

Shit.

A flash of Ryder pulling another female off her while they were...

Shit.

Shit.

Motherfucking shit.

Had she been so fucked up that Slash had convinced her to have sex with another woman?

She shoved her still-full bowl away. She'd never been a big fan of chili or having sex with other women and that shard of memory just destroyed any appetite she'd had.

She stared at the man across from her, just casually eating chili for breakfast like he did that on a daily basis. The man had seen her in the middle of a threesome with another woman.

Would a normal woman be embarrassed about being caught in that kind of situation? Well, she never said she was normal.

Ryder would probably agree.

"How long are you keeping me hostage?"

"As long as it takes for you to be clean."

"Of what?"

"Booze. Drugs. Strange dick."

"Did I not just tell you I'm not an addict?" she yelled, stopping herself before she slammed her hand on the table. "There's nothing wrong with having a little fun. You should try it. And the dick isn't considered 'strange' if you know his name."

He lifted his head and she could finally see his eyes. Oh, yes. That's how she was used to seeing them when he looked at her. Narrowed and full of annoyance. Though, they were shadowed from the bill of his baseball cap. "Keep your voice down. If you're gonna take attitude with me, you're gonna get it back. Promisin' you that, darlin'. And I keep my promises. Unlike you."

"You don't know shit about me," she grumbled.

"I know more than you realize."

What did that mean? She knew Diesel's crew had access to information on people. Stuff not even cops could get. Had he done some sort of background search on her?

What did he think he knew?

He continued, "You're drinkin' to dull the pain. Know

it, since I did it myself. But there's no reason for your self-destructive behavior. None."

"You don't think I have a good reason?"

"No, darlin', you don't. What you're doin' isn't makin' you feel better. It's makin' it worse. You've got people who love and care about you. You've got family. The DAMC sisterhood. You're not your father. You didn't even know Pierce was your fuckin' father for most of your life. Yeah, he was a dick and did fucked-up shit. But none of that affected you directly, so stop playin' the victim in all of this. What he did to Zak, to Diamond, to Brooke, was so much more fucked up. And you don't see them spreadin' their legs for anyone while high and drunk."

When she found out the truth—that Pierce, the former president of the Dirty Angels MC, was her father—her life had taken an even uglier turn.

Pierce had been a monster. A cancer that rotted the DAMC from the inside out. A traitor. A child molester. A rapist. And he tried to have his own daughter raped and murdered. A woman herself born out of rape. Kelsea's half-sister, Brooke.

She had no idea Pierce was her father for her first twenty-seven plus years. All she knew was he'd been the leader of their "family." But it turned out the only reason he'd become the club president was because he set Zak up to go to prison for ten years, so he could nab the top spot instead.

Ten whole fucking years.

That asshole's blood was running through her veins. And her mother *knew*. She knew all that time she was Pierce's daughter and told *no one*. Not even Pierce. She had locked down that secret and let it fester for decades.

"Know you're fucked in the head with all the truth that came out about Pierce. I got it, darlin', I do. But there's no reason to destroy yourself because your DNA donor was a piece of fuckin' shit. And that's all he was, a sperm donor. He was never a father to you. But even so, you worry about his tainted blood runnin' through your veins? You forget your granddaddy's sittin' in SCI Greene for fuckin' *murder*. And for not just a single count, either. So, you're worryin' for nothin'."

Yep, her biological father had been a scourge on the earth, and her grandfather on her mother's side was doing life in prison for murdering a few rival MC members. She was doomed with that family tree.

He thought she was worrying for nothing. She didn't agree.

She also hadn't agreed to staying in the cabin under duress with this man. "I want to go home."

"Which home? That shit hole apartment you share with two other skanky bitches who have all kinds of strange dick coming in and out at all hours? Or back to your mother's?"

"How do you know about my roommates?"

Ryder snorted. "Is that what you call them?"

"How do you know?"

"Because you're my fuckin' job, Kelsea. You. I'm the sucker who's forced to watch your ass. Me. And do you know how much that fuckin' sucks? I told D to go fuck himself a thousand times, but I stayed. Don't know why, but I did. I'd rather be back in Kabul than be here with you."

"You'd rather be back in the Middle East than keep an eye on me? Is it that bad?"

"Fuck yeah, it is. Watchin' you be stupid is insultin' to not only my intelligence, but my skills. D's given me a bump in pay four times. But your shit's not worth it. So like I told you before, this is the last time, woman. The last. I'm done. If your ass doesn't straighten up and fly right after this, my ass is gone. And then you can face your pissed-off bull of a cousin to explain why he lost one of his men."

If she was the cause of Diesel losing one of his highly skilled men? "He'll kill me."

"That's my guess."

It wasn't long after that discussion, he had cleaned up breakfast and she watched him move around the cabin.

Most of the times Ryder was sent to drag her back to Shadow Valley, he'd simply deliver her to Diesel. D would give her hell, she'd go back to her apartment and a few weeks later, she'd find herself being dragged out of a party, another MC's clubhouse, or a bar by Ryder once again.

This time he'd done the unthinkable. Dragged her ass hundreds of miles from home and took her somewhere she couldn't leave. Unless she hiked out. And she'd never hiked in her life. Plus, she had no shoes.

Until she had clothes, shoes and a sense of direction, she needed to stay put. But that didn't mean she couldn't plan.

Now she sat on his bed in one of his T-shirts and boxer shorts, which actually fit better than expected. Probably because his hips were slim and hers weren't.

She lifted his shirt up and pressed her nose into the cotton. He had no washer and dryer here, so she wondered if he had to head into this "town" to do laundry. Even so, his tee smelled like him, which made her traitorous nipples pebble.

She recalled bits and pieces from yesterday. She remembered her exhaustion becoming overwhelming to the point of crippling her when she went to take a shower.

It had been one thing she agreed with. She had stunk. But as she stood staring at the water falling from the shower head, her body had become lead. Heavy. And the darkness began to drown her.

She tried to escape it, crawl away from it, but she couldn't. This was why she drank and partied. This was why she didn't care what happened to her or what people thought of her.

She couldn't pull free from the garbage that rotted her bones and she could no longer try.

She just didn't give a fuck anymore.

As she sat across the table from him this morning, she had studied his hands. Those hands had touched her everywhere, including intimate spots as he helped her shower. He touched places he would've only touched a lover, but it wasn't like that. It was methodical. He had a job and he did it.

Unfortunately, she could do nothing to help him, even though she didn't want him washing her hair or soaping her up. Or rinsing her off.

And this morning, after he left for town, she'd climbed back into the shower under her own power and made sure he hadn't missed any important places. She washed away the tattered memories of being in that house, on that mattress, with Slash and the woman, a sweet butt she thought was named Shelly. Being a sweet butt meant Shelly got around and was used by any of the Demons who wanted her. She was there to service them, to do whatever they asked. Almost like a slave.

That meant by being with Shelly, Kelsea had potentially been with every Demon Shelly had ever fucked around with.

She shuddered. Then she wondered how many other club sweet butts Slash had been with.

Funny. Now that she was clear-minded, she really didn't care. Slash was nothing but a distraction for her. Nothing serious. A biker who she partied with and had sex with whenever she was in the mood.

She wasn't loyal to him. Nor he to her.

After Ryder busted in on them, she doubted Slash would be open to her coming back down into Demon territory, anyway.

No loss. Though the man had an awesome cock, his technique was awful. And he was a selfish lover, more worried about getting himself off than helping Kelsea achieve that goal.

She knew Ryder had to be naked when he'd forced her into the shower last night, but she didn't remember anything about him. And now she regretted that. She wished she'd seen him naked at least once. If he was half as amazing naked as he was clothed, then... *phew*.

But, regretfully, she'd never see him naked. She was getting the hell out of Dodge as soon as she could.

When she asked him this morning how he'd located her, he hadn't answered. She'd guessed after a few minutes. The same way he'd found her every other time.

A tracking device. Somehow, someway, her cousin had been able to track her cell phone. So maybe she was glad it was gone. That meant when she escaped this cabin, no one would be able to find her.

She'd have no money, no phone, but she was resilient. She'd find a way, either back to Shadow Valley or somewhere else.

Maybe she needed a fresh start.

And not one determined by the man who owned this cabin and whose rules she was supposed to follow.

No. It was her life. Her rules.

He could go fuck himself.

Chapter Four

Kelsea paced the cabin, wringing her hands and gnawing on her bottom lip as she heard his Scout slowly coming up the dirt lane.

He'd been gone for hours. *Hours*.

She was no longer bored, but instead, climbing the walls. She needed to get out of this prison of his. She needed to get back home... Or wherever. Somewhere, *anywhere*, other than here.

There was no TV, no Wi-Fi, no phone. No connection to the outside world. She'd come across a battery-operated radio and the few stations it picked up were mostly country.

Argh! She pulled at her hair, her skin felt as if tiny bugs were crawling all over it, her heart raced, while her pulse attempted to escape her throat.

She had searched the cabin for alcohol and came up empty. Not one fucking drop. What man didn't keep at least whiskey tucked somewhere in a cabinet?

She'd only found cold coffee, a few bottles of water, along with a half-kicked bottle of pop that went flat a long time ago.

She needed a fucking drink. She needed to beat back the garbage trying to bubble to the surface.

She wasn't an addict, she wasn't, but she needed to bury those thoughts, those memories somehow.

Ryder had been right. He had said out loud what she knew all along. She was using alcohol and drugs to self-medicate herself, to keep things buried so they wouldn't hurt. She just hadn't wanted to admit it to herself.

None of the drugs she'd used in the past were what she considered hardcore. Pot mostly. X, whenever it was offered. Sometimes a little blow when Slash had it. Once, and only once, Special K.

But right now, she was ready to crawl out of her own skin. Things she wanted to keep buried were fighting to the surface. With that, a sharp edge of panic sliced through her. And a whole lot of annoyance was directed at the motherfucker who brought her here.

She spun on him as he opened the front door, carrying a few plastic bags of what looked like groceries.

Maybe the grocery bags had a name and address on them.

Fuck. That wouldn't do her a bit of good since she didn't have access to a GPS.

He was humming some crappy country song under his breath as he dumped the bags on the counter.

Within a few steps she was standing directly behind him, her hands planted on her hips. "I need a drink. Did you bring anything back with you?"

His humming stopped and a muscle in his jaw worked as he glanced over his shoulder at her. "No."

"No booze at all?"

He cocked a brow at her, which made her grind her teeth. "Told you that your life was no longer your own and things were gonna change. Your stubborn brain must've missed that part."

No, she'd heard it. She just didn't want to believe it.

She blew out a breath. She needed something. *Something...* "How about a blunt, then?"

"A what?"

"A blunt! A joint! Pot. Weed. *Fuck*! You're a fucking veteran. Don't you all smoke pot to deal with your PTSD?"

He spun on her and she stepped back in surprise and with a little worry at the expression on his face. She couldn't miss his body become as tight as a stretched wire, his hands clenched into fists at his side.

"Jesus fuckin' Christ. I don't have any goddamn pot. You're here to straighten your ass out, not fuckin' get stoned or smashed."

She pressed her fingers against her throbbing temples. "Then I need aspirin. Something." She winced as she heard herself. The whine. The helplessness.

When had she become that person? When had she spiraled to the point that she became someone she, herself, didn't even want to be around?

With a sigh and a shake of his head, his long legs ate up the space between her and the bathroom, and he returned a few seconds later with a bottle of generic aspirin.

She held out her hand. But instead of handing her the bottle, he popped open the child-proof lid and shook out only two pills, holding them out to her.

Two. *Fuck.* She wanted to take the whole damn bottle. Then chase it with a fifth of vodka.

With a scowl, she plucked them off his palm and popped them into her mouth, swallowing them down dry.

Aspirin wasn't going to help. Being in this cabin wasn't going to help. Ryder being her glorified babysitter wasn't going to help, either.

Nothing would help.

Nothing.

Her fingers curled into fists as she lifted her face and

screamed. Not words. Not at him. Not at anything. Just screamed at the top of her lungs.

Unfortunately, that didn't make her feel any better, either.

She felt like a caged circus animal. Trapped. Hopeless. She needed to dull that anxiety. That pain. That deep-down fear eating at her like acid.

"Aspirin's not going to help make me forget," she yelled at him, even though he didn't deserve to be screamed at. It should be the other way around.

Ryder stood frozen, unable to hide the surprise on his face. "Forget what?"

"Forget!" she screamed again, hugging herself. Trying to keep herself from shattering.

He grabbed her arms and shook her. "Kelsea, forget what?"

Fuck.

Fuck. Fuck. Fuck.

She squeezed her eyes shut, tried to inhale a breath, but she couldn't. It felt as if her lungs had seized. She could no longer suck in any air.

She didn't care. She didn't care. She didn't care.

She just needed to forget.

She needed to purge herself of the memories.

And if she had to die to do it...

So be it.

HE HAD no idea what that meltdown was about. Besides her body possibly detoxing. She wasn't hooked on drugs. He knew that. Otherwise, he would have driven her ass directly to a rehab. Kicking a drug habit was more than he'd be able to handle.

But he knew she dabbled in them. He'd pulled her out of places when she'd smelled like weed. There had been times where he'd go find her and she was mellowed out between the pot and booze. Other times, she'd fight him, and be wound as tight as a spring.

Drowning herself in alcohol and lots of gratuitous sex was more her speed.

Why the fuck was he taking this on? He was only being paid to snag her and take her home to Diesel to deal with.

When he called his boss yesterday, Diesel hadn't been happy about his plan, but he was resigned to it. D said Ryder had a week to do what he could. If not, he was going to have Kelsea start seeing a therapist.

Ryder was surprised to hear that from him. D was not the kind of man who took private business outside of his "family," whether it be blood, the club brotherhood or his own crew.

But when Diesel mentioned Mercy's woman, Rissa, who was a therapist, it all made sense. Rissa was now a part of the ever-expanding "family." And even though she was a sex therapist, she was still trained to deal with emotional issues.

And if anyone had emotional issues, it was Kelsea.

While she'd been wild before, after finding out Pierce was her father, something had snapped inside her. At that point, she began to push everyone else away.

Everyone.

She'd moved out of her mother's house and shut out everyone else who loved her.

"Go outside, take a walk, cool off," he said softly. Her blue eyes were still wild, her face pale and she was rubbing at her temples.

It was killing him to watch her fall apart bit by bit. Every time he rescued her, she was a little worse. A little more unraveled.

His teammates, his fellow Shadows, had wanted her to hit rock bottom first. But Diesel wasn't allowing it and Ryder understood why. Her cousin couldn't watch her crash and burn, that's why he kept paying Ryder to find her.

For fuck's sake, Ryder couldn't watch her crash and burn, either.

He shouldn't care, but he did. He couldn't watch her take a similar path that he had.

If she was nothing to him, a nobody, simply a paying job, he wouldn't have brought her here. To his space. To the place where he himself went to escape. To not only recharge his batteries, but to get a hold of his own mental health.

It always worked for him. He had hoped it would work for her.

Now, he wasn't so sure.

A simple detox, a time away from a bad influence like Slash. Time away from the family that constantly reminded her of her piece of shit father and everybody that man had hurt or tried to hurt.

Nobody held the sins of her father against her.

She hadn't known.

Nobody had.

But even so, the truth about her father had sent her spinning.

"I don't have shoes," she said, her voice raw from screaming.

She sounded a little calmer. These mood swings, though... While he understood them—he'd seen it all too often with his buddies coming home after their military service—he questioned himself on whether he'd be able to deal with them. He was a little worried she might trigger something in him. Something he'd worked hard to keep packed down tight himself.

He released her arms now that she seemed to have leveled out a bit and went back to the bags he'd carried into the cabin. Plenty more remained in the Scout. Maybe she could help him carry them in, a good excuse to get her outside to inhale some fresh air.

Being on this mountain, in his woods, in the quiet, away from the hustle and bustle of everyday life, could be healing.

He pulled out the pair of flip-flops he'd bought so she'd at least have something to put on her feet. He snapped the thin plastic tie that bound the pair together and tossed them in her direction. She didn't even bother to try to catch them, instead simply watched with empty eyes as they landed on the roughhewn wood planked floor at her feet. She stared at them for a long moment, her long, unbrushed hair falling about her face, hiding it.

Ryder cleared the rough from his throat. "They're flip-flops," came out of his mouth because he didn't know what else to say.

He wasn't good with this emotional shit.

Watching her struggle internally, for whatever reason she was, was tugging at things hidden deep inside him, too.

Yeah, maybe bringing her here wasn't the brightest idea he'd ever had.

Even Diesel, when Ryder had called him, had barked out a laugh and called him a dumb fuck before hanging up the phone.

A dumb fuck was right.

"I got you clothes. They're out in the truck with the rest of the groceries. I need help bringin' shit in, darlin'."

She poked at the flip-flops with her big toe until they were right side up and she slipped her feet into them without a word. He had guessed at her size and had picked out a pair of medium and they looked about right.

Didn't matter. She wasn't going to do a ten-mile march with a loaded rucksack in them anyway.

He went back out through the open front door and called over his shoulder, "Comin'?"

He didn't wait and jogged down the steps of the deck to the Scout, grabbed a few more bags, including the bag with more clothes for her. As he was heading back inside, he was relieved to see her coming down the rough-cut wooden steps, even if slowly.

"More food and shit. Grab whatever you can," he said in passing.

Again, she said nothing and headed toward the Scout.

As he unloaded the bags on the table this time instead of the crowded small counter, he was glad he'd pulled the keys from the truck. Just in case. Then as it hit him, blood drained from his face as he realized he'd thrown them on the counter when he'd first walked in. He slowly turned, his eyes sliding over the old, scarred shellacked wood countertop for what he knew he'd see.

Nothing.

His keys were gone.

Fuckin' son of a bitch!

He heard the rumble of the Scout's engine as he unfroze his feet and ran out the door, just in time to see her doing a quick K-turn in the driveway.

He leapt down the three deck steps, almost eating the dirt as he landed.

"Kelsea!" he yelled as she took off down the lane, faster than the truck could handle since the lane was rutted more than normal from last spring's torrential rains.

"Son of a fucking bitch!" he shouted to the sky. Without another thought, he ran around the side of the cabin, jerked open the shed door and found his hidden ATV key. Now, he hoped the fucker would start since he hadn't run the four-wheeler in months.

He plugged in the key and turned, thanking the good fucking Lord that the engine turned over after a few seconds of it complaining.

He twisted the throttle and shot out of the shed,

bypassing the dirt lane. He knew the twists and turns the lane took like the back of his hand. And he also knew where he could conceivably cut her off. The only problem was he'd have to blaze a trail through the woods.

That might slow him down.

It also might hurt a bit.

But whatever pain he ended up enduring, he was going to make sure she felt the same.

Someone needed a lesson.

And someone needed it badly.

―――

Kelsea's heart thumped in her chest and her knuckles turned white as she gripped the steering wheel. She hadn't driven stick in forever. But she was headed down the mountain on a path that was so rutted, she couldn't take it out of second gear. In fact, she let the Scout coast down in neutral most of the way, dodging the deeper ruts when she could.

Even so, she smelled freedom.

She didn't have any idea how long this dirt road was, how long it would take to get to pavement or how long it would take to get to civilization. But her brain was clearing with every foot slowly traveled with just the thought of that possibility.

She needed to find the closest town and call someone who could Western Union her some cash. She flipped through her mind like a Rolodex, wondering who would be willing to help her.

Probably not too many. She had alienated a lot of people lately within the DAMC family and unfortunately, her roommates were flat broke. Slash didn't have two nickels to rub together, either, so calling him would be useless.

And she refused to call her mother. Or her sister.

Fuck. She had no one.

There was no one left.

She couldn't let that thought cloud her mind, she had to concentrate on navigating the hairpin curves of the steep lane. If she flipped Ryder's truck, she'd be screwed.

Holy fuck, this lane was never-ending!

As she maneuvered around what she hoped was the last sharp corner, she slammed on the brakes bringing the Scout to a sliding halt in a cloud of dust.

In front of her, blocking the path, was none other than one pissed-off Ryder. The man stood in front of a four-wheeler which was parked across the lane, effectively closing it off from travel. His muscular arms, scratched and bloody, were crossed over his chest and the worn Johnny Cash T-shirt clinging to his torso now had some fresh tears. His jean-encased legs were spread, his baseball cap sat on his head backwards like he was ready for battle. But what she couldn't miss the most was his thunderous expression.

Damn it!

There was no room to get around him to either the left or right because of large trees hugging the lane. The only path of escape was to plow right through him and the ATV.

They stared at each other through the windshield as she revved the engine a couple of times in warning.

He didn't move. In fact, he looked more determined than ever not to let her escape.

She cranked the window open. "Don't make me do it!" she shouted.

"Try it," he challenged, his eyes narrowing.

"Just let me go."

"The fuck if I'm gonna let you go. That's my fuckin' truck!"

"If I leave the truck, you'll let me go?"

Even from where she sat, she could see his lips thin and his jaw tighten even more. If it got any tighter, he'd probably shatter his teeth.

No, this man was not letting her go. Truck or no truck.

"Think you can walk to town in those fuckin' flip-flops?"

"I can damn well try." Even though she had no idea how far town was. Hell, she'd hitch a ride. Someone would pick her up.

A serial killer or some sort of Hannibal Lecter, most likely.

But at this point, she didn't care. Death might be a blessing. It would be easier than dealing with the scribbled mess that was her mind.

It would also be easier than dealing with the stubborn man before her.

The one that wanted to tell her how to live her life and how she should feel.

Bullshit.

No one... No one knew how she felt. No one knew the shit she had to deal with.

Ryder thinking he did was nothing but a joke.

He didn't know shit.

With a scream, she slammed her hands against the steering wheel.

He didn't know shit. How could he know anything about her? He couldn't.

She hadn't told anyone.

No one knew.

Just her and a dead man.

"Fuck," she squeaked in a panic as his long legs ate up the distance between them as he wore a determined expression that would probably scare the piss out of most people. "Oh, fuck."

She smashed her foot against the clutch, but her flip-flop got caught on the pedal and by the time she freed it, the driver's door was flung open. She jammed on the clutch again while desperately trying to shove the shifter in reverse.

His long arm reached in, yanked the keys, then he

slammed the emergency brake pedal with his hand. She was helpless to stop him from jerking her out of the truck by her arm.

A cry slipped from her lips as her bare knees hit the rough dirt and stones. That was going to leave a mark. His fingers tightened on both of her arms as he hauled her to her feet. That was going to leave a mark, too.

"Does that make you feel like a powerful man? Manhandling a weaker woman?" she spat out.

"You're hardly fuckin' weak," he said through gritted teeth. "You're just actin' stupid."

"Bringing me here was stupid!"

"I'm beginnin' to see that," he said, his voice tight as he escorted her to his ATV with a jerk.

Did he expect her to ride on that with him? If so, she might get the chance to jump off the back and—

She squealed as he sat sideways on the wide seat and jerked her hard enough she went off-balance and fell over his lap.

"What the fuck!"

He pulled his T-shirt she was wearing up and yanked his boxers down over her ass until it was exposed.

"What the fuck are you doing?" she screamed, struggling to break free.

"Let me tell you somethin', darlin'. You just committed a felony by stealin' my truck."

"You mean a felony like kidnapping?" she snapped. "What are you going to do? Spank me like a fucking child? Teach me a lesson? Let me tell *you* something, *darlin'*, I *love* being spanked. So, go ahead. Do it. You think it'll be punishment? It'll be just the opposite."

Beneath her, his thighs tensed. And that wasn't the only reaction she had pulled from him. *Jesus*, his erection was hard against her hip.

"Do it! I'll love every fucking second of it. The harder, the better," she sneered.

He still hesitated.

She waited. She wanted to feel that sharp sting against her flesh. She wanted to experience that pleasurable pain. Any pain he'd create would drown the pain that hovered from the past.

"Do it. I know you'll enjoy it, too."

"Fuck you," he drawled, his southern accent thicker than normal.

"Yeah, I know you want to do that, too. I can feel your dick. The thought of you spanking me has your blood pumping. Your heart racing. Your hard-on throbbing. Hasn't it?" When he didn't answer she continued, her thoughts spinning out of control. "You were just looking for an excuse to take me over your knee. And you now have it. So, do it."

When the flat of his hand came down on her ass, she bit back a whimper of pain. That also would leave a mark.

But she didn't care. She'd take whatever he could dish out. "Harder. Don't be a pussy. Show me what you've got. Show me how a 'real' man spanks a woman."

The second strike was just as hard as the first one and she jerked over his lap, the oxygen rushing from her lungs. She sucked in a sharp breath and forced out a laugh. "You're disappointing me, *darlin'*. I thought with all those bulging muscles, you'd be stronger than that."

He grunted with the power of his next strike and this time it hurt like fuck. Her eyes widened and she caught her bottom lip between her teeth to keep from crying out. But she quickly released it, afraid if he struck her again, she'd bite it through. "Pussy," she managed to whisper, but couldn't keep the shake from her voice, the tremble from her lower lip, and the sting from her eyes. Her last, "Do it," came out on a broken sob.

She tensed as she felt his arm lift again, and she closed her eyes and waited.

Nothing but air brushed over the burn of her flesh. No man had ever spanked her like that during sex. No man had spanked her like that, period.

Her legs were shaking, and the blood was rushing to her head as she hung over his lap.

This wasn't sex. This was punishment, according to him. He didn't want to have sex with her, he wanted to teach her a "lesson."

Like he had any right to do so.

But... if he didn't want to have sex with her, why was he so hard? Why was his cock like a steel rod beneath her? Why was his breathing hitched and coming faster than normal? Spanking her couldn't have been that much of an effort for him. The man was in shape, he worked out hard and often, he lived and played hard, too. Slapping her ass shouldn't have taxed him. Not one bit.

"Do it," she forced out on a breath. But this time it meant something else. As much as she embraced the pain, now she wanted the pleasure. It was another way to fill her head with something other than her tainted memories.

"Do what, darlin'?" He sounded out of breath, his words as strained as his zipper.

Did she have to explain? Would she have to tell him what she wanted? Needed?

Her own mind fought with herself and she said the exact opposite of what she wanted. "Let me go."

"That's not what you want."

No, it wasn't. It had been. But she wanted something completely different right now. Something she never expected.

He wrapped his fist in her hair and tugged her head up until their eyes met. His green ones shadowed, hiding something. "You use sex like a drug, and you want to use me."

"Is that so bad?"

"It is when the user becomes the used."

"So, use me. Take from me what you need, too. It'll be mutually beneficial. We're both consenting adults. I want it. So do you."

He shook his head slowly, his eyes never leaving hers. "No."

"You can't hide the proof."

"Many soldiers get hard during combat. It's not sexual. It's adrenaline."

"This isn't combat," she reminded him.

"No?"

"If that's all it is, let me go," she whispered, finding it difficult to catch her breath.

"We're not done here."

"Aren't we?"

"No, darlin'... we're not." With his one hand still fisted in her hair, he used the other to grab her upper arm and pull her up.

As she opened her mouth, he smothered her words, trapping whatever she was going to say between them as he crushed his mouth to hers.

She groaned and gripped his T-shirt within her fingers, holding on for dear life. Or maybe she was trying to hold onto the thin threads of her sanity. Sweeping through her mouth, his tongue twisted around hers, making her hungry for more.

He tasted so good. Who would've thought an asshole would taste so delicious?

No, he wasn't an asshole. He'd done nothing but try to help her and she'd just thrown it back in his face. Over and over again.

That thought swirled away as he shoved his tongue deeper, forcing her head back and another groan to slide up her throat.

Because she didn't have a bra, the tight tips of her nipples brushed against the worn cotton of his tee that she wore, making them more sensitive than normal.

She jerked herself free from his hands, letting the boxers drop to the ground. When he scrambled to catch her again, she slammed both palms into his chest, knocking him off balance and sending him backwards over the seat of the ATV. He landed on the ground with a grunt and she rushed around the ATV to shove her foot into his chest to pin him down.

"Don't move," she growled, jerking his T-shirt over her head and tossing it aside.

He could easily escape her, snap her ankle, tackle her to the ground. He didn't. He laid in the dirt, staring up at her, panting as hard as she was. Now his eyes weren't shadowed, they held a gleam.

She let her gaze roam over him from the top of his light brown hair, now hatless, over his strong jaw covered in whiskers, over those lips she had studied earlier this morning and tasted just seconds ago. His shoulders were broad, his arms corded, his Levi's fit him perfectly. His hips, his length of thigh, the hard line of his cock covered in denim.

Combat, my ass.

She licked her lips as his fingers curled lightly around her ankle and traveled in a caress up the calf of the leg she used to press him to the ground. Then, before she could react, he jerked her leg and she fell backwards. He surged up, wrapped his arms around her waist and twisted her until it was she who landed hard on her back in the dirt this time. All the air rushed from her lungs from the impact and she couldn't catch her breath when his weight held her down.

"Like it dirty, do you, darlin'?"

"The dirtier the better," she could barely get out.

Suddenly, she could breathe again, because he was up on his feet, staring down at her with hands on his hips.

She had no idea how he could move so fast. "I'm not desperate enough for Slash's sloppy seconds," he growled. "Get up."

He grabbed his baseball cap, smacked it on his thigh twice, and pulled it over his hair with a jerk, then picked up his discarded T-shirt and threw it at her. "Get dressed, too."

The cotton tee had landed on her chest and she balled it within her fingers. "Slash didn't get a chance to fuck me the other night. You rudely interrupted us beforehand."

He yanked the bill of his cap down lower. "Yeah? Sorry to mess up your romantic evenin'."

She rolled up to a seated position. "Sometimes it isn't about the romance, it's about wanting a good fuck."

His lips thinned and his nostrils flared just enough so she caught it. "He must be an expert then, since you keep goin' back to him."

She pushed to her feet and brushed her bare backside off, taking her time to do it since she could feel his eyes boring into her.

He could deny it all he wanted, but he wanted her.

"It's foolish to turn down a good fuck."

"'Good' is relative, darlin'."

She continued to run her hands over her body, brushing away the now non-existent dirt and debris.

She lifted her head, pushed her hair out of her face, and met his eyes. "You're right. 'Good' is relative."

"And you're up to no good," he grumbled as she approached him.

"Being up to 'no good' is a lot more fun than being 'good.'"

"You'd know."

She got so close to him that her bare toes were now touching his boots. "And you want to know, you're just resisting."

"I don't need someone else's leftovers."

"Isn't that what we all are? Someone else's leftovers? Or are you a virgin?"

"Cover yourself up and get in the truck."

She stared at him and he stared back, neither of them breaking their locked gaze. "I want off this mountain."

"We don't always get what we want, darlin'."

Wasn't that the fucking truth.

Chapter Five

WITH EVERY RUT she hit with his baby, he cursed. She had to be hitting the deepest ones on purpose now as his Scout slowly crawled back up the lane. He followed behind her on the ATV, ready at any moment for her to make a run for it. He had a gun safe with a combination lock in the shed and he would throw both sets of keys in it so she couldn't steal them again.

He'd never dealt with such a hard-headed woman before and, while he didn't mind a challenge, he wasn't sure he liked this one.

He'd been a cunt hair close to fucking her over his four-wheeler. And that would've been a mistake he might not have recovered from.

He was already regretting spanking her. He'd never taken a hand to a woman before, except for when they'd begged for a few playful slaps on their ass during sex. But he'd never fucking hit a woman as hard as he'd struck Kelsea.

Did she deserve it? Hell yes.

Did he feel like a bastard afterward? Unfortunately, also yes.

He'd always had a natural instinct to protect women, but he wanted nothing more than to throw the woman driving his truck right now off of a cliff.

What pissed him off the most wasn't her attitude. It was his response to her.

He'd lost his temper, but he'd reined it in in time before they'd taken a step he didn't want to take.

He didn't want to fuck Kelsea.

He didn't want to fuck Kelsea.

Fuck. He wanted to fuck Kelsea.

He roared with frustration as the Scout's brake lights lit up when she maneuvered around the last curve before coming to the clearing where his cabin sat.

He stopped his ATV at the narrow part of the driveway before it widened. Once again, so she couldn't try to escape. When she parked the Scout in front of the deck of the cabin, he waited until she got out and looked in his direction.

Jesus Christ. Her hair was a wild mess, his old tee she was wearing did nothing to hide her curves or the hard tips of her nipples. His boxers she wore did nothing but show her bare legs that he wanted wrapped around him. Smudges of dirt dotted her arms and legs, including a large one on her cheek.

There shouldn't be anything about her right now that would make her desirable to him.

But, fuck him, it was the exact opposite. He pictured her in his bed, her lips swollen from his kisses, her hair messy from having sex, her attitude sweet and mellow from multiple orgasms.

He snorted and shook his head. Now he was expecting miracles. He couldn't imagine Kelsea ever being sweet and mellow.

The woman was as stubborn as a fucking hellcat with claws that could rip a man's sac wide-open with one swipe.

And he liked his balls just how they were, thank you very much.

When she plugged her hands on the hips he wanted to grab onto while he fucked her hard from behind, he realized she was waiting for some sort of response from him.

Besides his dick being rock hard.

Motherfucker.

"Bring the keys to me," he yelled over the noise of his four-wheeler's exhaust.

She tilted her head and lifted one hand, his keys hanging off one finger. "Come get them."

He set his jaw. "My order wasn't a request."

Her eyes narrowed and her lips curled up slightly at the corners. Then she shrugged and headed in his direction.

Damn. That was too easy. Scheming, that was what she was doing.

When she got close enough, he snagged his keys from her and stuffed them deep into his pocket. Right next to his hard-on that was pulsing with every beat of his heart.

Her eyes landed on the evidence of his bad judgement and she smiled.

"You steal my truck again, and you will not enjoy the punishment. Guaranteed."

Her smile fell and she began to turn.

He grabbed her arm to stop her. "Get on. You're not leavin' my sight and I need to put the ATV away."

She gave him a look that was way too innocent. "You have the truck keys."

"I'm not chasin' you through the fuckin' woods when you decide to run."

She lifted one foot. "Can't run in these cheap-ass flip-flops."

"Knowin' you, you'd try. Get on."

She sighed and planted a hand on his shoulder as she began to climb on behind him.

"No. In front. You'll jump off the back." He pushed himself to the very rear of the vinyl seat and made room for her.

Without a word, she climbed in front of him and settled between his legs after a few wiggles of her soft ass against his traitorous dick.

"You done?" Without waiting for an answer, he hit the throttle and the force threw her back into his chest as he sped past the cabin and around to the large outbuilding behind it. The barn doors still hung wide open, so he drove right into the dark interior.

He shut down the engine, but kept his hands on the handlebars, effectively keeping her trapped between his extended arms.

"You done?" she echoed, her voice huskier than normal.

She shifted and his nose ended up in her hair which now smelled not only of his cheap shampoo but of the outdoors. When she went to sneak out from under his arm, he wrapped it around her waist, holding her there.

Against him.

Everything about her was soft. Except her attitude.

He wondered if that could soften, too.

The woman was fucking up her life. Either she couldn't see it, or she just didn't care.

Probably the second. And if she didn't care, neither should anyone else. But too many of the people around her did.

She needed to see that.

And why the fuck did he feel the need for it to be him to show her?

"Ryder?" she breathed.

"Yeah?" he breathed back.

"Are you going to let me go?"

Before he could think too hard about it, he nuzzled his nose deeper into her hair and answered, "No."

He spread his fingers wide until the tip of one brushed the bottom curve of her breast, then he slid his hand down her belly and under the worn cotton of one of his favorite T-shirts until her warm skin met his. He traced along the edge of the elastic waistband from one side to the other.

Her breath hitched and she held herself still in his arms. Both of them waited, his fingers right there at the top edge of his boxers. The ones that clung to her hips and ass better than he would've imagined.

He wanted her to demand he stop.

He wanted her to beg him to continue.

She reached behind her, wrapping her arms around his neck and arched her back as his hand slipped under the loose waistband and continued lower.

"Tell me to stop," he whispered roughly.

"Don't stop," she whispered back.

"Tell me you don't want this."

"I want this," she breathed.

He snagged her earlobe between his teeth, sucked on it, then traced the delicate shell before letting his warm breath sweep over her ear. She shivered against him.

He slipped his hand a little lower until the tip of his middle finger touched the very top of her pussy, right before the soft flesh split in two.

She was surprisingly smooth.

"You shaved," he murmured.

Her soft cheek rubbed against his much rougher one. "You didn't."

"You used my razor." Now it would be too dull for his face. He'd need to buy more on his next grocery store run. *If they didn't kill each other first.* "Did you ask if you could use it?"

"No, but I didn't ask if I could use your toothbrush, either... Ryder..." she said his name on a groan.

He was rock hard and trying to fight the temptation. But it seemed to be a losing battle.

She knocked his baseball cap off his head, and it dropped to the floor, then she combed her fingers through his hair, her nails scraping against his scalp. Luckily, he kept it short so she had nothing to grip, otherwise he was sure she'd be pulling on it as hard as she could.

She would love for him to submit to her. To hand over that power.

She had no idea that would never happen.

If anything, he was suddenly bound and determined to make the woman in his arms submit to him. To crack the hard and reckless exterior to get to the center where he was sure she was soft and caring.

She got lost along the way and forgot who she was.

She'd become someone else in an effort to ignore things she didn't want to deal with. But she needed to deal with them, or she'd only bottom out and possibly never recover.

He'd seen it. He'd been headed on that path himself a while ago.

Until he found Diesel and his teammates. A reason to keep himself above the drowning water. A reason to fight, to kick his legs and swim hard to keep his head above the surface.

After he left the Army, he had floundered and working as a Shadow gave him a purpose.

Kelsea simply needed a purpose.

Something to keep her breathing air instead of inhaling that water.

He couldn't do it for her, but he could hand her a lifebuoy and teach her how to kick her legs until she got back to land.

She curved one hand around the back of his neck, while the other trailed down his cheek, over her own breast, down her belly until she found his hand, which still hovered right there on the edge.

Because if he went farther, there was no going back.

They would both have to live with their actions.

And if her cousin Diesel found out... Neither might be breathing for very long.

She spread her hand on top of his and it was then that he realized hers was so much smaller than his.

She was tough, even thought she was invincible. But no one was indestructible.

Her nails dug into the skin of his neck and she rolled her head along his shoulder until her lips were right under his jaw and he could feel her warm breath beating against him. "Ryder," she groaned.

"Tell me what you want, darlin'."

If she said, "To forget," he was pushing her away, getting off that ATV and putting some distance between them until his head cleared.

He didn't want to be used to "forget."

If she wanted this, it should be because she wanted him and no other reason.

She used drugs, alcohol and sex with Slash, as well as others, to "forget." He didn't want to be lumped in with any of those things.

Her next words were the last thing he expected to hear from her.

"I want a man who tells me I'm beautiful. A man who doesn't look at me like I'm crazy. A man who can see past the mess I made to see who I really am. A man who doesn't look at me and see the monster whose blood runs through my veins. One who can see past the damage he caused. I want a man who sees *me*."

An ache filled his chest. "I see you, darlin'."

"You've seen me at my worst. I've fought you. I've cursed at you. I've ignored everything you've said. You kept coming. You kept showing up. You never gave up on me. Not once."

Hearing the rawness in her words, he closed his eyes.

"I don't want you to regret it," she finished.

"Regret what, darlin'?"

"Everything you've done for me. Everything I never appreciated. Everything you'll do for me. No matter what happens from here, even if I act like I don't appreciate it, I want you to know that I do. Please, no matter what, don't forget that. I know you've wanted to throw your hands up and walk away, but you didn't. I need you to know that means something to me, even if it doesn't seem like it."

Her words made him lose his breath and he released the ATV's throttle and, with his thumb, gently brushed away the smudge of dirt on her cheek.

"I just want you to know something, too... I don't give a shit who your father was. I don't give a shit about a man who was a problem that was handled. I care about you."

"Why?"

That was a good fucking question. Why did he care so much about the woman in his arms? Especially after everything he'd seen, everything she'd done. Why did she haunt him?

"Why, Ryder? Why did you continue to care besides being paid to by D?"

"Guess my head's as fucked up as yours. It isn't about the money, darlin'. It's because I can't sit the fuck back and watch you destroy yourself. None of us can."

He traced his fingertips along her jaw and down her throat, pausing on her pounding pulse. His beat just as fiercely. His hand skimmed over the soft cotton until he cupped her breast, his thumb brushing back and forth over the tight tip.

"Tell me what you want, darlin'."

"I told you."

"No." Catching that nipple between his fingers, he twisted it gently and her back arched once more.

"Tell me what you want, darlin'."

"This," she said on a hitched breath.

"No, darlin', tell me what... you... want."

"You. I want you."

His finger slipped down to separate her folds and he slid it inside. She was warm and slick as he slipped in another. With a groan, she ground down on his fingers, pushing them deeper.

He continued to tweak her nipple with one hand as the thumb from his other pressed and circled against her clit.

She bucked against him and began to rock back and forth. With her hand still on his beneath the boxers, she encouraged him to move faster. He didn't. He kept a lazy pace, amazed by how responsive she was just to his touch.

Had she been like this with all the others?

No, he couldn't think like that. He needed to remain in the here and now. He had to remember this was him and her. No one else. This moment was theirs. Fuck everyone else.

Her head slamming back into his chest and just missing his chin pulled him from his thoughts.

"Ryder," she panted.

"What do you want, darlin'?" He knew what the hell *he* wanted. He knew what he wanted to give her. "Tell me."

She ground even harder against his hand and he started to worry that she might break every bone in it in her chase for a climax.

"Do you want to come?" he murmured into her hair.

"Please," she groaned.

"I like hearin' that word come from you. Shows me you can be humble when you wanna be." He circled her clit harder, faster and he plucked roughly at her nipple over the cotton. "I wanna hear it more often. Yeah?"

"Yes," she hissed. "Please. Oh, please."

"Please what, darlin'?"

"Please... make me come."

"No one's holdin' you back but yourself. What you want's right there. Reach out and grab it."

Her body hiccuped against him as she planted her hands on his thighs and her hips shot up off the seat. He struggled to stay with her, to feel her reaction, the warm gush, the muscles convulsing around his fingers.

Yes, that was what she wanted. What he could give her, if nothing else.

When it was over, her head flopped forward, her blonde hair falling around her face. He could hear her ragged breath.

Or was that his?

He was rock hard before, now he was like titanium steel. His balls were tight, his dick pulsating. The urge to sink into her wet heat so strong it actually scared him.

He never wanted a woman so much as he did right now.

It made no sense. He had seen her at her lowest, but all of that didn't matter right now. He could push that aside and see her as she wanted someone to see her.

It was dangerous territory he was wandering into.

He should know better.

But that didn't stop him from digging out his wallet and pulling out a condom.

He placed it on the ATV's gas tank where she could see it. He wasn't going to do anything she didn't want. She needed to be the one to take that next step.

She needed to be a hundred percent sure.

Because this could change everything.

And if either of them would end up questioning their actions, he wanted it to be him, not her.

She lifted her head and plucked the condom off the tank. She braced her hands on his thighs again and with a flexibility that he hadn't been expecting—which was not only surprising but impressive—she had turned on the seat until she was facing him.

Her cheeks were flushed, her eyes held determination, and she had the condom wrapper tucked between her teeth. Without breaking their gaze, she unfastened his belt, the large, heavy buckle falling to the side as she quickly made work of the button and zipper on his jeans.

Just the thought of her reaching in and grabbing him made his cock flex. He didn't know how this would work since he was still straddling the seat with his thighs spread so there was no way to shove his jeans down too far.

Again, with skill that was a little startling, she worked both his jeans and boxers down enough for his cock to spring free.

He clenched his teeth as she ran her fingers up and down his length. But what was killing him the most was that she hadn't dropped her gaze at all. He continued to stare into her pretty cornflower blue eyes, and he waited, forcing himself to take one breath then another.

When her thumb brushed over the head, his hips twitched, and she smiled around the condom.

Reaching up, she grabbed the wrapper and tore it open with her teeth, spitting it to the floor. Looking him straight in the eye, she rolled the condom down his throbbing length.

Fuck.

Grabbing onto his shoulders, she rose and shifted forward. His heart was beating so hard, she had to hear it, too.

She dropped one hand to his dick, and he bit back a groan when she circled her fingers around the root and held him in place.

This was it.

If he didn't stop this now, there was no going back.

They were going to do something they couldn't undo.

He needed to consider all the consequences of what that would bring.

But as she lined him up and the head of his dick touched her soft heat, anything he had to consider, anything he should think about, was now gone...

He was gone.

There was nothing left but the need for him to bury himself in her.

Consequences be damned.

Chapter Six

His green eyes were dark, hooded and something flashed behind them that made a shiver run down her spine.

"What do you want, Ryder?" she asked softly as she hovered above him.

"You're holdin' the evidence. It's clear what I want."

His voice was deep and gruff and the man she was holding onto was nothing like any of the men she'd been with before.

There was a difference between a man and a... *man*.

Most who she thought were men turned out to be anything but. However, she'd only had one purpose to be with them and, not surprisingly, it was the same with them.

Ryder wasn't like any of them. He'd lived a lifetime already. He was seasoned. He was serious about his work and his play. He probably didn't take having sex lightly, either.

So, this could change things. For her. For him. Between the two of them.

She should consider that risk before following her instinct to lower herself and make that connection.

Normally, for her, sex was just that. Sex.

Suddenly, this seemed so much more.

Usually, the man she was with would rush to fuck her, and she'd hope to come before he did. If she even got that chance at all.

Ryder had held back. Waited. Wanted to make sure that *she* was sure.

She was. She wanted this. She wanted it this morning in the kitchen when she purposely came out naked to tempt him. He resisted.

She wanted it when he pulled her over his lap and spanked her. He resisted.

She wanted it when she shoved him to the ground and stood over him naked. Again, he resisted.

Now, he wasn't resisting but instead, waiting for her. He was giving her a choice to back out, to rethink all of this.

For her, there was nothing to think about. She knew what she wanted. And there was no denying what Ryder wanted, either. Like he'd said, she held the proof in her hand.

"Darlin'..."

"Yeah?"

"I've only got so much patience. You need to either climb onto the saddle or get off the horse."

He made her smile. It had been a long time since anyone had made her smile like that. Not a forced smile, but a true, spontaneous one.

She'd almost forgotten what that felt like.

"I haven't ridden a horse since I was little, and even then, it was a mechanical one outside of the local grocery store. Am I going to get my quarter's worth?"

A slow grin of his own crossed his handsome face and made her heart skip a beat. "Only way you're gonna find out is if you put that quarter in the slot and take a chance."

She held her breath as she slowly lowered, forcing herself to keep her eyes locked with his. The lower she went, the more heated his eyes became. His hitched breath escaped between parted lips. And when she couldn't lower herself any more, when he was fully seated, filling her, stretching her, they looked at each other in surprise.

Maybe they both felt that the shed—or, hell, the world—would come tumbling down around them if this actually happened. But it *was* happening and the shed still stood and they hadn't been struck with lightning, either.

Yet.

As long as Diesel didn't find out, they'd be good.

"Darlin'," he groaned.

"Hmm?"

"Don't just sit there. You're killin' me."

She smiled again at his pained grimace and circled her arms around his neck. She began to rock back and forth on his lap, driving him even deeper. "Are you going to make me do everything?"

"That's the plan."

That was a plan she could go along with. If he wanted her to drive, she'd drive. She did so by putting her lips a fraction away from his and answering, "Fine."

She slid the tip of her tongue across his lower lip and then dipped it inside his mouth, teasing.

Suddenly, her hair was clutched in his fist and he was crushing his mouth to hers. So much for her driving.

His other hand grabbed a handful of her ass and he used his feet on the ground and his powerful thighs to drive upward. Every time he slammed into her, her breath rushed from her mouth and into his.

But she didn't pull away, didn't tell him to stop. Because she liked it, she liked him. She liked this.

There was something right about it all. But she had no time to figure out what. Instead, he continued his onslaught, holding her against him and thrusting upward hard and fast.

She liked it like this, but she wanted more. She wanted

to feel his bare skin on hers. She wanted to feel the wiry hairs on his thighs tickling her skin. She wanted to see the flex of his muscles as he fucked her.

Because even though she was on top, he was the one doing the fucking. Not her. She was just hanging on for that ride. She had slipped the quarter in the slot and the mechanical horse was now doing the work.

Next time she'd get more. Next time she'd get all of him. Not just a quick fuck in a barn or shed or whatever it was, on the vinyl seat of an ATV with both of them wearing his T-shirts, with the boxers she was wearing wedged to the side, with his jeans just pulled down enough to access his cock.

Next time.

Because this time it was simply to break the tension between them. To get past that point of contention, so they could both breathe.

He said he saw her, but did he really?

Or did he see what everyone else did?

He broke the kiss and shoved his face into her chest, his breath coming hot and heavy, even through the thin cotton of the tee she still wore.

"Fuck, darlin', *fuck*," he groaned against her, his fingers digging even harder into her ass, his thrusting turning into a pounding, which jarred her each time his hips lifted.

The fabric from the bunched boxers scraped over her clit with each rise and fall, causing a shudder to sweep through her.

She wanted to come, to let go, but she wasn't there yet. And he seemed to be getting close.

If he came without her...

"Ryder..."

"What do you need, darlin'?" came muffled from between her breasts.

"Everything."

"Can't give you everything. Not here. Not now," he said on a broken whisper.

When? Where?

He lifted his head from where it had been planted. His frantic thrusting slowed, and he met her eyes. His grip loosened on her flesh. "Lift your shirt."

She grabbed a fistful of cotton and tugged it up until he had access to her bare breasts. He dropped his head once more, this time to snag one of her nipples between his lips, plucking at it a few times before sucking it deep within his mouth, sucking hard enough that she could feel that pull all the way to her core.

She clenched around him and he groaned against her skin, the vibration of that making it more intense. His teeth scraped along her skin and over the taut tip of her nipple, making her jerk within his arms. Arching her back, she encouraged him to continue, one hand tightening around the back of his neck and the fingers of the other brushing through his hair.

He couldn't suck her breast into his mouth any deeper and when he let her go, her nipple was swollen and wet and he blew over the tip, making it bead even more.

"The other one," she groaned, pushing his head over.

"Please," he reminded her.

"Please," she whispered.

Their gazes remained locked as he tugged on her other nipple with his lips, then opened his mouth wide and sank his teeth gently around the whole areola. The tip of his tongue alternating between flicking and circling the pebbled nub.

Fuck.

Ryder squeezed her ass cheeks and held her down as he lifted his hips and ground against her.

"You wanna come?" he asked while kissing up her neck, along her jawline, his lips blazing a path to her mouth.

"Please," she breathed in anticipation of her not only having an orgasm but of him taking her mouth again.

And when he did, she wrapped both of her hands around the back of his head and held him there, taking over, riding him by circling and grinding against him. Until she felt it, that buildup deep within her. She wanted to tell him, but she didn't want to let his mouth go, either.

He was the best kisser. His lips were soft but firm, his tongue skilled. And she couldn't wait to feel his mouth elsewhere.

Another time.

Next time.

She only hoped there would be one.

He grunted in her mouth as she rode him faster, determined to reach the end of this ride successfully before her quarter ran out.

She gasped, but he kept their mouths connected when she did so, kissing her harder, his fingers flexing against her ass.

He was close, but now she was even closer.

Then... she was there...

She landed hard on his lap and their kiss broke when he grunted. As he surged up one more time, her orgasm raced through her, her muscles contracting around him, squeezing him as he came.

Once again, with their gazes locked, both of their eyes widened with shock. Surprise. Disbelief that sex could be so good between them.

Their eyes held for one pounding heartbeat. Two. Until...

She dropped her gaze from his when something behind his eyes changed.

"Kelsea," he said, his voice raw.

She couldn't look at him. Not yet. Whatever happened was too new, too fresh for her to deal with. Instead, she shoved her face into his neck and wrapped her arms tightly around him, leaning into him and holding on.

"Darlin'," he whispered, his breathing still fast and ragged, his accent thicker than normal.

He wrapped his fingers around her forearms, ready to peel her from him. To expose her vulnerability.

But she wasn't ready.

She wasn't ready to deal with what just happened.

To try to figure out what it all meant. If anything.

When she resisted, and begged, "Don't let me go yet... *please*," he sighed softly, and his broad palms smoothed down her back until he was holding her just as tightly.

She just needed a few minutes like this. She needed to be held. To feel secure in his arms.

Maybe it was just a fantasy that he might care about her. But even if it was, she wanted to hold onto that fantasy for a little while longer.

"Don't let me go yet... *please*."

There was something about her request and her saying the word "please" that gave him a sliver of hope. It was stupid since it was only a word, but her asking instead of demanding, instead of being a brat, made a world of difference to him, made him look at her differently.

She wasn't saying it to be smart or sarcastic. It came from her honestly.

A little common courtesy went a long way, especially after the way he had to deal with her so many times in the past.

She wanted someone to see *her*. But he wanted her to see *him*, too. Not just as a guy who would show up and ruin her fun. Not as the one tasked with dragging her drunken ass out of a bad situation and delivering her home safely.

Every. Fucking. Time.

For this moment, she wasn't his "job." She was simply a woman and he was simply a man who wanted that woman.

In truth, wanting her wasn't smart.

He had told himself he wasn't going to fuck her.

He did.

Where they went from here, he had no fucking idea.

But even so, he wasn't letting his guard down. At this point, he still couldn't trust her not to do something stupid.

This short span of time in each other's arms was just a positive in the midst of a whole bunch of negatives. He'd seen it before. He'd lived it before.

One moment of sunshine in the midst of a storm. You enjoyed the warm light while you had it before the next dark cloud blew in.

Because he knew the sunshine never lasted.

So, he needed to be prepared to get caught out in the rain.

Chapter Seven

Ryder stepped out of the bathroom, a towel wrapped around his hips, and stopped to watch Kelsea digging through the bags on the bed.

After she had showered, she apparently stole a clean pair of his boxers and another one of his shirts. At this rate he wasn't going to have any clean clothes of his own.

"I bought you some clothes."

She pulled a three-pack of white underwear out of one of the bags and held it up. "You mean *these*?"

Okay, he had to agree, what he could find might as well be granny panties. What did she expect out here in the mountains?

"Do you think the local grocery story has a rack of fancy undies? This is what they got. Take it or leave it. You're not wearin' it to go fishin' for dick. It's to cover that revolvin' door that took all that strange."

She raised an eyebrow and dropped the package on the bed. "You mean that revolving door you just walked through yourself?"

Yeah, that one.

She turned with her hands on her hips and ran her gaze

from the top of his still wet hair, down his bare chest and then hovered on the place the damp towel clung to. Which was his half-chub after seeing her bending over the bed, his boxers clinging to her generous ass.

"You clean up nice," she murmured, slowly walking toward him. He held his breath when she reached him and picked up his dog tags, turning them over in her hand.

"Army," she read as she ran a thumb over the raised metal. "I didn't think Ryder was your real name. This tells me otherwise."

"Name I was born with."

She lifted her head and her blue eyes held a twinkle. "Dwight?"

"Was born with that one, too."

"Dwight Ryder," she repeated like she was tasting it.

His chest tightened at his name on her lips. "You don't like it?"

"Do you care if I don't?"

Yes. "No."

She shrugged and let the tags drop back to his chest. "Then it doesn't matter."

It mattered.

They stared at each other for a few moments. Finally, she stepped away and went back to the bed. "So, you bought me socks but flip-flops instead of shoes. Granny panties, but no bra." She snorted and lifted a sweatshirt from the bed.

He saw that one and had to buy it for her. It was too good to pass up.

"This all they had?" she asked with a raised eyebrow.

The sweatshirt had a big brown donkey on the front with the word "smart" over it.

It truly fit her.

"You realize it's too hot to wear a sweatshirt?"

"I know, but it was perfect for you."

"I take it you're saying I'm a smart ass?"

"Don't have to say it, darlin'." He smirked as he moved closer.

"Guess you bought a matching one, then," she said as she continued to dig through the bags. After a few seconds, she lifted her head. "Well, I guess I'm stuck with wearing your boxers and shirts. But since we won't be in this cabin for a long time, I'll get by."

"Walmart's about an hour away. I'll try to get there on my next run. You'll just have to give me your sizes."

She frowned. "I'm sure I can last another couple of days."

Facing his dresser, he yanked his towel off and dug in his drawer for a pair of clean boxers. He didn't keep a lot of clothes at the cabin, so if she kept wearing his stuff, he'd also need to hit a laundromat. "I'm sure you can, too, but it ain't gonna be a couple days, Kels."

"Ryder..."

He lifted a hand over his shoulder, not bothering to look in her direction. "Don't wanna hear one word."

"I've got a job."

He snorted. "Right. A job you don't bother to show up for. Left your sister in the lurch time and time again. Think she's about done with your bullshit. If it wasn't for Dex, she'd have fired your ass months ago. You better kiss that man's feet next time you see him."

He yanked the boxers up his legs and adjusted his dick into place before grabbing a pair of camo cargo pants out of another drawer. He pulled those on, too. He still didn't glance behind him to see what she was up to.

Probably silently cursing at him.

He found an old olive-green T-shirt and dragged that over his head before turning around.

Her eyes were heated as she stared at him.

Well, that wasn't what he expected. *Fuck.*

He adjusted his dick again.

"You have a nice ass," she murmured.

"So do you, darlin'."

"Maybe you shouldn't have gotten dressed."

He steeled himself against the purr in her voice. "Got things to do. Just because we're out in the middle of nowhere doesn't mean I get to lounge around in bed all day."

"I bet you're never lazy and take a day just to spend it in bed."

He tipped his head but didn't answer, because he'd done it only once. But then, he had a really hot brunette in his bed that day at the Inter-Continental Hotel in western Kabul and she was a very good reason to stay there.

He doubted Kelsea wanted to hear about his hookup with a British war correspondent. Or the sexy French photojournalist that joined them.

Nope. He doubted she'd want to hear that story.

But it was a good one. He had turned on his southern charm real thick-like. They ate that shit up. That wasn't the only thing they ate—

"Where are you going?"

He'd been walking toward the front door, adjusting himself once more when her question made him pause. He glanced over his shoulder. His breath caught as he took in her wild blonde hair and... When had she changed into one of his wife beaters?

Fuck.

He'd bought them to wear under his flannel shirts, so they were white and, apparently, practically see-through since he could just see the pink of her nipples that were pressed against the thin fabric.

Fuck. He didn't need to get her any more clothes from Wally World. What she was wearing right now was perfect.

The only problem was, her wearing that made it way too

tempting to take a day and be "lazy" in bed. That was after fucking her until his balls were drained dry.

And then fucking her all over again.

She lifted her eyebrows at him.

What? Oh yeah. "To get dinner."

"Already? It's early yet." Her blue eyes lit up. "Is there a burger place locally?"

"Somethin' like that."

"Really?"

"Got a smoker out back. Gonna make some smoked whistle pig sandwiches," he announced with a grin.

"Is that a specialty around here like Bangin' Burgers at home?"

Ryder turned his head away, pinning his lips together. "Mmm hmm."

"Can I go with you?"

"No."

"What am I going to do while you're gone?"

"Clean."

He slammed the door shut behind him and began to hum Luke Bryan's *Huntin', Fishin' And Lovin' Every Day* as he headed toward the shed to get his ATV and Remington Varmint .223 rifle.

Today was going to be a good fucking day.

HE EXPECTED HER TO CLEAN. Like she was his maid or something.

Suuuuuure.

She'd get right on that. Maybe tell him to pick up a little maid outfit from the costume section at Walmart.

She scowled at the toilet brush in her hand and after one last swipe around the rim of the toilet bowl and a quick flush, she tossed it into the sink.

What was she doing? Why did she feel the need for his praise? Or the need to see a smile from him directed at her?

Why did she even care?

He'd been gone for almost an hour already and when he got back, he probably wouldn't even notice that she put away all the remaining groceries and the clothes he'd bought. As well as made the bed and scrubbed the tiny bathroom.

She was done. If she was going to remain here for a couple more days, she needed to spread out his "chores," otherwise she'd get so bored she'd start climbing the walls.

While the sex earlier had relieved some of the tension and frustration—at least for a little while—that tended to be deep-seated in her bones, it was now starting to creep up on her again. The edge she traveled was beginning to narrow and turn razor sharp.

She glanced around the cabin and found a pile of old magazines on a rough-cut built-in shelf. She went over to thumb through them and wrinkled her nose when she realized they were all about hunting or fishing.

Yawn. She had no interest in camo-colored rifles or tree stands. She hoped she was out of this cabin long before she got desperate enough to start reading them.

She had snooped around the cabin this morning when he'd done his grocery run, so she knew the cabin was completely dry. Which made her wonder if he ever drank.

And if he didn't, why not?

Her gaze landed on the pair of flimsy flip-flops he'd bought her, and she rushed over to slip her feet into them. Peering out one of the back windows toward the shed, she checked to see if he was out there.

He wasn't.

But she noted the glass certainly needed a good cleaning. However, that would have to wait. She'd put that on the *what-to-do-when-she-was-bored-to-death* list.

Right now, she had more snooping to do.

She quickly escaped the cabin, passed something that looked like a metal barrel positioned on its side and mounted to a stand with smoke rising from a little chimney. Whatever wood was burning smelled really good.

But if he was planning on smoking a deer in that thing, she figured it would be difficult. One, it was too small to hold a whole deer. Two, they wouldn't be eating that tonight since she assumed it would take a long time to smoke that much meat.

She shrugged. But what did she know about hunting?

Her mouth watered at the thought of having some really tender venison. She'd had it plenty of times since her Uncle Ace was always stocking the freezers on his farm with deer and sharing it with his family. She never turned her nose up at his deer bologna.

When she got to the large double doors of the shed, she noticed they were cracked open and slipped into the darker interior.

Hesitating just inside, she stared at the spot where his ATV had been parked earlier. The spot where they'd had sex. That memory made everything within her clench.

She only hoped he'd want to repeat that performance tonight. But this time in his bed with both of them fully naked.

Yes, she'd like to explore his whole body with her tongue. Especially after seeing his naked, muscular ass earlier when he'd been getting dressed.

He certainly hadn't been self-conscious of his nudity. But then he had no reason to be. He was put together well. Very well.

Using her thumb, she wiped a little bit of saliva that had caught in the corner of her lips.

Back to the task at hand...

Before they had left the shed earlier, he had thrown both

sets of keys, for his Scout and the ATV, into the large gun safe standing in the corner on a cement slab. She hurried over to it and tried the handle.

Locked.

She let her gaze slide around the shed. The only light in the building came from windows that were even dirtier than the ones in the cabin. Well, she wasn't cleaning those. It was a storage building, after all.

A few metal cabinets hung from one wall over what looked like a work bench. Her gaze roamed over a couple chainsaws, garden and hand tools, and a few red plastic gas cans nearby.

Then her eyes landed on an old free-standing, rustic cabinet built from wood. Covered in dust, it appeared to have been in the shed for a very long time.

As she approached it, she noticed it had a little wooden latch and no lock on it, unlike some of the other cabinets which probably held more expensive tools and the like.

She blew on the wooden handles, coughing as the dust cloud blew back in her face. Flipping the latch with her finger, she opened one side and peered into its dark interior.

Bingo!

She swung both doors wide and grabbed her discovery. She clutched the old bottle of whiskey covered in years of grime like it was a prize. She retrieved what appeared to be a somewhat clean rag from the work bench and wiped off the top before unscrewing it and taking a sip.

She let the liquor slide down her throat and then released a long, relieved sigh.

Yes, that's what she needed to smooth out the edges. She took a longer sip the second time and then gauged the level of amber liquid in the bottle. She'd have to ration it since it wasn't full. And she had no idea how long this little "vacation" on this mountain would last.

Okay, just one more little sip. The warmth swirled

through her as the whiskey landed in her belly. She screwed the lid back on and put it back into the cabinet in the exact spot where she found it, then searched for more.

She found an old flask at the very back of the shelf but when she shook it, she was disappointed to find it empty. With a frown, she put that back and her hand knocked into a wooden box. Instead of sliding it back into its place, she pulled it out and stared at it.

It appeared hand-made and had the initials DBR skillfully carved into the lid. She ran her finger over the letters, wondering what the B stood for.

She could think of a few things.

Bossy. Bastard.

No, that wasn't fair. More like badass or brave.

She was starting to look at him in a different light than she'd ever had before.

Had he always been hot? Fuck yes.

And that slight southern accent of his? Just made certain parts of her quiver.

But in the past, she'd never been thrilled to see him. When she did, that meant her ass was about to be dragged out of somewhere she most likely didn't want to leave.

Funny, her cousin had six *bad-to-the-bone* men working for him. But every single time it had been Ryder who'd shown up to get her. She was pretty sure he didn't volunteer for the job.

It was like he was being punished for something.

She moved back to the workbench, put the box down and stared at it for a few seconds.

Why did she feel that if she opened it, she'd be getting a glimpse into Ryder's life he hadn't planned on sharing?

But then... why wasn't it locked up? Why was it just sitting in an unlocked cabinet in the shed where anyone hiking by could take it?

It could be just an empty box. One he made in Boy

Scouts or something. Maybe she was making more of a deal out of it than she should.

She turned her head and listened carefully to make sure she didn't hear the ATV.

It was quiet. The only noise coming from the birds in the surrounding trees.

She held her breath as she unclipped the little metal latch, then slowly and carefully raised the lid like something was going to jump out and bite her.

Well, if any spiders were hiding in there, she was going to lose her shit. She shuddered.

The little rusty metal hinges creaked as she finished lifting the lid and she sucked in a breath.

Three patches laid on top. She carefully pulled each one out like they were made of glass and breakable. The first patch said "RANGER" in the center of a ribbon-type banner and had the numbers "75" to the left and "RGT" to the right. Under that was a worn patch of the American flag that was backwards. She ran her thumb back and forth over the last one which simply read "RYDER."

She chewed on her bottom lip. Why would he keep these personal items not only here, instead of at home in Shadow Valley, but out in a shed?

Did he forget they were out here?

She placed his name patch to the side but had a hard time dragging her eyes from it back to the box.

When she did, she noticed that under the patches sat a medal.

She frowned, trying to make sense of what she was seeing.

This medal wasn't a typical medal. Not one she'd seen on the news or in a movie.

Or, hell, anywhere.

It was special. And personal.

This "medal" was created from aluminum foil, beads, and dried globs of glue.

It was messy. Crude.

Clearly made by a child.

Did Ryder have kids? Was he keeping that a secret?

Her fingers shook as she carefully lifted it and tilted it toward the muted light coming through the yellow-hazed window.

"Metal of Value" was written in black permanent marker across the top.

Metal of value.

She had no idea what that meant. What any of it meant.

But she was afraid of breaking it or knocking even one bead off. Someone somewhere put time and love into creating this object.

As she went to put it back in the box, a piece of yellowed paper at the bottom caught her eye. She placed the "metal of value" to the side with care and pulled out what looked like a letter.

As she unfolded it, it was clear that this handwriting wasn't from a child. It was neat and most likely written by an adult. The writing was slanted like the person was left-handed, but the handwriting was bold and readable.

She skimmed the note, saw a man named Benjamin had signed it. Was that his last name? First name? Did it matter?

No, what mattered was the content of that note as she started again from the top and read it more slowly.

> "I know our mission was a black op, but you deserve the Medal of Valor, bud. You saved my ass when you came back for me, even knowing you were putting yours on the line by stepping into a direct line of fire. You could have died, given up your life to save mine. It was selfless and there aren't a lot of people like that left in the world.
>
> "I wish they'd give you that medal, because you

EARNED it. But since we weren't officially there, you'll never get the recognition you deserve.

"You don't know what it was like to come home to my family, bud. What it meant to me to see my son for the first time after I thought I'd never see him again. I'm not ashamed to admit that I bawled like a fucking baby. It freaked my son the fuck out, but when I got my shit together, I explained how my friend saved my life and helped me return home to him and his mother. I told him you deserved a medal but would never receive any kind of recognition. So, he decided to make you one himself to thank you for bringing his dad home. I know it ain't much and certainly not enough, but it's something...

"If you ever need me, my friend, I'm there... Anything, Anytime, Anywhere. Sua Sponte."

Sua Sponte.

She had no idea what that meant or what language it was.

She gently refolded the letter and carefully put it back in the bottom of the box. She added the rest of the contents back the way she found it. After sliding the box back on the shelf, she secured the cabinet.

She stared at the closed doors for a moment.

Fuck. Ryder had saved a man's life.

He'd probably saved a bunch of people's lives.

The man had done so much in his life. Hell, he was a hero.

What had she accomplished?

Nothing.

She was almost thirty years old and had not a goddamn thing to show for it.

She'd been nothing but a waste.

She quickly reopened the cabinet, grabbed the bottle of whiskey and shut it once more.

She untwisted the top again on the bottle and lifted it to her lips.

She was no better than the bastard whose sperm made her.

The rotten apple hadn't fallen far from that poisoned tree.

She was nothing but a burden to her family, to the club... Hell, even to Ryder.

If it wasn't for her, he'd be home doing whatever the man did instead of holed up in this cabin on a mountain alone with her.

She lifted the bottle again and took another swig.

She was such a waste of space. Why the hell did Ryder want to fuck her? Was it because she'd pushed him to it? Would he have done it otherwise?

She took another drink, twisted the cap back on and headed back to the cabin.

She needed to brush her teeth and hide the whiskey before he returned.

Chapter Eight

Ryder put two plates on the table and stared at Kelsea. She'd kept herself busy since he came back into the cabin about an hour ago.

She'd been cleaning, like he asked. Though, he never expected her to listen.

He pursed his lips as he watched her ass wiggle back and forth in his boxers as she scrubbed at one of the windows.

What had gotten into her?

This wasn't the Kelsea he knew. In fact, her behavior made him a little suspicious.

"Dinner," he called.

"I'm almost done with this one."

"No, you're done now. You can finish tomorrow. It's late and we need to eat."

By the time he returned with two field-dressed groundhogs, had skinned them and threw them in the smoker, the sun had already started to set.

It took the pigs two hours to smoke just right. Which made it a lot later than he wanted to eat. Which meant he had no patience for her dawdling right now.

He had shredded the meat off the bones outside and

buried the skin, bones and everything else they wouldn't use out in the woods away from the cabin.

Now he had perfectly smoked, shredded whistle pig mixed with a hickory BBQ sauce, topped with a bit of local homemade coleslaw, and a touch of horseradish all piled up on a fresh roll on their plates. To the side of that, he'd spooned a healthy portion of bean salad he'd picked up at the grocery store's small deli counter. The two glasses of sweet tea he'd put out earlier were starting to sweat.

Between the chili and the bean salad, no one should be lighting a match in the cabin any time soon.

He pulled his seat out and glanced over to where she was still working. "Darlin'. Dinner. Now."

"In a sec."

His brows furrowed and in a few long strides, he was at the window she was cleaning, yanking her off the chair she'd been standing on to reach all the panes.

She squealed in surprised.

He met her wide eyes as he held her in his arms. "When I say now, I mean now. Not when you feel like it. This ain't your mother's place, it's mine. I make the rules. It'd be best if you remember that."

"It'd be best if you remember that I'm here against my will. So, your rules don't mean shit."

He pursed his lips as he considered her. "What happened to the Kelsea who was ridin' my dick earlier?"

"Dick only goes so far. Maybe you need to remember that, too."

He raised a brow. "Do I?"

"You can put me down now."

"Down over my knee again?"

Her chest rose and a shaky breath slipped from between her soft, kissable lips. It was not only hard to ignore those but also her pebbled nipples visible under the undershirt she was wearing.

His dick couldn't ignore those, either. He let her slide down his front until she was on her feet. "Spankin' you won't be punishment, so go." He pointed toward the table. "Let's eat while I think of a better punishment for one, when you lie to me, and two, when you talk back."

"I'll like it all," she said as she headed to the table, a flush in her cheeks and a sparkle in her eye.

"Brat," he mumbled under his breath. Problem was, he'd like to give it all to her, too. Too much so.

He watched as she pulled out the other chair and plopped her ass in the seat. Without even a glance in his direction, she lifted the sandwich and took a big bite.

"Must've forgotten your manners," he grumbled as he moved to the table and settled across from her. "I'm sure your momma taught you some."

"What she should've taught me was not to fuck assholes. That was a life lesson she and I both could've benefited from."

He tilted his head as he watched her shove the thick sandwich into her mouth and take another big bite. "No one's forcing you to fuck assholes."

She swallowed, then shrugged. "You're right. I guess I prefer them. Must take after my mother in that regard."

He dropped his gaze to his plate, picked up his sandwich and took a bite of his own. Damn, that shit was good.

"I don't like beans."

He swallowed his mouthful and chased it with some sweet tea. "And?"

"Next time get something else."

He sucked on his teeth, waited for a moment for his blood pressure to settle, then said, "Next time you're makin' the meal. I gave you enough time to settle in, now the cookin' is on you. You want me to smoke meat, I'll do it. But other than that, it's all you, darlin'. You turned your nose up at my chili, now you're turnin' it up at the best bean salad in a hundred-mile radius. You make a list of what I need to pick up on my next run and I'll do so. But I can tell you it's not gonna be a box of cereal and a gallon of fuckin' milk."

"I don't cook."

"You do now."

"I don't have any recipes and don't have the internet to look any up."

"Gotta binder full of my granny's recipes. Don't need the internet." He picked up his glass and took another sip of his tea. She was going to have to make that, too. And learn just how sweet he liked it.

"I can borrow your phone."

"No service up here."

"How did you talk to Diesel, then?"

"Carrier pigeons."

She put the remainder of her sandwich down and stared at him. "I'm not allowed to lie but you are?"

"You're catchin' on, darlin'."

She opened her mouth, then shut it and picked up her sandwich again.

"Good choice."

She lifted a brow. "What?"

"Not talkin' back."

She rolled her eyes and shoved the last bite of her sandwich into her mouth. "Damn, that was good. I need another one of those."

He tipped his head toward her plate. "Soon as you eat your beans."

She shoved her plate away, patted her belly and lied, "I'm full."

"What'd I tell you about lyin'?"

"I forget."

He snorted and shoveled bean salad into his mouth.

She eyed his sandwich. "That was good meat. You might

have to tell Ace how to smoke his venison like that. It's never been that good."

"I would if it was venison. Ain't deer season, darlin'."

Her gaze lifted to his and she pursed her lips. "Rabbit?"

He smiled down at his plate and picked up his sandwich. "Nope."

She sat back in her chair and stared at him. "What was it?"

"Said I was makin' smoked whistle pig, proof that you don't listen."

"That wasn't the name of the recipe?"

"It is, but it's also the source of the protein." He lifted his head again and met her eyes. "Your uncle likes to hunt, then?"

"Yes... Ryder... what is it?"

"Dinner."

"Well, whatever it is, it's good. I'm sure the leftovers will be even better tomorrow night for dinner. If we're careful enough, it might even last until we go home in a couple days."

"Better dig through those recipes and make a grocery list. This groundhog will only last for our lunches, not our dinners, too." He forked more beans into his mouth, chewed slowly and waited.

He heard the scrape of her chair but concentrated on his plate to hide his grin.

When he heard her making noise in the kitchen he looked up, expecting her to be having a hissy fit about eating an oversized rodent that could predict the weather.

What he saw surprised him. She was scooping more groundhog meat from the aluminum pan onto a roll.

"What are you doin'?"

"Well, since it's not going to last, I'm eating another one. And fuck those beans."

He shook his head and bit back a laugh. "You're just itchin' to be punished for disobeyin', aren't you?"

She glanced over her shoulder and winked at him. "Abso-fucking-lutely."

He winked back at her and no longer hid his grin.

She held up the plastic bag of rolls. "Want another one?"

"Abso-fucking-lutely. But you're gonna eat your beans."

She turned back to the counter. "We'll see."

Yes, we will.

HIS FINGERS SKIMMED over her ass as she laid naked on her belly on the bed.

"I thought you were going to punish me for disobedience, back-talking and lying."

"Maybe the punishment will be not givin' you what you want."

"Well then, I don't want to be spanked."

"There you go lyin' again."

She buried her face into the pillow, her body shaking next to him. Good to see she was easily amused.

He continued to trail his fingers over her ass, his eyes following his hand's movement. "Does it hurt?"

She stilled and turned her head to face him, her left cheek now on the pillow. "A little but nothing I can't deal with."

"I've never struck a woman like that before."

Kelsea drew herself up on her elbows and glanced down at him. "You've never spanked a woman before?"

"Oh no, I have. Just not with the fury I was feelin' when I spanked you."

Her brows furrowed slightly. "I drove you to it," she said softly.

"Darlin', that does *not* make it right. That's not the man I am nor is it the man I ever want to be."

"Then you can make it up to me."

"Well, I was already plannin' that, but now that you mentioned it—"

"Now I mentioned it, you won't give me what I want. I mean what I *don't* want!" she quickly corrected, then muffled a curse into the pillow and kicked her feet against the mattress in an overly dramatic display.

He bit his lip to keep from laughing out loud. She was a pain in his ass, but, *fuck*, if he'd be able to keep his hands off her for the next week or so. Or however long he deemed it necessary they remain holed up in his cabin.

He shouldn't touch her. By touching her he was stepping into some potentially sticky shit. Shit he might not be able to wipe off the sole of his boot.

Once again, he thought about how he shouldn't have lost his temper. The first time by bringing her here instead of delivering her directly to Diesel. The second by spanking her on the ATV.

He hardly ever lost his temper. But the woman naked on his bed had pushed him to do it twice in two days.

He knew her well enough that she might never get her shit together and any intention he had to help her may be wasted.

He liked a soft, pliable woman. One who enjoyed tending to his needs without a lot of back-talk or headache.

Kelsea was not that. Not even close.

Probably never would be, either.

And, to be honest, if she did become that, he might be a little disappointed. He didn't want to extinguish that wild fire, he just needed to reduce it to a controlled burn.

The only problem was, he didn't want to end up scarred for life from touching those flames. And with the dumpster fire Kelsea was, he was taking that risk.

Fucking her once could be chalked up to an error in judgement. Doing it a second time was no longer a mistake. It was a conscious choice.

A bad one.

He needed to get off the bed, pull on some clothes and go sleep on the couch.

Was he going to do that?

Fuck no.

Stupid motherfucker.

But was the pussy worth the problems?

At this point, also no.

He'd dealt with a lot of shit in his life. Especially during his time in the military as an Army Ranger. He'd dealt with shit that even had its own shit.

But it made him who he was today.

Kelsea was the exact opposite; she'd always had it easy. And sometimes acted like a spoiled brat. Maybe her family wasn't rich—not that the Doughertys were hurting financially—but she'd always had someone looking out for her. Maybe not a parent, but her cousins, her club "sisters," and the whole damn DAMC family. Her mother, Annie, wasn't as bad as Kels made her out to be. The woman had just made a couple mistakes. And one of those mistakes was Kelsea's father.

The fact was, someone was always there for her if she needed it and, in turn, she just spat in all their faces.

Finding out who her father was, was a low hit. Knowing what a rotten motherfucker he was, was also hard to swallow. He got that. But it wasn't enough reason for her to spin out of control like she had.

Her life was a million times better than a lot of the women he'd seen overseas during his tours. She didn't realize just how good she had it.

Somehow, she needed to see what she did have and

learn to appreciate it. He had no idea how to go about even beginning to open her eyes to that. None.

While he was on the outside and could see it clearly, she was in the midst and was blind to it. Or maybe she was just ignoring what she'd had all her life. Support. Love. Family.

Things some others would kill for.

"Are we naked for a reason?"

He turned his head to study her. "You in a rush? Got somewhere to go?"

She had finally used the brush he'd bought her, since her hair now laid like golden silk across her bare shoulders. It was long enough to drape over her arms and onto the bed.

Fuck, did he want to fist that hair and fuck her smart mouth.

In fact, that might be the perfect punishment. And it at least would keep her quiet.

He grinned.

Her blue eyes narrowed. "What?"

"Think I just figured out your punishment."

"Oh yeah?"

"Yeah."

"Am I going to like it?"

"It's punishment, darlin'. "

"Oh yeah, right. I'm definitely not going to like it then," she said.

Not sure about you, but I fuckin' will.

"So now what?"

"So now you get off the bed and get on your knees on the floor."

"Now?"

"I'm pretty damn sure I included that word in my instructions."

Did she just roll her eyes at him?

As she climbed off the bed, he asked, "Ever been tied up before?"

She hesitated but didn't turn to look at him. "Once."

"Did you like it?"

"No."

"Why?"

She finished getting off the bed, took a few steps away before turning and slowly getting to her knees. She met his eyes as she answered, "I just didn't."

"I need a reason, darlin'."

"I just didn't."

She was avoiding the truth for some reason. For now, he'd let that go. But they might have to revisit that again in the near future.

"Well?" she asked as she perched on her knees, naked as the day she was born.

"Well what?"

"I'm waiting."

"Maybe that's your punishment."

"Your hard-on is trying to reach the ceiling, so I doubt me sitting here is the punishment."

She was right. He was rock hard in anticipation of what he was about to do next. "Maybe I'm gonna jack off while you watch."

"That wouldn't be any fun."

He sighed. She was right about that, too.

He rolled off the bed and onto his feet. As he studied her kneeling on the floor, her blonde hair falling softly around her face and shoulders, her lips curved in a naughty grin and her blue eyes holding some wicked thought, he wondered what she'd be like if she was always so compliant.

Again, would he want that? Would that be Kelsea?

Her eyes followed him as he approached her slowly, his fingers gripping the root of his dick.

He stopped directly in front of her. The crown of his cock just a few inches from her parted lips.

"How is this going to be punishment?" she whispered, her tongue darting across her bottom lip.

He bit back a groan at that. "Because you won't be able to speak, whether to back-talk or otherwise. And I'll get to enjoy some blessed silence."

"That won't be the only thing you'll be enjoying."

"Depends on how good you are."

Her eyes flicked up from his dick to him. "Never had a complaint before."

"Had a lot of dick in your mouth, darlin'?" *Damn it.* He really didn't want to know, so he hoped she didn't answer it. And luckily, she ignored it, once again focusing on his cock, which now had a bead of precum at the very tip.

In fact, when she finally opened her mouth to answer, he stepped forward and pressed his dick in between her lips to stop that answer. Her hand came up and gripped him. And, *fuck*, she was right, he wasn't going to complain. Not yet, anyway.

He grabbed two tight handfuls of her hair at the back of her head and ordered, "Hands off."

Her eyes flicked up to his again and he was surprised when she listened and dropped her hands to his thighs. He was okay with that because she was going to need to hold on, he just didn't want her controlling the pace or how deep he was about to take it.

Her eyes widened as he began to do what he fantasized about, fuck her face. With a tight grip on her hair, he plunged his dick in and out of her hot, wet mouth with each thrust of his hips.

He figured if she gagged, he'd back off slightly, but until then, he was going to give her everything he could without hurting her.

She made a noise around his length and he watched her carefully to make sure it wasn't too much. When her hand came up, he grabbed it and placed it back on his thigh.

"If it's too much, you tap twice, darlin'. But do your best not to tap out."

Her eyelids got heavy but her eyes heated as she stared up at him, her mouth a stretched *O* around his cock, her cheeks expanding and contracting with each thrust.

He guided her head with two hands wrapped in her long hair and, *fuck*, he hadn't had head this good in a long fucking time.

Too fucking long.

Between the wet heat, the suction and her tongue, she was wreaking havoc on him. His heart was pounding, his mind racing, his hips twitching, and his balls were ready to explode.

Damn. She was good. So good that he was going to blow his load too quickly. She knew just what to do with that mouth of hers to take him there.

He wasn't sure if he should be happy about that or disturbed. Now was not the time to think about her history.

He began to thrust so deeply a tear escaped the corner of her eye. But she didn't tap her fingers against him. She wasn't indicating he should stop, so he didn't. In fact, she sucked more enthusiastically, moaning around him like it was the best thing she'd eaten in a long time.

Good thing she liked dick more than she liked beans.

A groan vibrated up her throat and she dug her nails into his skin.

He released her hair and began to pull out, but she grabbed the back of his thighs and leaned forward, keeping him deep.

Jesus fuck. He thought she was suffering, but now he was.

He was about to lose it. "Darlin', gonna make me come doin' that. You can let go if you want."

She didn't. She began to suck more intently.

"Darlin'," he groaned. "Gonna come."

That would end up being his last warning.

With a grunt, he thrusted forward and spilled himself at the back of her mouth, down her throat and she didn't stop, she continued to run her tongue up and down the thick ridge of his cock and sucked even harder.

He jerked and his fingers found her head again. This time to pull her off.

His head fell forward with his eyes closed and he was doing his best not to pant like one of his late grandpap's hounds after it treed a squirrel.

"That was quick," he heard.

He opened his eyes and stared down at her, still on her knees, amusement on her face.

"Been a while," he grumbled with a frown.

"We just had sex earlier. You should've been able to hold out longer than that."

Fuck.

He tucked a finger under her chin and lifted her face up. "Next time it won't be your mouth, it'll be your ass."

A slow grin crossed her face. "I'll like that, too."

He dropped his hand and headed to the bathroom, slamming the door shut behind him.

AFTER HEARING THE SLAM, Kelsea got to her feet and stared at the closed door. She curled her fingers into fists and ground the heels of her palms into her eyes as she fought the urge to scream.

She was struggling to keep from crawling out of her skin. She needed to take the edge off, but there was no way he was going to stay in the bathroom that long. Maybe the sharpness would dull once he came back out and fucked her.

She looked with longing over to where she had hidden the whiskey. Her gaze slid back to the closed bathroom door and then to the bed.

Her decision was made for her when she heard the water stop running in the sink. She hurried to the bed and climbed on, not bothering to get under the sheets. Instead, she propped two pillows under her head, draped her hair around her shoulders, and pinched her nipples until they were peaked.

He wouldn't be able to resist her.

Would he?

No. Impossible.

She heard the door open. *Look natural. And sexy. Sultry. And not like the pain in the ass he thinks you are.*

Kelsea snorted. She was losing it.

Well, that was to be expected when she was stuck on a mountain somewhere in Kentucky without any connection to the outside world.

As Ryder stepped out of the bathroom, she lost her breath as she watched him approach.

His broad chest, his muscular arms, the slight ridges in his stomach, his sexy, defined obliques—*phew*— which pointed in a V to all the goodness below. She'd had bigger, but she'd had smaller, too. And he was no slouch. He kept the wiry hair trimmed around the root of his cock, which was semi-soft at the moment as it swung between lean, but muscular thighs with each step he took.

He might be some former Special Forces badass, but he was also a country bumpkin and that made him endearing. However, he was stubborn, too, and that made him frustrating.

Good thing she was just as stubborn.

Her mouth opened as he turned off the light on the nightstand on his side of the bed and climbed in. Her head jerked up as he yanked one of the pillows she'd been using out from under her and stuffed it under his own head. He squeezed and hit it a couple of times to get it just right, then, with a sigh, settled in.

She snapped her gaping mouth shut. "Uh..."

"'Night, darlin'."

"Um..."

"'Night," he said more firmly, wiggling deeper under the covers.

"I think you forgot something."

"Nope. Turned off the bathroom light, didn't I?"

Her gaze slid over to the open bathroom door. "Yes."

"Then I didn't forget anything."

"Me."

"What about you?"

"You forgot to do me."

"Up here, it's not all about you. One of the lessons you're gonna learn while here."

"Are you serious? You're going to leave me hanging like that?"

He flipped over onto his back, tucking his arms under his head and yawned loudly, not even bothering to cover his gaping pie hole.

"Oh no."

"Oh yeah, darlin'. Like I said, from the moment I dragged you outta that Demons' cum-stained bed, your life was no longer your own. I own your ass right now. And until I think you're ready to head back to Shadow Valley with a new attitude, that's the way it's gonna be."

"But I—"

He waved a hand half-assed toward where she gave him head. "That there wasn't for you. It was for me."

"Well, that's fucking selfish."

He turned to his side and propped his head on his hand as he stared at her. "Damn right it was. Gettin' a little of your own medicine."

"I'm not selfish."

He snorted and flopped onto his back again.

"I just gave you head." Not only that, she swallowed. That was far from selfish.

"Thanks."

"I don't want thanks."

"Okay, then. I take it back."

"I want fucked."

"Oh darlin', you're going to get fucked. But you don't get to decide when. That head job was punishment, not to get you warmed up."

"But it got me 'warmed up.'"

He didn't say anything.

"Look how hard my nipples are."

"Saw 'em."

"You don't want to—"

"Nope," he cut her off. "It's late. Time for bed. Turn off your light."

She glanced at the lamp with what looked like a deer skin shade on her side of the bed. Oh no, she wasn't turning that off. And she wasn't done.

Not only had her blood been humming since giving him that blow job, she'd also been wet and throbbing with anticipation. He wasn't going to be the only one who went to bed sexually satisfied. She still needed not only a release, but to tamp down her edginess. And that wasn't going to happen just by closing her eyes and trying to go to sleep.

If he wasn't going to help, then...

She'd help herself.

Chapter Nine

What the fuck.
What. The. Actual. Fuck.
He was *not* going to react. Fuck no, he was going to pretend he was sleeping. That's what he would fucking do.

She was not lying next to him touching herself, squeezing her own fucking tits, moaning, sighing, groaning.

No, she wasn't.

He inhaled a deep, slow breath, trying to remain as quiet as possible. Not that it would matter, she was making so much noise, she wouldn't have heard the whimper he released.

His cock was like a steel rod, throbbing as if it had a heart of its very own. He wasn't going to touch it. He was going to ignore it.

Because if he reacted, she would win. She would get what she wanted. And she wouldn't be learning a lesson which she needed to learn.

One being, the Earth didn't revolve around her. Another being, some of her actions affected others.

Right now, her actions were affecting him. *Godfuckindamnit.*

He turned his head just slightly until he could see her out of the corner of his eye.

Big mistake.

Huge. Just like his erection, which was tenting the sheet. But it wasn't like he could hide it. For fuck's sake, if he turned to his side it would be like the kick stand on his Harley.

Her head was thrown back on the pillow, her neck arched, her eyes squeezed shut. Her mouth parted and all kinds of dick-hardening sounds were rising from those lips.

The ones that had been wrapped around that dick so expertly not even ten minutes ago.

Her knees were cocked, and she had one hand on her breast, her fingers twisting and pulling on her nipple and the other...

The other was tucked between her legs but he couldn't see what she was doing.

Not that he needed to see it.

He knew.

He knew exactly what she was doing because her hips were rocking back and forth on the mattress.

He dug deep to find the willpower he knew he had. Somewhere. It was there somewhere. Willpower honed from years of sacrifice while in the military.

The self-control he'd learned from being in some of the shittiest places on the face of the earth, dealing with some of the shittiest humans for the shittiest reasons.

Kelsea was just a female. A woman. A brat. A bratty woman trying to get her way.

He could ignore her.

She'd be done soon... hopefully... then she could turn off the light and go to sleep.

Yep, that was going to happen. Anytime now.

For fuck's sake.

He carefully rolled to his side, away from her, and muffled his groan into the pillow.

Why? Why did she tempt him so much?

She shouldn't.

She was the opposite of what he liked.

Pliant and pleasant. Sweet. Happy. Uncomplicated.

However, that wasn't what his dick liked. Not right now, anyway.

No, his dick would be perfectly fine with complicated, smart-mouthed, stubborn and reckless.

His brain and his dick warred with each other. Unfortunately, his dick was winning.

No, it wasn't that his dick was winning, it was pulling his brain over to the dark side, convincing it that they were two consenting adults and what happened in this cabin remained in this cabin.

It would go no further.

Once the time here was over, he was taking her home to Shadow Valley and, if she was lucky, he might be kind enough to slow the car down before pushing her out when he delivered her back to Diesel.

No lingering. No explanations. No nothing.

He was done after that.

She'd be out of his hair. No longer his job. Because if it was last thing he did, her ass would be straightened out.

And this was why he had to resist her.

He couldn't give in.

He couldn't step in that muck.

But his dick wanted to get dirty. Really dirty.

He sank his teeth into the pillow and struggled not to scream.

He'd suffered before. Plenty of times. He knew what it was like to suffer. This should be a piece of cake.

It was just pussy.

Just pussy.

He didn't need it.

Fuck.

She wasn't just pussy.

No, she was a blonde-haired, smart-assed vixen who had tempted him one too many times.

He'd been wanting to teach her a lesson for months.

Every other time he'd saved her ass, he'd resisted doing so.

He'd been strong.

He'd known it would be a mistake.

But he'd already made one too many missteps these last couple of days.

What would one more be?

He was a man after all. Who could blame him for making another mistake? No one.

Fuck.

He jackknifed up in bed, not daring to look at her. It had sounded like she came once and was working on number two.

His eyes slid to his jeans, which were draped over a chair in the corner. He had one condom left in his wallet. He didn't keep them in the cabin because he'd never brought a woman here before. This was his sanctuary. His escape for when the world started closing in.

Note to self: pick up more condoms on that trip to Walmart.

Because there was no way he was fucking her without one. Not after seeing some of the situations he'd pulled her out of.

She hadn't been picky. And that was putting it mildly.

Though, that needed to change, too. No more reckless, random fucks.

She needed to get on the straight and narrow and settle down like that rest of her club sisters. She needed to find a good man who could deal with her ass and bring her to heel.

She also needed to reconnect with her blood and club family. She needed to toe the line with them.

But right now, she needed to get fucked.

With a curse under his breath, he grabbed his wallet out of his jeans, found the last condom and stared at it.

He should slice it with his knife was what he should do, then that would stop what he was about to do next.

He slowly turned back to the bed and even with only the one small lamp, he could see the flush in her face, her bottom lip tucked between her teeth and the pebbled peaks of her nipples caused by her own fingers. But her blue eyes were on him. Heated. Beckoning him.

As if he was a puppet and she held the strings, he slowly moved to the end of the bed, so he could clearly see what she was doing.

With the condom in a death grip in one hand, he climbed onto the bed, between her legs, and after spreading them wider and removing her hand, he dropped his head to take one long lick from the very bottom of her pussy all the way up to her clit.

She was slick from at least one orgasm, possibly two. Her taste and musky scent were all woman. He sucked the hard nub into his mouth, not being gentle at all.

Kelsea cried out and bucked against him. He did it again, making sure his teeth scraped her roughly. Her hands grabbed his head, encouraging him to continue.

But this wasn't about her getting what she wanted.

He wasn't her puppet. He would never be her puppet. She might have had that control with other men.

But not him.

Never him.

This was his fucking cabin, his rules.

He lifted his head. "Hands off."

Her fingers flexed against his scalp then dropped to her sides before sliding up to her breasts.

He shook his head slightly. "Hands off. Palms flat on the mattress at your sides. Keep them there. You do not touch yourself, you do not touch me."

He expected her to bitch or whine, but she didn't. She just smiled.

Which should worry him.

Starting from the bottom, he licked her again like he was catching the drip from a melting ice cream cone. When he nibbled at the top, her hips jerked.

He did it again, this time letting the tip of his tongue separate her plump folds on his way up. All the while he'd kept his eyes tipped up to her.

Watching.

Waiting for her to disobey.

Waiting for any reason to take her over his knee again. This time not in anger, but simply to teach her a lesson.

He flicked the tip of his tongue against her clit, then alternated sucking it hard. He didn't stop until she was writhing on the bed, though she managed to keep her palms planted on the mattress as she was told. Her head lifted as she stared down at him and he met her gaze, watching her carefully. Shallow breaths escaped through her parted lips like the steam from a locomotive.

When her head slammed back into the pillow, he released her and rose to his knees.

Her eyes opened wide and her expression of disbelief quickly morphed into one of anger. "No!" she screamed, her hands no longer flat but balled into fists and she pounded them into the bed. "No! You don't get to do that. Not again."

He wiped the back of his hand across his mouth and reminded her, "My cabin. My rules. While here, your ass is mine, Kelsea."

With a frustrated growl she began to roll over, kicking

him hard in the process while he was still perched between her calves.

After catching his balance, he grabbed her flailing ankle and yanked it hard, pulling her all the way over until she laid flat on her belly.

"I just told you your ass is mine." He slapped one of her cheeks hard. He watched her ass ripple under his palm. "Get it up."

"Fuck you!"

"Yup." He grunted and grabbed the ankle of the other foot that made solid contact with his solar plexus. *Fuck*, that hurt.

He had to hesitate for a second. Catch his breath. Gather his control. Because what he really wanted to do might hurt her.

He'd hurt her once, even though she denied it, but he wanted to make sure he didn't hurt her again. No matter how much she was driving him to it.

But she wanted it. She wanted to antagonize him to that point of anger.

He had no idea why.

Had she done it with others? Pushed them until they got rough with her? Got physical?

Why?

Why did she need that? Did she get off on it?

There was a sweet edge of pain that he could give her without taking it over the top. If she needed it, she could ride that edge, get off on it, but still enjoy the pleasure that went along with it.

That was if he wanted to give her any pleasure. Right now, he wasn't feeling so generous.

He smacked her ass again. "Ass up. Not gonna tell you again."

"Fuck you."

"Darlin', words aren't gonna hurt me. Roadside bombs,

land mines, fifty caliber weapons will. Tellin' me to go fuck myself is child's play. Gonna let your ankles go, if you kick me again, you *will* regret it."

With a muffled scream into the pillow, as soon as he released her ankles, she pulled her knees under her and lifted her hips off the bed until her ass was in the air like he demanded.

Her pussy was open and shiny. She could fight him all she wanted but there was no denying she wanted him. He dragged a finger through that wetness and instead of a scream this time, she muffled a groan into the pillow.

Fuck me. She was getting what she wanted in the end. She knew how to play the game and he had fallen right into it.

She was smart and cunning. And all of that she wasted by not putting it to good use. If she only put all that energy into something worthwhile...

Damn fucking shame, it was.

"You keep your head down and your ass up. You don't touch yourself. You don't touch me. You take what I give you and nothing more. You got me?"

"Fuck you."

He used his teeth to rip open the condom, then spit the wrapper out after pulling the condom out. He rolled it on, his cock flexing in anticipation as he did so.

Instead of his finger, he used the head of his latex-covered cock to slide through her wetness a second time. He held on tightly to her hips so she wouldn't push back and impale herself on him.

She wasn't going to take control. It was his. His cabin. His rules. She needed to get with the fucking program.

He pulled away slightly and ran his thumb next through her slit, gathering the slickness before finding the tight hole that was tempting him.

It would serve her right if he took her there instead, not letting her come.

He pushed the pad of his thumb against her and she relaxed, inviting him in.

She wanted it there. *Fuck.* Now he should deny that want.

Or at least show her what she could have if she decided to stop being a brat.

If she did, he'd give her anything and everything she wanted.

He pressed the tip of his thumb into her and buried it up to the first knuckle.

She groaned again, turned her head and hissed "yes" at him. "Give it to me that way."

He ignored her because if she kept encouraging him, he just might do that. He pushed forward until his thumb was completely inside the hot, tight canal.

"Ryder," she groaned, jamming her hips back.

He plunged it in and out of her as her fingers gripped the sheets and she cried out.

Fuck. What hadn't this woman done? What didn't this woman like?

A shudder swept through him when she begged, "Please."

He steeled his resolve. This wasn't supposed to be for her.

This was to teach her a lesson.

Wasn't it?

Damn skippy.

He slipped his thumb from her and, once again, gathering her own wetness first, he slipped one finger back in and then a second. She was so tight. He scissored his fingers in an attempt to stretch her. She cried out, her sphincter squeezing him even tighter.

"Relax," he whispered, watching her body tense. Maybe he was wrong. Maybe she hadn't done this before.

Could there actually be one part of her that remained untouched?

He wasn't going to ask because he didn't want to hear the answer. He'd simply believe that was true.

"Ryder," she groaned. "Please."

He loved that word on her lips way too much.

"Please what, darlin'?"

"Fuck me."

"You askin' or demandin'?"

Her hesitation was too long for his liking.

His fingers slipped from her as she dropped her hips to the mattress. "Are you trying to break me? Is that your goal?"

He curled over her back, pressing his mouth to her ear, growling, "Yes, darlin', I'm tryin' to break you. Of bad habits, of an attitude that alienates those who love and care about you. Of not caring about yourself."

He traced the tip of his tongue around the delicate shell of her ear. He pushed her hair out of the way and scraped his teeth down her neck and over her shoulder. He paused for a moment then sank his teeth deep into the curve of her neck.

She bucked underneath him as she cried out. With one hand tangled in her hair, he grabbed her hip and plunged inside her.

She was soft and hot and wet... Her core squeezed him tight as she gasped and groaned and hitched her hips up to an angle he knew would help him hit all the right spots.

He warred with himself whether to leave her hanging this time or to let her have the release she so wanted.

He wanted to teach her a lesson of patience, but how could he when he had none of his own right now.

He wanted to teach her a lesson of being malleable, but

how could he when he wanted nothing more than her to be a wildcat.

He wanted to teach her a lesson of selflessness, but how could he when denying her release appeared more selfish on his part.

He couldn't deny her when he wanted to see her squirming in ecstasy. With pleasure, with an orgasm.

He unclamped his teeth from her flesh, kissing the spot where he bit her, working his way back down her neck. He sucked on her skin at the top of her spine and her hips pushed back against him with every slow thrust he took.

Because he wanted it to be unhurried, careful and worthwhile.

Yes, she needed to learn life was more about just her, but sex was not the way to teach her.

He needed to find another way. Some way to open her eyes. To show her that life could be good, great even, if she actually cared.

She needed to care.

About herself.

About the people that surrounded her.

Not about him.

No. He didn't belong in her life.

Not now. Not ever.

This was such a bad idea.

Bringing her here.

Fucking her.

Because, *fuck him*, being inside her was pulling something from him. Something he didn't want to acknowledge.

The desire to take care of her was strong. Seeping into his pores, running through his veins, fogging his mind, squeezing his heart.

His head was fucking with him. That's all it was.

Sex caused a biological reaction, not an emotional one.

He needed to remember that.

Dig down deep for that willpower. To resist.

To resist that urge to want to take care of her. To resist feeling something other than sexual attraction. To resist the urge to do more than just help drag her from that dark pit she'd been wallowing in. That recklessness, that obvious cry for help.

He didn't need a headache like her. Someone who fought him at every turn.

Pliable. Pleasant. That was what he wanted.

That wasn't who was beneath him.

He pressed his forehead into her back and after a moment of trying to settle his thoughts, he dragged his tongue up her spine. Tucking his arm under her hips, he hitched them higher and his fingers found where they were connected. Found where she was so soft, and he was very hard.

They were so different.

One doing his best to be responsible. The other doing her best to be the opposite.

Finding her clit firm, swollen and slick, he circled it, grinding the pad of his finger against it, feeling her muscles squeeze and ripple around him with each touch, with each thrust.

It became a mindless rhythm, his body automatically moving, bringing the both of them forward until they stood on that cliff, holding hands, waiting...

Waiting to plunge off the edge.

Over and into the abyss that called to them.

He squeezed his eyes shut as she released his hand and fell without him. Her climax convulsing around him, dragging him to that same precipice, where his toes hung over the edge and he teetered.

But he resisted. He held back. He fought the urge to follow her.

"I want to come again. Make me come again." She wasn't demanding. She was breathless and begging.

Instead, he pulled out and without thinking, pressed the head of his cock against the hole he stretched earlier. For a split second, he waited until she clearly knew what came next.

But she was tense, and he had a hard time pushing past that tight ring of resistance.

"Darlin', relax. Let me in."

Her head rolled back and forth on the pillow, her hands still fisting the sheets, a moan escaping her.

"I want to come again," she pleaded.

"You will, just listen for once. Relax. Trust me."

Would she? Trust him?

"Lube," she groaned.

"Darlin', my dick is drippin' with your response. You're wetter than a Louisiana swamp."

"That doesn't sound like a compliment."

"Believe me, it is." He pulled away enough to gather more of her arousal on two fingers and slide it over her puckered hole. He gathered even more, and this time dipped his fingers inside. "Push against my fingers. That's it, darlin'. Push again." As she was still pushing, he slipped his fingers from her and replaced them with his cock, sliding inside with not a lot of resistance this time.

He took it slow, first just the head, then a little more.

The tightness, the heat was making his head spin, but he needed to keep his wits about him.

She lied. If she had anal sex before, it had maybe been once. An experiment, perhaps.

She was not used to this. This was new to her.

Her head lifted off the pillow and she turned to look at him, her blue eyes glassy, her face flushed.

"Okay?" he forced out. For fuck's sake, she needed to say yes.

She nodded. "Keep going..."

Thank fuck.

He pulled her hips up as he moved to his knees. "Keep your head down unless it's uncomfortable." He pushed farther, deeper when she didn't respond but simply listened to his instruction.

He pushed a little deeper, her tight canal squeezing him until he thought either his brains or his balls would explode.

Something had to give.

He wouldn't last long but he did want her to come again. However, she needed to hurry. He was dangling by a frayed thread.

"Darlin'..."

She made a noise, he wasn't sure if it was an answer. Hell, he wasn't even sure if she was listening. He had to assume she was.

"What do you need..."

"Keep... doing what you're doing," she managed to answer.

That he could do.

"On your belly," he commanded, pushing her back down to the mattress.

Digging his knees into the bed, he held on tighter to her hip with one, while he continued to circle and massage her clit with his other. But it was when he slipped two fingers inside her to find her soaked, was when she tensed and cried out.

Thank fuck.

Because when she came, she squeezed him so tightly, he thought he saw stars.

With a grunt, he drove deep one last time and then there was no doubt, he did see stars.

After a few moments, with his heart still thumping, his breath still rapid, he did his best to relieve her of his weight.

He didn't pull out, he wanted to keep that connection just a little longer.

This was when she was pliant and pleasant. When a smile curled her lips, when her eyes were soft. When she wasn't fighting him.

This was who Kelsea was at the core.

He wanted that to last just a little while longer, because while he hoped it would last, he knew it wouldn't.

It was too soon. She was only at the head of the trail, she had a long trek to the end.

"Ryder..."

The men he worked with called him Ryder. His fellow Army Rangers also called him by his last name, among other things. The woman sleeping by his side in his bed should call him by his first name.

"Dwight," he murmured.

"Dwight," she echoed sleepily, snuggling deeper into the bed. "Can you grab me a washcloth or something?"

"Please," he reminded her softly.

"Please, Dwight."

Fuck.

It wasn't said sharply. It wasn't said in her typical smart-ass way. It was genuine.

But it was the next thing she said that got him in the gut. "Thank you."

That was the first time she ever thanked him for anything.

He rolled out of bed to go dispose of the condom and clean up. Halfway to the bathroom he stopped and turned to stare at the woman he thought might never change.

In two days, she had already started to transform. Not completely, but she was headed down the right path.

She just needed to free herself of the heavy chains of drugs, alcohol and bad company that had been dragging her down.

She still had a long road ahead of her. But if she wanted him along for the ride to help, he'd be there.

Because having her in his bed, sleepy and satisfied was a thousand times better than him kicking down doors and dragging her ass out of some questionable situations.

He sucked in a deep breath, pushing a strange ache out of his chest, and headed into the bathroom.

He stood in that tiny room a lot longer than he should have, staring at himself in the mirror. Reevaluating his decisions.

His choices.

His sanity.

Because that woman that was in his bed right now was a threat to it. He'd worked hard to level out. To keep himself that way.

And right now, he felt anything but.

Chapter Ten

THE CABIN WAS dark and quiet except for the slow and steady breathing of the man who slept.

When he'd come back out of the bathroom earlier, he brought a warm, wet washcloth like she'd asked and instead of just handing it to her, he gently cleaned her up.

Afterward, he'd climbed back into bed, and with one arm wrapped around her waist, he'd pulled her tightly against him. Her back to his front. His nose in her hair. His warm breath blowing across her skin as it got slower and louder.

She only wished she could fall asleep that fast. She couldn't. Her brain wouldn't allow it. For when it was dark and quiet, her thoughts began to spin. Her memories fought their way to the forefront.

The ones she kept trying to beat back.

At night it was difficult. And that was the main reason why she found things to do all night. Parties, clubs, a one-night stand, whatever.

It kept those memories at bay. It kept her brain busy. Once the booze or drugs, or exhaustion from sex hit her, she could sleep. Or pass out. Whichever happened first.

It was only then she wouldn't dream.

But tonight, while the sex with Ryder had made her sleepy, when his arm held her like a vise against him, her brain began to spin. Thoughts swirled as if they were debris stuck in the vortex of a funnel cloud.

Every time she tried to get free, his arm tightened even more until she felt as though she was being smothered.

She held herself as still as possible, waiting, hoping he'd eventually sleep so deeply he'd loosen his hold.

After what felt like an eternity, his arm finally dropped, and she carefully wiggled herself free.

She didn't just move to the other side of the bed. She got out, slipped into one of his discarded T-shirts and tip-toed across the cabin.

To the only thing that would help her.

The only thing in the cabin that might stop her racing thoughts.

She moved over to where Ryder hung his hunting gear along the wall. And underneath, a pair of high rubber boots was lined up next to hiking boots, what looked like combat boots, and sneakers.

She grabbed the whiskey bottle from inside one rubber boot where she'd hidden it earlier and took a quick glance over her shoulder to make sure he hadn't moved.

He hadn't.

Bottle in hand, she moved over to the couch and slid to the floor, sitting back against the end he couldn't see from the bed. Slowly, she unscrewed the lid and, putting it to her lips, she took a mouthful, careful not to breathe so she wouldn't cough.

The whiskey's burn as it went down was familiar and she closed her eyes, waiting for the warmth to hit her stomach, the prickle of her nerves to dull.

She lifted it again, this time to judge how much was left. About a third. Maybe enough for tonight, but not enough for tomorrow. She'd have to deal with that when the time came.

She had no idea how.

With no booze, no pot, no other drugs, the only thing left was sex.

Her thoughts went back to the man who slept on the other side of the cabin. She needed to remain quiet, let the booze do its work, so when she got back in bed with him, she'd be able to fall asleep and avoid the nightmares.

Because if he found out about those...

No, he couldn't.

No one could.

No. One. Could.

Not ever.

She lifted the bottle again and took another long swig. The heat in her belly intensifying. She put the bottle down between her feet, and scrubbed her hands over her face, hoping the booze started working soon. She needed to get back in her bubble, where things weren't so painful, so raw.

He didn't understand why she needed this since she wasn't an addict. That wasn't the reason. But she couldn't tell him the truth.

He would never look at her the same again.

No one would.

Everyone would look at her with horror or pity. And she didn't want that. She couldn't handle seeing that in their eyes. It would make everything so much worse.

She needed to protect herself from that. To bear the burden alone.

But that hadn't been working, either.

She had a hard time fighting that darkness alone, even though she kept trying. No one knew just how hard she worked at it. They only assumed she was reckless and out of control.

That she was a brat. A bitch. A dumb cunt.

And yes, she knew D's crew had a nickname for her. DC.

They could claim it stood for "Diesel's cousin" all they wanted, but she was sure that wasn't it.

Ryder wanted to help her, but she was afraid of spreading that darkness to him, of dragging him into that abyss. It wasn't fair he was forced to deal with her time after time, she knew that. Especially when he'd probably dealt with so much in his life already. Why would he be willing to take on her shit, too? Some DC who couldn't get her life together.

He shouldn't. No one in their right mind would.

She grabbed the bottle and took another long sip, regretfully looking at what little remained at the bottom. Not enough.

She finished it off and after quietly placing the bottle back on the floor, she dropped her head to her knees to wait for the alcohol to flow through her system, to dull that sharp edge.

The cabin was too quiet. The noise in her head too loud.

A rush of air hit her and before she could react, a hand grabbed her elbow and hauled her roughly to her feet like she was a rag doll.

"What the fuck!" Ryder roared in her face, making her flinch at his raw fury. He reached down, picked up the empty bottle and shoved it in her face. "What the fuck, Kelsea?"

She opened her mouth, but nothing came out. She had even stopped breathing.

How did he move so quietly? How did she not hear him coming?

He whipped the bottle across the room, and she winced when it exploded against one of the walls.

"I—"

His fingers dug painfully into her arm as he hauled her across the room back toward the bed. "I was stupid to think that I could trust you not to sneak out of bed and do somethin' stupid. Now I'll rectify that by tyin' you to the bed at night."

What?

No. No. No.

"No," she whispered.

"Yes. I can't trust you. And that fuckin' disappoints me..." He spun her around and pointed to the bed. "Sit."

She sat, her body beginning to tremble. "Dwight, please."

"Please what?" When she didn't answer quickly enough, he barked, "Please what?" He scrubbed a hand over his hair and blew out a breath. "I'm so fuckin' disappointed in you."

She bit her bottom lip to keep it from quivering. She tried to steel herself against that disappointment. Because disappointing him disappointed her, too. She lifted her head, fighting back the sting in her eyes. "Join the crowd. You're not the only one."

He shook his head and shoved a finger in her direction. "Don't move. I need to find somethin' to tie you up with."

"No!" she shouted.

"Trustin' you was my mistake. I won't do that again. I have no idea where you found that fuckin' whiskey. I'd cleaned everything out of this place years ago. Everything. I don't know how I missed it. Fuck!"

He began to pace, his eyes searching the dimly lit cabin. He was looking for something to use to restrain her. She must convince him not to do that.

She sucked in a breath when his eyes landed on her again. Searing. Agitated. "Where did you find it?"

Fuck. If she told him, he'd know she'd been snooping around.

He stopped in front of the bed and grabbed her arms

again, giving her a rough shake. "Where did you find that bottle?"

He wasn't going to stop asking until she told him. And he'd figure it out eventually, anyway. "In the shed."

His head shot up, his eyes narrowed. "Where in the shed?"

"In... In the wood cabinet."

He released her and stepped back. His expression changing to surprise when his brows furrowed. "It wasn't locked?"

"No."

His jaw tightened. The anger was back. "What else was in there?"

"Nothing."

"What else did you go through?" he growled.

"Nothing!"

His shoulders lifted slowly as he stared at her. Then he lowered them just as slowly. He was trying to rein in his anger. That wasn't hard to see.

His head spun toward his jeans, still hanging over the chair in the corner and in a few long strides he was there, grabbing the end of his belt and drawing it through the belt loops.

Holy shit. Was he going to strike her with the belt?

"Dwight." She cursed the shake in her voice.

"No, you lost that privilege. You call me Ryder and nothin' else."

"Ryder... You're not going to hit me with your belt." His buckle was large and would cause damage if he did.

His step stuttered on his way back to the bed, he glanced at the belt in his hands with his eyebrows pinned together. "Hit you?" He lifted his head again and looked at her. "I'm not gonna hit you. I'm gonna tie you to the bed."

Fuck. She'd rather feel the sting of that leather on her ass than be restrained to the bed.

"You—" Kelsea struggled to swallow the lump in her throat, because she was having a difficult time getting her words past it. "You can't tie me up."

His head tilted and his eyes narrowed once again. "Says who? You forgot. My fuckin' cabin. My fuckin' rules. You broke those rules. There are consequences for your actions. That's one of the lessons you need to learn. You want to act like a brat, you're going to be treated as one."

"Ryder," she whispered again, then swept her tongue over her dry lips. There wasn't enough booze in the world for her to be tied up. "I'm... I'm sorry."

His eyes widened just long enough for her to catch it, then he schooled his face. "I told you no booze or drugs while you were here. You totally shit all over that."

"I had to—"

"You *had* to? Only addicts 'have to.' You claim you're not an addict."

"I'm..." She dropped her head and shook it. "Just don't tie me up."

"Why, Kelsea? You didn't give me a valid reason earlier when I brought it up."

"I just... can't."

"Why?"

She squeezed her eyes shut.

"Hands out."

Instead of obeying, she curled them into her lap.

"Kelsea."

She turned pleading eyes up to him. Couldn't he see what this would do to her? Did he not have any idea? "Dwight."

He arched a brow at her.

"Ryder, please."

"Tell me why."

"I don't like not being able to escape," she whispered. "I can't escape when I'm tied up."

"That's the point, darlin'. Hands out."

Panic bubbled up from her gut and she felt like she was going to throw up. She slid off the bed and went to her knees at his feet. "I'm begging you. *Please.*"

"You should've thought about the consequences when you drank the whiskey."

"I only needed it to forget. So... So I can sleep."

He grabbed her chin painfully between his fingers and lifted her face to him. "Look at me and don't you fuckin' look away. What do you need to forget?"

She kept her eyes pinned on his and dug deep. She'd rather see the anger than the revulsion. "Nothing."

"Don't you fuckin' lie to me, Kelsea. I told you lyin' would have consequences." He closed his eyes as he blew out a breath, then let those green eyes bore into her as his words crossed his lips as slow as cold tar. "What do you need to forget?"

Her eyes slid to the side and her bottom lip trembled even more. "Nothing."

His fingers tightened on her chin.

He wasn't going to let this go. He'd never let this go.

Maybe he wouldn't tie her up if she told him...

"My father. I need to forget my father."

Chapter Eleven

"We all need to forget your father. He was a total fuckin' piece of shit. He set up what should have been his 'brother' to go to prison for ten years. He tried to have Dex and Brooke killed. He raped Brooke's mother. He raped Diamond, for fuck's sake." Ryder's mouth opened to continue listing Pierce's sins, but there was no point in reminding his own daughter of how horrendous the man was.

She knew.

Of course that was what bothered her, but enough that she couldn't sleep? It didn't make sense. And the escape thing. Why was she afraid of not being able to escape?

The hair on the back of his neck stood and dread landed in his gut like a ton of bricks.

There was something more. Something else that was making her spin out of control since finding out Pierce was her father.

Jesus fuck. He didn't want to know.

But he couldn't ignore it. He couldn't help her if he didn't know the truth. The complete truth.

But fuck him. Fuck him. Fuck him. He didn't want to

know. He didn't want to even begin to wrap his head around what he was thinking. He hoped he was wrong.

He needed to be wrong.

She was just being overly dramatic about her sperm donor being a total piece of shit.

He sucked in a breath in an attempt to tamp down the nausea.

He forced the next question past his lips. "What do you need to forget? Why are you afraid of not being able to escape?"

She jerked her chin from his grasp and turned her head away. She appeared defeated. This was not the Kelsea he knew.

"Kelsea." His heart was now pounding in his throat.

He didn't want to know.

He didn't want to know.

He didn't want to know.

But he needed to.

He couldn't actually get the specific words out, instead he could only ask, "Like Diamond?" hoping it was enough. Also hoping it wasn't, either. That she'd misunderstand and not answer.

Had Pierce done to Kelsea the same he'd done to her club sister? Had he gone that far with not only another underage female, but one who was his own flesh and blood? "Darlin', answer me. Like Diamond?"

She wouldn't look at him. That wasn't a good sign. "I should've said something. I know that now."

"Kelsea, please don't tell me he did the same to you as Diamond," he said in a pained whisper. His lungs seized, then he exploded, "*JESUS FUCK!*" He pressed a hand to his forehead, his blood roaring through him as he spun away from her and strode across the cabin.

He stopped in front of the wall where he'd smashed the whiskey bottle and stared down at the mess.

He understood it now. Kelsea was as shattered as the glass at his feet.

"I was lucky." Though those words were said in barely a whisper, he'd heard them.

He turned his head in her direction. "How's that?" Maybe he was wrong. Maybe it wasn't what he was guessing. For fuck's sake, he needed to be wrong.

But the raw words he didn't want to hear, the truth he no longer wanted to know, punched him right in the gut.

"It was only a couple times. It could've been worse. My mom interrupted him the third time. At the gun shop."

It could've been worse.

How could it have been worse?

Ryder scrubbed his hands down his face. He turned and headed slowly back to her where she still perched on her knees on the floor in front of the bed.

She suddenly looked so young. A broken child as her eyes tracked him as he approached, her face paler than normal. "The first time, I..." She swallowed so hard, he could see it. "I fought him. I scratched him. I bit him. I screamed. He... He got an electrical cord and... and tied my hands behind my back. He... he jammed a bandana in my mouth."

She needed to stop. He couldn't hear the details. Not without losing his shit and becoming a whirlwind of destruction. And that wouldn't do either of them any good. He needed to keep his head on straight. He needed to think clearly. He needed to remember to reserve his anger for those who deserved it.

It wasn't Kelsea. Not at this moment.

"Where was your mother? Why were you alone with him?"

"Because as part of her job at the shop, he'd send her on errands. She'd set me up in the back room with a movie or a video game."

"Your mom didn't know." He didn't pose that as a question because he sure as fuck hoped Annie didn't know. Because if she did and allowed it to happen anyway? She might end up in the same place Pierce did.

No, no "might" about it.

"No, she didn't see it. And she thought I was just being difficult when I refused to go back there."

"What about the scratches and the bites?"

"It was only the first time. I heard him make an excuse why his arms were bleeding."

"Why didn't you tell her?"

"Because he said he'd kill me if I did. And I believed him."

Of course, she did. Pierce had been a snake. Intimidating, manipulative and sneaky. If none of the club brothers knew what he truly was like, then of course, an impressionable young girl would believe anything he said.

"You didn't fight him after the first time?" He hated to have to ask that question, but he needed to know. It was one thing for Annie to believe Pierce's bullshit once, but a second time?

"He said if I kept fighting, he'd do it to someone else." She sucked in a breath and lifted her chin. She was trying to gather strength to say what she said next. He had to steel himself, too. "Ryder, I didn't want him to do it to anyone else. I wanted to save everyone else. But... but I couldn't let him do it anymore."

Jesus fuck. "You didn't save anyone. That was just one of his tactics to manipulate you."

"I know that now. But maybe it would've saved Diamond."

Hold up. That didn't sound right. "Diamond's older than you..."

Oh fuck. Diamond had been maybe fifteen at the time Pierce stole her virginity. Ryder wasn't sure, though. All he knew she was too young and it was against her will. That's all he needed to know. But if...

But if Diamond had been fifteen, it might have happened to Kelsea afterward. "How old were you?"

"Fourteen."

He caught his wince. "He did it to Diamond before you, darlin'. Don't think for one second you're the reason he... That you caused what he did to her. Pierce is the only one to blame in any of this shit. Not you, not Diamond. No one that bastard touched."

Annie should've told Pierce that Kelsea was his daughter. She never should have hidden that fact. Maybe he wouldn't have wanted to step up and be a father, but it might have spared Kelsea the rest. If he knew she was blood...

Ryder wasn't sure if Pierce would have even cared. The man might not have had one fucking shred of decency.

He reached down and helped her to her feet. She didn't need to beg him not to tie her up. He understood her resistance now.

He understood it all. Her behavior. Everything.

Fuck, he was such an asshole.

He pulled her into his arms and held her tight, pressing his lips into her hair. He was fighting back his rage. It was no longer aimed at Kelsea. It was now directed at Pierce. That day in the DAMC clubhouse when so much shit came to light because of Brooke showing up in town...

That truth not only devastated the members of the Dirty Angels MC, but also Diesel's Shadows. They all knew Diesel would want revenge and to remove Pierce from their midst. All six of them were willing to step up and do whatever needed to be done.

All of them. Any and all would have volunteered to take out that trash for the last time. But that choice was taken out of their hands when someone else stepped up and took care of that situation. Someone who felt the need to dole out retribution on Diamond's behalf.

His thoughts returned to the current room, the current situation, the woman in his arms when she mumbled, "I hate her," against his bare chest. "She lied to me. My life was a complete fucking lie."

He had no idea how widespread Pierce's evilness went. Who else besides Kelsea, Diamond and Brooke's mom had he raped?

Had Pierce abused Annie, Kelsea's mother, too? Is that why she kept the truth secret?

None of that made sense. And he couldn't begin to try to understand Annie's thinking. But she should've known Pierce was a dog. He never hid that fact. And she left her young daughter with him. Alone.

"You shut her out, darlin'. Maybe you two need to have a heart to heart. To learn why she did things the way she did. Why she hid the truth. Maybe you need to hear her reasoning."

Her arms looped around his waist, squeezed a little tighter. "I can't talk to her. I can't even look at her right now."

"I know, but she's suffering, too, from the mistakes she made. She loves you, darlin'. That I do know. She's the one who kept on Diesel's ass about findin' you when you'd disappear for days. It wasn't just your sister and Dex. Annie worried more than anyone."

He gave her a kiss on the forehead and released her, letting his hand slide down her arm until he grasped her hand. With a gentle tug, he urged her to climb into bed with him.

He tucked her under the covers and slid in next to her, spooning her close.

He was waiting for her to start crying, to release some of that pent-up emotion she'd been hiding, but she didn't.

And that worried him.

Because, for fuck's sake, he wanted to cry. For her. For Diamond. For everyone whose life Pierce touched and not in a good way.

She needed to find a better outlet to deal with what she was dealing with other than booze, drugs or random acts of sex. It was bad enough when she just thought it was a trusted club brother who violated her. But then to find out it was her own flesh and blood...

So, when she said it could've been worse, he wasn't sure how much worse it could've been. She had to live with that knowledge, those memories of a man who should've been trusted, blood or not, violating that trust.

"In the future, darlin', you need to be completely honest with me. I can't be walking into a situation blind like that. It's not good for me. And definitely not good for you."

She didn't say anything for the longest time. Her breathing was steady as he held her, nuzzling his nose into her hair, wishing things had been different for her.

But they weren't and they needed to move forward from there.

While he was thankful he now knew the truth, the root of her issues, he also knew that truth complicated things. And he wasn't sure what he could do to help her, though, he was willing to try. He used to be exactly like her. He also used to medicate himself with alcohol, pot and one-night stands. It was an easy way to avoid reality. To also avoid the past.

That's why it had been difficult for him to see her in those same situations. Why he hated to be the one to drag her ass out of them. Eventually, he woke up and realized what he was doing.

What he had been doing was destroying himself. Because while trying to wipe out the bad memories, he realized he was wiping out the good ones, too.

While doing everything in her power to forget, she alienated a lot of people who loved her along the way.

But then, no one knew.

Only Kelsea. And now him.

She probably didn't want to tell anyone else, but maybe she needed to. Like Mercy's woman, the therapist. Rissa would probably be willing to help.

"Was it you?" she asked softly.

"Was it me what?"

"Who stripped him of his colors. Who... Did you do it?"

"You know I can't talk about that shit. That goes against our code. Just know this... That man will never hurt anyone again."

Her ribs expanded and contracted under his arm.

"Darlin', you bein' reckless by doin' drugs, gettin' smashed and fuckin' guys you shouldn't, isn't hurtin' him. It only hurts you. I sure hope you were protectin' yourself out there. There was no reason to make things worse."

"If you mean by protection..."

He cut her off because it drove him mad to think of how many guys she'd probably been with. "That's exactly what I mean."

"Always."

"With Slash?" His jaw got tight with the urge to pound his fist into the middle of that guy's face.

"Especially with him."

He should be relieved but picturing her on that filthy mattress with him still got his blood boiling. "Why?"

"Because I knew I wasn't the only one in his bed."

"You mean like that other bitch?"

She took another deep breath. "And others."

"Then what were you doin' with him?"

"Because I didn't care."

"Darlin', you need to start caring about yourself."

She didn't say anything else for the longest time and he thought maybe she had fallen asleep.

He discovered he was wrong when her fingers squeezed his arm. "You're a good man, Ryder."

He closed his eyes. If she only knew.

"Dwight," he corrected her.

"Dwight," she repeated softly. "Hold me until I fall asleep."

He waited for the "please" and it didn't come. But fuck him, he didn't care. He'd do it anyway.

"I'm gonna hold you all night. Not gonna let you go, darlin'."

He kept his word and didn't get a fucking wink of sleep himself. Not when he couldn't get what Pierce did to her out of his head.

Death had been too good for that man.

Chapter Twelve

KELSEA PRESSED her face against Ryder's warm, broad back. She could feel his muscles flexing under her cheek as he steered the ATV up a steep, rocky path. A few times she'd closed her eyes and just enjoy holding onto him. Touching him gave her a sense of security.

Even if it was a false sense, it still felt good.

He had woken her up when it was still dark outside, and she had no idea why. She'd been surprised she'd fallen asleep at all, especially after their conversation and her confession last night.

But she had slept. And like he said he would, he held her all night. In fact, when he woke her by combing his fingers through her hair and whispering her name, he'd been flat on his back, her head on his chest and his arm still around her waist, pinning her to him.

Even though her knee had grazed his morning erection, he didn't do anything about relieving it. She hoped it wasn't because he looked at her any differently after last night.

Or actually, she did.

She hoped he didn't look at her in disgust, a victim of

not only rape but incest, but instead, with understanding and not only of her being a pain in his ass.

She didn't have time to judge his current opinion of her since he had her rush to get dressed. She only had a chance to pee and splash water on her face before he disappeared from the cabin, telling her to meet him out front in a couple minutes and that those two minutes weren't negotiable.

Which basically translated to—as Diesel would say—"No lip."

He didn't say a word when he pulled around to the front of the cabin. He kept the four-wheeler running as she climbed on behind him, wrapped her arms around his waist and he gunned the gas.

That had been ten minutes ago. At first, the path they took was narrow because of the thick of the woods and the overgrowth choking their travel. Now, the trees were thinning out, the path becoming even rockier and the night sky starting to recede.

She had no idea where they were going besides up.

A few minutes later, after her bones and teeth had been rattled loose by the rough ride, they came to a clearing of sorts. A spot only large enough to park the ATV and for them to stand.

That's when she realized he was humming low. Not quite singing but every now and then a word would slip past his lips.

Probably another country song.

Blech.

"Where are we?" she asked as he grabbed her hand and intertwined her fingers with his. He didn't answer, but only kept humming as he jerked his head toward a large boulder that rose out of the earth.

Was she expected to climb that? She only wore flip-flops. Actually, she was wearing socks with her flip-flops because that was one thing he insisted on, even though it was an unattractive look. But it was something to help protect her feet from the underbrush going up the mountain.

She just knew she would not be continuing that fashion statement once she got a real pair of shoes to wear. Hopefully later that day, after his trip to Walmart.

She followed him and realized there was a very narrow foot path around the boulder that couldn't be seen until you were right on it. They skirted the monster rock only to come across more. Actually, a rocky cliff.

Even though dawn wasn't quite upon them, she could see the view was spectacular. The peak of the mountain where his cabin was built overlooked a deep valley and some distant mountain ranges.

She didn't get to appreciate it for long, because he tugged her along, eventually letting her hand go so they could scramble over a few more rocks. Until they came to one that they could stand on at the edge.

Where it seemed she was standing on the very edge of the world.

She could only imagine the beauty of it all when the sun was up.

Fuck. That's why he brought her here at this fucked up hour. The sunrise.

He settled himself down on the boulder and raised his hand to her. Once she took it, he guided her to a seat between his spread legs. She wiggled until her ass couldn't go back any further and his heat enveloped her. Leaning back, she rested against his solid chest.

And, *holy shit*, he began to sing so softly. His deep baritone vibrated from his chest into her back, the melody not only surrounding them but filling her.

She had no idea what the song was or who it was by, but the words made her heart do a somersault.

The lyrics he sang talked about letting him help her get out of the place she was currently in and wiping away her tears. Being safe in his arms and how he wouldn't ever let her down. That eventually her heart would come around and how her life would change one sunrise at a time.

He had his arms around her, clasping her hands on his thighs and he was slightly swaying back and forth.

The words that affected her the most had to be the chorus because he sang those same lines three times.

By the time he was done, the sun was peeking over a distant mountain range and the sky was painted in hues of pink, orange and even a little yellow mixed in with shades of blue.

Absolutely breathtaking.

Just like his voice when he sung softly in her ear.

Just like him.

She wasn't lying last night when she told him he was a good man. He *was* a good man.

And she regretted all the times she gave him a hassle. When her recklessness forced him into situations he didn't want to be in.

She shivered when he swept her hair away from her neck and pressed a line of kisses from a spot behind her ear to the top of her spine.

Reaching behind to cup his face, her fingers brushed along the short, wiry whiskers covering his cheek. He hadn't had time to shave since he was in such a rush.

She liked it.

He probably didn't.

She tilted her head to the side and gave him better access to where he was nibbling, which was the tender spot where her shoulder met her neck. Her nipples pressed into the soft cotton of one of the shirts he had bought her. Cupping the weight of her breasts, his thumbs brushed back and forth slowly over the hard tips.

She leaned her head back against his collarbone and

sighed. It wasn't an impatient sigh, but one of contentment and happiness.

She had always thought telling anyone about what happened to her would make her feel worse. But telling Ryder last night had changed something inside her. As though she now had someone to share that burden with her instead of carrying the heaviness of it on her own.

"I'm not a country fan, but that was beautiful. What song was it?"

"Would you know it if I told you?"

His voice was so low that with his hands on her breasts and lips on her neck, she might orgasm. If that happened, she was going to make him a homemade medal just like the one hidden away in his shed. "No. But it was perfect."

"I know. That's why I sang it. It's called *Sunrise* by Rascal Flatts."

She let her gaze slide over the valley and across the skyline which was beginning to turn more blue with white puffy clouds.

She felt at peace here.

On his mountain.

In his arms.

With him.

Her soul had settled. She wasn't sure how long it would last, but she'd take it while it did. "Thank you."

"For what?"

"Bringing me here." She let him believe she meant to see the sunrise. But it was so much more than that.

"You need to open your eyes to what's around you, darlin'. That's why I did. There's so much beauty surroundin' you, you just need to see it. So many people love you, but you've been blind to it lately."

He was right. Finding out that the man who had molested her when she was young was actually her father made her feel even more dirty. Unclean. Ruined. Tainted. All of it. And she couldn't talk about it with anyone.

Not with her mother, not with the club sisterhood. Not even her half-sister, Brooke, who might understand the most. Who was only born because her mother was raped by their father.

So, no one.

Even though, like Diamond, she had pushed away what happened to her at fourteen, it all became fresh again when she found out that man was her blood. That discovery had festered inside her, ate at her until she couldn't take anymore.

Until she felt like she had splintered into a million pieces and she'd never be whole again.

The truth? And she'd never tell this to anyone, not even Ryder... She wanted to die. She thought that was the only way she'd ever get peace.

But she found it.

Here.

However, she needed to remember that she was his "job." A job he was tired of doing. And had also claimed he wasn't going to do it anymore.

He wanted her to stop her wild ways, so he didn't have to deal with her anymore.

He stated in no uncertain terms, he was "done."

"Do you come up here often?" That sounded like a bad pickup line.

"Whenever I need a reminder that life is worth livin'."

She had no idea why he would need such a reminder. "Why?"

"'Cause, darlin', I've seen things that would make anyone question every aspect of their life. Why some have so much, while others suffer so greatly. We all grow up bein' told life can be unfair, but when you witness that shit day after day, it can get overwhelmin'. That shit starts to drag you down. Sometimes to where that hole is so deep and so dark, you don't know if you can ever climb back out."

His chest pressed into her back as he took a long, deep breath.

Before she could say anything, he continued, "I have questioned many a time if what I did in the Army did more harm than good. I enlisted and took my military career seriously. I wanted to do good. I'm not sure I accomplished that."

"What did you do in the Army as a Ranger?"

He hesitated a little too long. "Whatever they told us to do."

"Like?"

"Missions."

If he didn't want to talk about it, she wouldn't push him. Though, she was curious about the mission that got him that homemade Medal of Valor. "I'm your current mission."

"Yeah, darlin', you are."

Once again, his answer reminded her that she was just his assignment. Nothing more. So, she shouldn't read into anything that occurred during this time on this mountain. "You take your missions seriously."

"Yeah, I do. Not only back then, but for your cousin, too." All the Shadows took their jobs seriously. Diesel had a good crew. A team of men he could rely on. And Ryder was proof of that.

"Have you ever saved anyone's life?" While she knew the answer, she was curious on whether he'd acknowledge it.

It took him a long time before he responded. "Saved a life. Took a life. Did what needed to be done."

"Are you a hero?"

"No, darlin', I'm just a man."

She doubted he was "just a man." The author of that letter she found wouldn't have gone home to his wife and son if it wasn't for him. And she was sure he wasn't the only life Ryder saved.

He was just that type of guy. He was a good man at the core. She couldn't say that enough.

She gave him more of her weight and he accepted it, wrapping his arms around her even tighter.

"When I hit the store later, I'll pick up more condoms. And a pair of shoes for you. You'll just have to jot down your size when we get back."

She wasn't ready to go back. Sitting there on that rock at the top of a mountain in his arms, her head was the clearest it had been in the last couple of years. She could look past the darkness and see that light. Just like the sunrise.

Life at that very moment was simple. A man. A woman. A quiet and peaceful place.

Their own little world.

She didn't want it to end.

"We should get back so you can make breakfast and I can head out."

She trailed her fingers over his forearm. "Not yet. I want to hear you sing another song."

She didn't glance behind her but when his body jerked against her, she knew he was probably shocked at her request.

She was surprised, too, but she knew it would delay their departure and even though she wasn't a country fan, to hear his voice in her ear was as beautiful as the sunrise they'd witnessed. "Do you know anything other than country?"

"Sure, darlin'." Then he started singing in a twang so strong she winced. "My pickup broke down, my hound dog died, my wife left me for my neighbor..." His pitch went off-key, and she covered her ears. "My barn burned down, and my gosh-darn cow ran away from home. Now I'm fresh outta milk."

She whacked his arm. "That's not a song."

"Sure is." His laughter shook her.

That made her smile so big her face ached. "Come on, now."

"Okay, fine. You don't like my Ryder original? Then I'll stick to somethin' someone with more talent wrote. How about this one? It reminds me of you."

What song could possible remind him of her? *Crazy Train* by Ozzy Osbourne?

But what he sang, she recognized. She knew the song well, but she never would have applied it to herself.

Because it was *Warrior* by Demi Lovato.

It wasn't country at all, and she was surprised he knew the words. But he did. He knew them all.

However, that wasn't what surprised her the most. She couldn't believe he thought she was a warrior.

As she listened to the song, concentrated closely on the lyrics, she understood exactly why it reminded him of her.

Like the song *Sunrise*, this one was just as perfect because it was about a story that had never been told before. It talked about how she was ashamed, confused, broken and bruised but now she was a warrior and ready to take back her life.

And she was. She was taking back her life today just like the song stated. Her father stole a part of her she'd never get back, making her grow up too fast. But the lyrics reminded her that she needed to rise out of those ashes and burn like a fire. Become strong again by growing thicker skin and wearing steel armor.

She grew up in an MC. She had MC running through her veins. Even though it was from both her mother and her asshole father, it was there. The women in the club sisterhood were strong. Each and every one of them. She needed to draw on that strength.

Not one of them would turn her away if she needed help. Not even now.

She knew that deep down in her heart.

Ryder was right. She needed to look at what surrounded her. Not the bad, but the good.

When the song came to an end, Ryder followed up with, "And he can never hurt you again, darlin'. Even if he wasn't gone off this earth. I wouldn't let him."

I wouldn't let him.

He was a true warrior. Not her.

Chapter Thirteen

His instinct to protect the woman who sat in his arms, leaning on him, wisps of blonde hair getting caught in his early morning whiskers, was growing at an alarming rate.

It was one thing to be sexually attracted to her, but that wasn't all it was.

Which was troublesome.

If he was being honest with himself, he shouldn't even be sexually attracted to her. Not with some of the situations he'd found her in. If anything, it should be the opposite.

Made him wonder if he'd lost his damn mind.

Yes, that's what it was. Temporary insanity. Once he delivered her back to her cousin and she was moving forward with her life as it should be, he'd forget all about her.

Right?

Fuck me.

A low grumble came from his gut. He needed not only his head examined but food in his stomach. "Time to get back, darlin'. Need to eat."

He also needed to get more condoms. There was

nothing he wanted more than to fuck her right there on that rock, especially while the sun had been rising.

Maybe once he got some, they could take another early morning trip to catch it again, this time better prepared. Like with a blanket. And maybe breakfast. Also, take her for a hike once she got more appropriate shoes. Show her not only the beauty of a sunrise, but of the Kentucky wilderness. Show her how much he loved that mountain.

If she wanted, it could become her place to decompress when needed, too. Whether he was there or not. Though, he wasn't sure he'd want her up here alone.

And he definitely didn't want some other man up here with her, fucking her in his bed.

Fuck no.

So, scratch that.

"I don't want to leave."

Me neither, darlin'. "We can come back."

She twisted her head. "When?"

"One of these mornings."

"How long are we staying up here?"

"We'll head home when you're ready." *When I know you're appreciatin' life and not takin' it for granted.*

"And if I'm ready?"

"You're not ready, darlin'." *And I'm not ready to head back, either.* Not yet.

"It's not fair that you're here stuck with me because of the way I am."

"I'm not sacrificin' shit. I love it up here." That was one hundred percent true.

And I love sharin' it with you.

Fuck him, that was one hundred percent true, too.

Before he said something stupid, he disengaged from her and got to his feet, then helped her up. As she went to turn away and climb back over the rocks, he snagged her arm and hauled her back to him, slamming her into his chest.

Her blue eyes held amusement as she looked up at him. "Thought you were hungry."

"Oh, I'm fuckin' hungry all right," he murmured, then took her mouth.

He slipped his tongue between her parted lips and as their tongues tangled, she groaned, pressing herself against him harder.

With her not wearing a bra, the only thing between her tits and his chest was a little bit of cotton.

He wrapped the arm he was holding around his waist and took her jaws in his hands as he deepened the kiss. Her other arm circled him, too. And that felt right.

For fuck's sake, she might be shorter than him, she might have curves where he didn't, but they fit together perfectly.

Fuck him where his thoughts were going, too. That wasn't ever going to happen.

First of all, if Diesel knew he was banging his younger cousin, he'd pound Ryder into the ground. Ryder would put up a fight, but he doubted he could win against the bigger man, especially when that man's beast was raging.

Second, Kelsea had a long way to go to get her head together. Just her confessing to him what Pierce did wasn't a magic elixir. It would take time and effort for her to get straightened out. In fact, there hadn't been one whole day yet where she hadn't had liquor or drugs in her system that he was aware of.

Today might be that first day. Yesterday would have been if she hadn't found that bottle in his shed.

How he missed that one when he trashed the rest, he had no idea. He hadn't been in that old cabinet in years. He had no reason to get in there, so he didn't expect whiskey to be stored in it.

Maybe it was best he hadn't known. Otherwise, he might have hit that bottle himself a time or two. Who was he fooling? He would have polished it off in one shot.

The day he woke up from one bender and began searching for his next was the day he rid his life of that shit.

Drowning out his memories, his guilt, his regret wasn't a permanent solution. Death was a permanent solution, but even as fucked up as his thoughts were, he wasn't ready for that final step.

Instead, he took twelve other steps. And when he found that direction wasn't working, he'd found himself back in bars night after night. Bar fight after bar fight. Until he picked the wrong bar. The wrong fight.

Stupid drunk, he got into a fight with a fellow veteran. Though, he didn't know it at the time. But he went head to head with a former Marine Raider.

That night he lost his ass.

The next morning, he found himself again.

And he also found a buddy he'd now give his life for.

Someone he was proud to call his friend, his teammate, and fellow Shadow.

He owed Steel everything.

Including dragging his reluctant ass in front of an MC Sergeant at Arms and club enforcer named Diesel. Convincing him to join D's crew. Surrounding himself with like-minded men who had seen and did the same sort of missions he had. Some even worse.

They understood.

They supported each other.

They had each other's six.

For life.

So, as much as he bitched about being sent to retrieve Kelsea time after time, as many times as he threatened to quit, he never would. D, and the rest of his team, knew he was bluffing.

In the end, Steel saved his life, so Ryder felt the need to pay it forward.

Which was why he was currently swapping spit with the beautiful blonde in his arms.

While he only meant to pay it forward, this was turning out to be so much more.

And, again, that was worrisome.

Her moan and her fingers squeezing his ass brought him back to the here and now, making him realize how hard his dick was.

They needed to get rolling and there was no doubt they needed condoms.

He broke off the kiss and stared down into her hooded eyes. He freed his gaze and jerked his chin toward the direction of the narrow foot path.

"Let's go." His voice was rough because he was struggling to keep from bending her over a nearby rock, ripping his boxer shorts down her legs and fucking her without a condom.

And that would just be plain stupid.

Instead, he sucked at his teeth, set his jaw and smacked her on the ass. "Go."

Then he stood back, flipped his ball cap forward for the trip, and watched that ass as she began to climb over the uneven rocks, taking her time in those ridiculous flip-flops he never should've bought her. But at the time he hadn't planned on taking her anywhere. Also, never in his life had he shopped for women's clothes.

He held his breath when she slipped a couple of times, then forced himself to move and stop gawking at the scenery. He needed to help her back to the ATV before she broke her damn neck.

As she climbed on all fours over one steep boulder, he hesitated once again to watch her ass.

Fuck.

That was not helping.

Suddenly, she was out of sight.

He hurried to follow her and came around the next large rock to see her working her way over another one. She was almost to the narrow dirt footpath.

As she reached her foot down toward the ground, he saw her wobble.

Fuck! Those fucking flip-flops!

He leapt from one boulder to the next in his attempt to catch her before she fell, but as he landed, his boot ended up caught in between the two boulders and as if in slow motion, his ankle twisted first before his whole body followed. His weight propelled him forward at the same time his foot held him back.

He cursed as he only saw grey rock and then nothing.

"Fuck!" she yelled at the same time Ryder did.

She pushed herself to her feet, brushing dirt and debris off her bare knees. Her eyes landed on one of her flip-flops that had fallen off and she grabbed it, jamming it back on her foot. She turned to complain once again about him buying her stupid shoes and gasped.

"Dwight!" she screamed.

He was face down on the boulder.

She scrambled back up the rock to where his head was. "Dwight!"

He wasn't moving. He wasn't responding. She had no idea what happened. She thought he was right behind her and then she lost her balance when her flip-flop slipped off her sock.

She was too busy trying not to break her own neck, so she hadn't been paying attention to where he was.

She squatted down next to him. His eyes were closed.

Was he dead?

He couldn't be dead!

Holy fuck, what would she do if he was dead?

Fuck! Fuck! Fuck!

"Ryder! Dwight!" she shouted again, tapping her fingers lightly on his cheek. "Wake up."

She ran her gaze over his body and when she got to his feet, she noticed his boot stuck in a crack.

She crawled in that direction and carefully began to unlace the boot that was caught. When she got it loose, she gently pulled on his leg until she worked his foot free.

Once he was no longer trapped, she moved back to his torso and carefully rolled him onto his back.

"Oh fuck," she groaned. She knew nothing about first aid. He had a gash up near his hair line which was already beginning to swell. And it was bleeding like crazy! "Fuck. Fuck. Fuck," she muttered. At least he was breathing.

She needed to keep her wits about her and figure out what to do. Of course there was no one probably within miles. So, she had no help. She grabbed for his cell phone which was on his hip, and when she pulled it from the holder, she realized not only was the screen cracked but the body of the phone was crushed. She tried to power it on anyway, with no luck.

She whipped it into the woods with a curse.

His leg didn't look too twisted, his arms didn't appear broken, but they had a few scrapes. The half of his face that didn't have blood running down it, looked fine. The only major injury she could see was his head wound.

But head wounds could be dangerous.

How the fuck was she going to get him back down the mountain?

Should she take the ATV and go get help? Fuck, she couldn't leave him up there alone. And she had no idea how far the nearest help was. She had no fucking clue where in Kentucky they were. She had no phone. The cabin had no phone.

She tamped down the panic that was rising.

Think, think, think.

First, she had to stop the bleeding. She yanked up the pant leg of his jeans and pulled the tactical knife from its sheath he had strapped to his ankle. She used it to cut off the bottom of her T-shirt. It wasn't sanitary but it was the best she had.

Once she had a long strip of cotton, she gently wrapped it as best as she could around his head, hoping to at least stem the flow.

Now she had to get him on the ATV somehow and drive him back to the cabin to get the Scout.

How was she going to do that? She couldn't pick him up or carry him. And she certainly wasn't going to drag him.

She tapped lightly on his cheek again. "C'mon, Dwight, wake up. Please."

She lifted his eyelids and saw his pupils were blown.

Was that the sign of a concussion?

She had no fucking clue! Where was Google when she needed it?

After removing her flip-flops, she squatted by his head, hooked her arms under his armpits and pulled on his lifeless body.

Fuck, he weighed a ton.

She gritted her teeth and pulled harder, digging her feet in for leverage.

She landed backwards on her ass. With a curse, she scrambled back up and hooked him again.

She had to do this. She had no choice. He was relying on her to help him.

Finally, he was starting to slide. Slowly, carefully, she pulled him off the boulder and onto the dirt path. She didn't have far to go around the next boulder. The ATV was parked just on the other side of it. But she was out of breath already.

She couldn't give up. With a grunt, she walked backwards, pulling his dead weight. It seemed like hours, but it was probably only minutes, before she finally rounded the last boulder and spotted the ATV.

She wanted to cry with relief, but she needed to keep going.

She had no idea how she was going to get him on the ATV. None.

Even if she managed to get him on the back, how the hell was he going to stay on? He'd fall off and crack his head open again.

She chewed her bottom lip as she contemplated their current situation.

She propped Ryder up against the boulder and pulled his T-shirt over his head. With his knife, she cut it in half. She could tie him to her with the shirt.

She squatted next to him, touching his cheek. "Ryder. Please. Wake up. I need your help."

He needed to wake up. That was the only way she'd be able to get him on the ATV. She might have to wait it out until that happened.

The bleeding from his head wound seemed to have slowed, but the cotton over it was soaked with blood.

He was listing to one side, so she straightened him up and planted her ass beside him. As soon as he became conscious, she'd get him loaded onto the ATV and get him back to the cabin as quickly as possible.

She held his lifeless hand for fifteen minutes before he groaned, blinked his eyes open and groaned again.

"Dwight!" She jumped to her feet. "Are you okay?"

No, dummy, he wasn't okay. But she wanted to hear his reassurance anyway.

"Where... am... I?"

Fuck.

"Can you get up?"

He stared at her, his pupils still more dilated than normal.

"I have to get you back to the cabin."

"There's... two of you." He almost sounded drunk. He groaned again and reached up near his head wound.

"Don't touch it. Are you seeing double?"

"Lemme juss shake... it off."

"You aren't going to just shake this off, Dwight. You don't 'shake off' a head injury."

"What happened?"

"You got your boot caught and cracked your skull open on the rock."

"Been beaned in the head before."

"With a big rock?"

"Gonna be fine."

"Well, I doubt you're going to die." For fuck's sake, she hoped not. "But right now you're not fine."

He lifted his hand again.

"Don't! Don't touch it. You'll put more dirt in it. You've got a gash." That "gash" was really swollen now and she was sure it was bruising badly under the temporary bandage. "I need you to help me, Dwight. I need you to get on the ATV so I can get you back."

"I'm... fine."

"You're not fine. Your pupils are blown. I think you have a concussion. But I need you to try to stand up and sit on the ATV."

She held out her hand and he stared at it. "I'm fine."

Stubborn fuck!

With another groan, he tried to push to his feet, flopped back down onto his ass and turned his head in time to puke.

Kelsea wrinkled her nose and swallowed hard. *Ugh.* Someone else puking made her puke, too. She swallowed back the bile that rose. At least they hadn't eaten yet.

Once she was assured he wasn't going to puke again, she squatted back down beside him, draped his heavy arm over her shoulder and said, "On three." She took a deep breath. "One... two... three..." She grunted as he gave her a lot of his weight. But finally he was on his feet, but she was sure not for long. He wobbled a couple of times as she shuffled him the few feet to the back of the ATV and helped him mount it. With one hand on his shoulder to keep him upright, she scrambled onto the front and hurried to wrap his T-shirt around both of their waists tightly, tying it with a knot.

She grabbed both of his arms and wrapped those around her waist. "Lean on me, if you have to. Just don't puke on me. And, for fuck's sake, hang on as best as you can."

"I'm fine."

"You're not fine!" she screamed and hit the starter. "Hang the fuck on." She eased the throttle and slowly pulled away, hoping the shirt held. Hoping she didn't lose him when going over some of the rocks and ruts.

Hoping he wasn't bleeding internally somewhere.

"Gotta puke," he grumbled loud enough over the ATV's exhaust.

She slowed the four-wheeler to a halt and helped him lean to the right enough to expel the remainder of his stomach without them both wearing it.

After a few minutes, he managed an "okay" and she headed back down the trail, winding their way around the worst of the rocks and ruts.

It felt like hours to get back to the cabin, and she wanted to cry with relief when the small clearing finally came into view. She did it. She got him back to the cabin without him falling off the back. But almost all of his weight was pressing her forward.

She didn't care.

What she cared about was they had made it. At least this far.

Next step was getting him into the Scout and to the nearest hospital, even though she had no idea where that was.

She pulled the ATV right up to the front steps of the cabin and untied the T-shirt that bound them together. "How far is the nearest hospital?"

"Hour away."

"I can take you to the hospital. I just need the keys to the Scout. You locked them in the safe. I'll need the combination."

Holding him upright again, she got off the four-wheeler and helped him off, sitting him on the deck steps.

He still looked out of it. His skin was pale and his pupils still large. More black than green.

His words were still slurred when he said, "Nothin' they can do 'bout a concussion."

"Bullshit. They can examine you. Sew that gash closed. Make sure that thick skull of yours is still in one piece."

"I'll be fine. I just need to rest."

"If you say you're fine one more time..." she warned. "What's the combination?"

"Darlin'..."

"Ryder," she said between gritted teeth. "What's the fucking combo?"

He closed his eyes and said nothing.

Was he unconscious again?

"Ryder..."

He opened his eyes. "Don't know."

"What do you mean, you don't know?"

"I... can't remember it."

"Can you guess? Is it four-digits? Five? Your birthday?"

"Darlin', I don't know. My head's spinnin'... Just... help me inside. I'm—"

Kelsea lifted her face to the sky and screamed.

"Just help me inside."

"If you're *fine*, do it yourself."

"Someone needs a spankin' with that fresh mouth."

"Good luck with that."

She leaned over, hooked his arm over her shoulders and helped him back to his feet. They slowly made it up the three steps, to the front door, and finally inside.

They didn't stop until they reached the bed. She eased him onto it, then pulled off his remaining boot and both of his socks.

The leg that got caught had a swollen ankle and was a bit purple. It wasn't broken because he put weight on it.

Ice. She needed ice and a first aid kit. And to clean up the gash.

She propped up his head with a couple of the pillows and headed toward the kitchen. Under the sink she found a small first aid kit and she filled a couple Ziploc bags with ice. Finding two small kitchen towels, she took everything back to the bed, where he was leaning back against the headboard with his eyes closed once again.

She helped him out of his jeans, then placed one of the towels over his ankle with the bag of ice, making him hiss.

She eased the piece of her shirt off his forehead since it was now sticking to the wound.

"Are you still feeling nauseous?" *Oh, please say no.*

"A little."

"Do you need a bucket or something?"

"Just in case."

She hurried to the bathroom and snagged the small trashcan, as well as a warm, wet washcloth to clean his wound.

She tucked the can next to the bed, then sat on the edge of the mattress beside him. She gently cleaned the area around the gash.

His eyes were semi-focused on her as she worked. "Are you seeing two of me still?"

"No, but you're a bit fuzzy."

"As soon as you remember that combination, you let me know."

"I'm... Never mind."

"Right."

"Nothin' a little rest won't cure."

"You need stitches," she said, opening up an alcohol swab and continuing to clean his gash. He winced. She was sure it stung.

"Butterfly bandages in the kit."

She dug through the box and found four. Once she had him cleaned up and bandaged, she stared at him.

And he stared back at her.

She lifted her hand and held up four fingers. "How many fingers am I holding up?"

"Three." Before she could drop her hand, he snagged it and pulled it into his lap. "You did good, darlin'." His words were still a bit slow and sluggish but his pupils were beginning to recede.

"Why don't you lay down so I can put ice on that gash to reduce the swelling?"

He didn't let her hand go. "You did good, darlin'."

She stared at their clasped hands and nodded, swallowing back the lump that had risen in her throat.

"Better than most. Most would've panicked. You kept your shit together."

"I'm not sure about that."

"I am. You used your head."

"You did, too, to cushion your fall. Please don't do that again."

"You got it." His thumb brushed back and forth over the back of her hand as he held onto it.

"I was scared."

"Yeah," he answered.

"I didn't know what to do."

"Yes you did. You did what you needed to do. You persevered and got it done. That's all that's asked from any warrior."

"I'm not a warrior."

"Yeah, darlin', you are. You're stronger than you know."

She dropped her gaze from his. "You need to lay down and ice that hard head of yours."

He gave her a crooked smile and he let her help him lay flat on his back. She placed the towel and second bag of ice on his forehead, again pulling another wince from him, then sat back and studied the man in that bed.

"Guess I'm getting out of making you breakfast. I doubt you want to eat anything right now."

"I'll eat later when my stomach isn't doing somersaults. But don't think you'll get out of making me breakfast tomorrow."

"We'll see."

"Yes, we will."

Chapter Fourteen

BETWEEN HIS ANKLE and his noggin, he wasn't leaving that bed anytime soon. But he was okay with that.

He now remembered the combination for the gun safe, but he wasn't ready to give it to her. He needed her to believe him when he said he didn't need to go to the hospital. What she did by patching him up was the same thing any ER would do. Wrapping his ankle would've only made it swell worse. She had propped his foot up on a spare pillow and iced it. Enough said.

The butterfly strips worked just as well as stitches. He'd used them plenty of times. Not only on himself, but his fellow Rangers.

His fellow Shadows, too.

As for the concussion, he just needed to wait out the symptoms.

The dizziness and nausea came and went in waves. He hadn't puked again, but he also hadn't been able to eat. She insisted he drink water. Which he did. He managed to at least keep that down.

Now the cabin was quiet with neither of them saying much.

With one hand holding a half-melted bag of ice to his head, he turned it to stare at her. She laid in bed next to him on her side, her head propped in her hand, her eyes closed.

She had checked on him several times during the night, getting him more ice when the previous batch melted and letting him lean on her during the short trip to the bathroom when needed. He couldn't put his full weight on his ankle yet. And he still had bouts of dizziness.

He wasn't sure just how much sleep she got, so he wouldn't be surprised if she recently drifted off.

With his free hand, he reached out to brush her long blonde hair off her bare shoulder, letting his fingers trail along her smooth skin. She was once again wearing just a pair of his boxers and one of his white tank top undershirts.

She looked way better in them than he did. She looked even better out of them.

He needed to get his brain back in full working order so he could get to town and buy those condoms. There was no way he was taking her back to Shadow Valley without fucking her at least one more time.

Because once they got home... It would be best if that never happened again.

But... did he trust her enough to send her into town without him?

Did he feel comfortable enough to send her without any kind of cell phone? What if something happened to her along the way?

What if she got a hair up her ass and bolted with his Scout, leaving him stuck with just his ATV?

Her blue eyes opened and she smiled.

Jesus fuck. He couldn't think of any better way to wake up with that smile pointed at him. Well, maybe if she was smiling at him while riding his cock.

He pressed his palm against his morning wood. Her eyes automatically went there.

"Guess something *is* working properly this morning."

"The day it doesn't, I might as well just throw in the towel."

"They make pills for that."

"So I heard," he grumbled.

She laughed. "Studs like you think you'll never need them. That it's a sign of weakness."

When the fuck did she suddenly go from acting like she was barely twenty-one to her actual age of almost thirty?

He wasn't going to question her sudden onset of maturity. Could be just being away from the losers she was hanging and partying with. Could be her system becoming free of any unnatural substance.

Could be from his little "mishap" and her being forced to make mature decisions.

He was proud of her. While he *thought* he told her that yesterday, he needed to tell her that again. And again.

"We're human and we all have weaknesses, darlin'. Even me. Even your cousin, Diesel."

"Jewelee and his daughters are his weakness."

"Understandable." And that was why the big man kept those three females so close. As soon as he "claimed" Jewel, her ass was working at In the Shadows Security, helping D. Then once his girls were born, he hardly ever let them out of his sight.

Some might think he was too protective. Ryder understood the need to protect them. Jewel, Violet and Indigo were now the blood that kept that man's heart beating. If anything happened to them...

She pursed her lips. "Never thought that man had any kind of soft emotions in him."

"He proved everybody wrong. Even himself."

"Well, Jewel has always been a petite powerhouse and stubborn as shit."

He snorted. "Like someone else we know."

She jerked her shoulder. "When you're raised in a club full of hard-ass bikers, you tend to act like one, too."

"Not one of them acts a fool, darlin'."

"They've all had their moments."

That was certainly true. Not just bikers but former special forces. Sometimes it took a good knock upside the head to see things more clearly.

Not in his case, of course, but Mercy's. That man had found the perfect woman for him, but he let her slip from his fingers. He didn't want to burden her with his issues.

It only took two blows to the head for him to see Rissa was the right woman to deal with his shit. One from a steel pipe, the other from Jewelee's hard truth.

"You hungry?" he asked. While he meant breakfast, the look on her face clearly wasn't about food.

"Could be," she murmured, sliding closer to him.

Yeah, even with a concussion and a botched ankle, his cock was raring to go. Right now his injured brain needed all of his blood to heal. While normally he'd partake in a little self-help to redistribute that blood, this morning he hadn't woken up alone.

Which meant getting his erection under control could be a lot more satisfying.

If she was willing.

Watching Kelsea run her tongue over her bottom lip made his cock flex. Yeah, she might be willing.

"Must be a real pain when one part of your body is always giving away how horny you are."

"You mean like your nipples?" Because, *fuck*, the way they were pressing through the thin cotton, it appeared as if they could cut glass.

She glanced down at her own breasts, then cupped them, squeezing them together. "I could be cold."

"You ain't cold."

She smiled again and met his eyes. "No, I'm not." She

kneaded her breasts and brushed her own thumbs back and forth over the tips, making them stand out even farther.

"Can't fuck you, darlin', but you keep doin' that, I might get creative."

She shot him a wicked smile that went right down to his balls. "You need to rest."

"A man can't rest when you're doin' shit like that."

"Like what?" She sat up and tore the tank top over her head, whipping it to the bottom of the bed. "This?" She snagged both of her nipples between her fingers and twisted and pulled at the same time.

He groaned. And it wasn't from his head pounding, it was from his smaller head throbbing.

"Darlin', seriously, this isn't helpin' my situation," he moaned.

"Maybe this will..."

"Fuuuuck..." he groaned when she ripped his boxers down just far enough to wrap her little hot mouth around that throbbing head. One hand gripped the root while lightning shot into his balls with each suck of her mouth and lap of her tongue.

He leaned his head against the headboard and worked his fingers into her hair, closing his eyes. If he watched her, he might shoot his load too quickly. Instead, he let the pleasure surge through him. Tightening his fingers into her hair, he let her set the pace, not encouraging, not discouraging, just sitting back and enjoying what she was doing.

However, when her fingers released his cock and she moaned around him, he couldn't help but open his eyes. Her fingers still twisted her own nipple, which was peaked and darker than normal. Her other hand was now down the boxers she was wearing and she was rocking her hips back and forth.

"Darlin'," he breathed. She was going to kill him.

She tipped her eyes up to him and his chest tightened.

He might regret his next demand. "Boxers off."

Without releasing him, she shimmied out of them, then her hands went quickly back to work.

Yeah, he was going to regret that. But it would be worth her razzing him if he came too quickly.

And he was going to regret this, too. "Turn around. Let me."

She released him with a wet pop and scrambled around. As she took him into her mouth again, he pushed her hand away from her pussy and slid his fingers through her wetness.

Jesus. He wanted her to climb on his lap and ride him like a wild pony. That wasn't going to happen.

That wasn't going to happen.

Damn. That wasn't going to happen. Instead, he slipped his fingers inside her, and began to work his thumb over her clit. He had to put what he was doing on autopilot because her skills with her mouth and tongue was fucking with his concentration.

Curling his fingers, he found the spot which made her clench around him, both her inner muscles and her mouth.

"Don't neuter me with your teeth when you come, darlin'."

She didn't react to his words, but continued to work her magic, which made his head spin and not from his concussion.

The pressure in his balls increased to the point where he knew he wasn't going to be able to stop what was going to happen next. He was at that tipping point, where it wouldn't take much more.

He needed to get her to that same point and quickly. "Ease up a bit," he forced out.

She ignored him and increased her pace instead.

He set his jaw and with the hand he released from her hair, smacked her hard on the ass. "Ease up, Kelsea."

Again, she ignored him, without releasing him, she twisted her head and narrowed her eyes on him. The defiant look didn't go unnoticed.

He smacked her ass again, this time harder, and when he did, she groaned again around his cock and she squeezed his fingers tightly.

"Gonna play that game, huh?"

She smiled around his cock, sliding her tongue up the ridge.

"Gonna come and leave you behind then. Was tryin' to—"

Her mouth tensed around him but she managed to avoid sinking her teeth in as she clamped around his fingers and he felt the ripples of her orgasm. She moaned around the head of his cock.

And that was all he needed to push him over that edge as he came in her mouth and she took him all.

His eyes had closed when he came, but he opened them when he heard her chuckle after letting him slip from her mouth.

"When are you going to learn, I like it when you spank me?"

"Noted. Good thing I like to spank you."

She sat up, turned around and resettled against his side, curling around him, careful of his bum ankle. "Your accent gets thicker after you come."

He shrugged. "'Cause afterward I get lazy."

"Why would you try to hide it?"

"When you're called a dumb hick one too many times because of it, you learn to hide it."

"Who called you a dumb hick?"

"It was a long time ago." And a conversation that wasn't necessary. Between his time in the military and then living in Pennsylvania the last few years, he'd managed to diminish his southern accent.

"Well, you're hardly dumb. Can't say you're not a hick, though. Especially when you fed me groundhog."

He chuckled and wrapped an arm around her shoulder, pulling her closer. "Thanks, I think. Also, having an accent in Pennsylvania draws notice. Some of the shit we do, I need to do it without catchin' anyone's attention. A lot of times I need to blend in."

"Well, I think it's hot."

He glanced down at her, cuddled against his side. "Well, now you know what to do for it to come out."

She lifted her gaze to his. "Come being the important word."

He brushed his thumb over her cheek and studied her. "How you feelin'?"

"Shouldn't I be asking you that?"

"I'm talkin' 'bout up here." He tapped her temple lightly. "Any urges pullin' at you?"

She tilted her head and tucked her bottom lip between her teeth. After a moment, she shook her head. "No, not right now."

But could he trust her to go to town and not stop to pick up a bottle of liquor or simply take off, deserting him?

She pushed away from him, climbing from the bed. "I'm going to make you some breakfast since you haven't eaten in over a day. I'll do my best not to burn your eggs and toast."

"I'd appreciate it."

He watched her pull on his tank top and boxers and wander toward the kitchen.

"Darlin, you up to takin' the Scout into town after breakfast for a supply run?"

She stopped to peer over her shoulder and arch a brow at him. "You remember the safe combo?"

"Now I do."

"Did you have selective memory yesterday because you didn't want to go to the hospital?"

He grimaced. "No. I wasn't lyin' 'bout that."

"Do you trust me?"

Well, that was a loaded fucking question. He sucked in a breath before asking, "Can I?"

She turned all the way around back toward the bed, her hands on her hips, her head tilted as she looked at him. "Only way you're gonna find out is if you put that quarter in the slot and take a chance."

No doubt about that.

———

KELSEA BLEW OUT A BREATH. She did what she promised. She took his Scout into town with his hand-written directions and found the Walmart about an hour away. Bought a large box of condoms and decided to throw a second box in, just in case. Along with some lube, which he didn't request. She also purchased a prepaid cell phone.

Again, just like he asked.

She also picked up stuff for easy to make meals. One of them being a box of spaghetti and a jar of sauce along with frozen meatballs and garlic bread. She wasn't a cook at all but she could pull off a mean spaghetti as long as she didn't have to do it from scratch.

She had accomplished everything she came to town for. And now it was time to head back.

But, no, here she sat. Behind the wheel of his precious "baby"—his description, not hers—in the parking lot of some half-empty strip mall. She had pulled into a spot where she could see the sign above the door of one of the occupied stores. It read Blue Grass Spirits.

The "spirits" weren't of the ghostly kind, either.

Hence, her indecision.

She had been good so far. She fought and won against the temptation to buy a second burner phone. One for her that she could keep "just in case." But common sense won out since she was using his credit card, so he'd see the charge. And she had no doubt he'd check them.

He'd especially be looking for alcohol. He was smart enough not to give her cash.

Not that Kelsea blamed him.

But now the urge to take a risk, to buy a bottle of whiskey, vodka, rum, *something*, was winning.

She could have driven right past. She did it on the way into town without a problem, but leaving was a different story. She had automatically pulled in. It reeled her in like a fish on a line.

But a fish would fight more. A fish had the strong instinct to survive.

She was weak.

So weak.

She pressed her forehead to the steering wheel and closed her eyes.

She didn't know what to do. She didn't know how to scrub those awful memories from her brain.

For years she had buried them. She thought she'd been successful. That they were buried so deep they'd never resurface. But when her half-sister Brooke came to Shadow Valley searching for her biological father, only to find out her mother had been raped by Pierce...

She didn't know Brooke was her half-sister until the other secret came out. The secret her mother kept from her. That the man Annie worked with at the MC's gun shop was really her father. She had kept it from him, from her own daughter, from everyone.

And that's when things surged back to the surface. Where the shame prickled along her skin. Where the disgust churned her stomach. Where she had a problem looking in the mirror because when she did, she began to see some of the similarities to the man whose sperm created her.

She was blonde and blue-eyed, while the rest of the females on the Dougherty side of the MC family were all dark-haired, except for her cousin Ivy, who was a redhead. Ivy and Kelsea were the oddballs due to their fathers' genetics.

She lifted her head and watched as customers walked in and out of the liquor store. Walking in empty-handed, walking out with booze.

It would be easy. Walk in, use Ryder's credit card, walk out.

Drive away.

Disappear.

Find somewhere no one knew her. Where she could live without anyone knowing anything about her. Start a new life.

She ground the heels of her palms into her eyes and screamed, the sound filling the empty Scout.

She could take the easy way out. But would it really be easier? Or just more avoidance?

Would she just be re-burying her issues instead of facing them head-on?

By taking off and deserting Ryder, she would be kicking him in the nuts. Not only by leaving him to fend for himself up at his cabin, but by doing so, being unappreciative with what he was trying to accomplish.

Helping her.

He didn't have to do so. He didn't have to take time out in his life. He didn't have to deal with her being a pain in his ass.

He did it anyway.

He not only sacrificed for his country, but he sacrificed for her. Maybe it wasn't quite the same, but she should be more appreciative.

She had been gripping the steering wheel so hard, her hands were beginning to cramp.

She needed to head back. It was her turn to help him.

It was also time for her to start being responsible. Stop disappointing her family. Beg for her job back from her sister, Brooke. Maybe even take her up on being a partner in the interior design business. Get serious about life.

Have a goal. A purpose.

Do something to make everyone proud.

Brooke had offered her a partnership back in the beginning when she first set up her business in Shadow Valley after moving it from Harrisburg. But then Kelsea continued to disappoint her. Become unreliable.

Not a business partner anyone in their right mind would want.

Her gaze slid to the prepaid cell phone on the passenger seat. Picking it up before she changed her mind, she hit the power button and as soon as it lit up, she plugged in Brooke's phone number and sent a text.

I promise 2 B a better sister. ~K

She put the phone back down and stared at it. A minute later a text came through: *Where R U? Do U need help?*

"Yes," she whispered into the quiet interior of the Scout. *No, I'm fine. C U soon.*

"I'm fine." What Ryder kept repeating when he wasn't. "I'm fine" was a way to get people to stop worrying. To brush off their concern.

She also wasn't sure if the part about seeing Brooke soon was true or not. She wasn't sure what Ryder's plan was. But whatever it was, she would go along with it.

Instead of reaching for the door handle, she gritted her teeth and turned the key, his Scout roaring to life. She pushed in the clutch, shoved the shifter into first gear and pointed the vehicle back toward Ryder's cabin.

Chapter Fifteen

To say he didn't fret, wondering if she'd come back, would be a lie. A big one. If he hadn't been injured, he'd have been pacing. But then if he hadn't been injured, she wouldn't have gone to town at all.

He put a lot of faith in her to do the right thing.

And for fuck's sake, she did.

Though, as soon as she handed him the phone and went back outside to unload her purchases, he quickly logged onto his credit card account and scanned the locations where she'd used it.

The gas station just outside of town where he told her to fill the tank and Walmart. They didn't sell liquor at either place, so he was pretty sure she didn't do anything stupid.

He leaned his head back against the headboard and blew out a relieved breath.

She came back inside carrying several plastic bags full of stuff.

"Darlin', as soon as you're done, come on over here."

She glanced over at the bed, set the bags down on the counter and nodded. "'Kay." Then headed back outside.

After two more trips, she shut the front door and immediately headed over to him.

"Sit."

She sat on the edge of the mattress close to him, her brows furrowed. "What's the matter?"

"Nothin'. You did good."

His heart squeezed when her face lit up, but she quickly hid it.

"Gimme some sugar," he said. When she leaned in, he curled his fingers around the side of her neck and held her close while brushing his lips lightly over hers. "You taste good."

"Drank a pop on the way back. Want one?"

"Yeah. But in a minute. Need more of that sweetness first." His fingers slid up her neck, through her hair and wrapped around the back of her head to pull her closer. He nibbled along her bottom lip, then took her mouth completely.

Their tongues tangled for a few minutes and her palm pressed flat over his heart which was thumping strongly.

She was not good for him. No way, no how. But he couldn't deny that there wasn't something about her that did it for him.

More than something.

A lot of things.

But he needed to keep his boots planted securely on the ground and remember who she was.

She was a smart woman who just had done some dumb things. She was a woman who had been letting her past decide her future. She was a woman who had stopped caring.

She could have the world by the balls if she just reached out and grabbed them.

Speaking of balls... "You grab condoms?"

She pulled back and smiled. "Two big boxes."

"You did good," he repeated.

"I figured."

"A good pair of shoes?"

"Bought a pair of sneakers."

He nodded. "Finish puttin' the shit away and get back here double time."

"With the condom and lube?"

He cocked a brow. "You got lube, too?"

She pushed from the bed and shot him a smile. "Maybe. But are you sure you're up for it?"

His hand dropped to his erection that tented his boxers. "What's it look like?"

"I meant your ankle and your head."

"Not going to be usin' either one of those things."

"Going to get creative?"

"Sure am, darlin', so hurry up. In fact, get back here triple time."

"You in a rush? Got somewhere to go?" she teased him with his own questions.

"Yeah, I plan on goin' down on you while you straddle my face. Then you're gonna ride my cock. Sound like a plan?"

"Sounds like a damn good one," she answered with a grin.

He agreed.

———

SHE HAD one naked thigh tucked over his, her arm curled around his waist and her cheek on his chest as it rose and fell. Their hearts were now beating normally, their breathing steady, their damp skin now almost dry.

His fingers combed through her long hair, spreading the silky blonde strands along her bare back.

Normally, he'd be trying not to nod off after sex. Especially with how active their sexual activities had been, now that his ankle could bear his weight and his concussion symptoms were gone. But he was wide awake from a fear he was doing his damnedest not to show.

He'd brought her to his cabin to help "save" her.

But now, who was going to save him?

That slippery muck he had been trying to avoid... He not only stepped in it, but lost his boot while doing so.

It was one thing to have sex with the woman in their little safe "bubble" of his cabin. It was another to continue to do so after they headed home to Shadow Valley.

No matter how he looked at it, it just wouldn't be smart.

And they needed to get back soon. He had no more excuses to keep them holed up in his cabin.

She'd been alcohol and drug free for over a week now. She hadn't had any more meltdowns. No, instead, she had woken up every morning and made breakfast without him asking for the past five days. The same with dinner. She also had cleaned the cabin from top to bottom. She had taken a long hike with him once his ankle had been able to handle his weight and there were no more twinges of pain.

They had returned back to the top of the mountain on the ATV twice and watched the sunrise. Though they missed part of the second one because he couldn't wait to be inside her while the sun was coming up over the mountains.

It had been the most beautiful thing he'd ever experienced in his life. The soft colorful hues of the start of the day lighting up Kelsea's face as she climaxed around him and cried out his name.

Fuck, if he could do that every morning for the rest of his life, he'd die a happy man.

But he couldn't.

They couldn't.

He couldn't hold her hand for the rest of her life, either.

He needed to let her go. Let her take control of her own life. It would now be up to her to continue on the right path. Either she would or she wouldn't.

But either way, he didn't want to be her crutch. That would do her no good.

When he stepped out of the cabin to call Diesel the other night, the man had ordered him to bring her home. He wasn't paying Ryder for a "fuckin' vacation."

He ended up telling the big man that he didn't have to pay him anything. He was fine with doing all of this on his own time. Diesel had grunted and not said anything for a few seconds. Finally, he warned, "She better not come back fuckin' knocked up. 'Cause then we're gonna have an even bigger fuckin' problem than me an' you do right now."

"She ain't gonna come back knocked up," Ryder assured his boss. Because at least that was true.

"She texted Brooke," Diesel grumbled.

She hadn't told him that and must have deleted the texts before handing over the cell phone to him. "And?"

"An' said she'd be a better sister."

"Sounds promisin'," was all Ryder responded. He hoped she'd stick to that.

"Yeah, we'll fuckin' see. Needs to keep her ass outta West Virginia an' away from that Slit."

"Slash."

"What-fuckin-ever. Otherwise..." D went quiet.

Ryder got his meaning, though. The war between the Dirty Angels and the Shadow Warriors MC had finally come to an end. But Ryder wouldn't put it past the club enforcer to start a new one with the Deadly Demons over his cousin.

"Don't think that's gonna be an issue," Ryder assured him. But he also never told D how he found Kelsea that night. He had been trying to avoid that war. Because even though it would be between the two MC's, he and his fellow Shadows would find their asses in the middle of it.

And a new war would put all the DAMC women and children at risk and possibly even Mercy's woman, Rissa. Ryder couldn't imagine the death and devastation that would happen if both Mercy and Diesel went on a rampage. It'd be like Godzilla and King Kong taking over the world at the same time.

"Anyway, get your ass back here. Got a couple jobs comin' in. Also, Slade's got a request."

"What kind of request?" Slade was a DAMC member, but also a former Marine. He had helped the Shadows a time or two in the past when it came to some assignments when they were short-handed. He was the only man Ryder knew of that could go head-to-head with Steel when it came to boxing.

"When Crow visited Rocky at Greene last time, the man mentioned another possible siblin'. Nothin' concrete, but Slade wants us to find him if he exists."

"Hunter's best for that."

"No fuckin' shit. But Hunter's on another job right now. Everybody's tied up 'cause you're up on that mountain twiddlin' your fuckin' thumbs. We're shorthanded."

"Is he in a rush? Can't he wait until Hunter's free?"

Diesel grunted into the phone. "Just get your ass back here, got me?"

"D..."

"Yeah," he grunted again.

"You mentioned gettin' Rissa to talk with Kelsea. I think that may be a good idea. I think she needs it." He also didn't tell D the truth about what Pierce did to Kelsea. In fact, he was going to leave that up to her. He would take that secret to his grave if she wanted him to, but it would be a good idea for her to talk to someone since Ryder wasn't a therapist. And he would have a hard time listening to her and not be furious with Pierce the whole time.

"Yeah."

"I'm serious."

"Said fuckin' yeah," D bellowed into the phone, which made Ryder wonder if D had a suspicion about why Kelsea was acting out. His boss was wicked smart, though he looked and sounded dumb as a rock. The man caught a lot of people off guard that way, so it wouldn't surprise him if D had figured it all out. Maybe that's why he would never let Kels hit rock bottom.

Now it all made sense. As the DAMC's enforcer and Sergeant at Arms, he was tasked with protecting everyone in that club. And any failure in that respect hit him hard, though he'd never say it.

Even though Pierce had been a long-time member, in fact before Diesel was born, whatever happened to any of the current generation of the DAMC fell on his shoulders, whether he was the enforcer at the time or not.

He just took his job that seriously.

"Gonna talk to Mercy."

"Do that. Givin' you two more fuckin' days, then get back here."

"Copy that."

The phone went dead.

That conversation had been yesterday. Which meant they needed to head back tomorrow.

Which meant one more dinner, one more breakfast. One more night together.

If it was up to him, they might not get much sleep.

"You got tense," came softly from the area of his chest.

He forced himself to relax when he tipped his eyes downward. "Yeah."

"Why?"

He took a breath. "Time for us to go home, darlin'."

She lifted her head and locked her blue eyes with his. "Today?"

He shook his head. "Tomorrow."

"I thought you said we'd go home when you thought I was ready."

"You're ready, darlin'. Can't keep you here forever." *Can't keep you forever.*

"I like it here."

He raised his eyebrows. "Yeah?"

She planted her cheek back on his sternum, her eyes turned towards him. "Yeah. I never thought I'd like to be unplugged from the world. But it's grown on me."

"I come up here as often as I can."

"How long have you had it?"

"My grandfather built the original cabin. My father built the shed. It's been in my family for three generations."

"Is your grandfather still alive?"

"No."

"Father?"

"No. I was young when my grandparents passed on. My parents had me when they were older. My mother was forty, my father fifty-one."

"Any siblings?"

He shook his head. "My mother didn't think she could conceive. I was a surprise."

"I'm sure I was a surprise, too."

He brushed a hand over her hair. "He never knew who you really were, darlin'. Not one of us told him before... Well, just before." Before Crow sliced the motherfucker's neck. Before any of them actually knew everything.

Kelsea didn't respond, just stared at the nearest wall.

"Darlin', you've got family who loves you. I wish I had the family you have. Think about your cousins, Dex, Ivy, Bella, Hawk and, hell, Diesel. Your Uncle Ace and Aunt Janice, who'd give you the shirt off their backs. Your Aunt Allie. And, I've told you this several times, your mother loves you, whether you believe it or not. You are so much more than the DNA your father donated. You're a Dougherty. Be proud of that. Even without them, you've got the rest of the club sisterhood standing behind you. One thing about your MC is that the loyalty among you all is intense. However, you also gotta remember, you need to reciprocate that. They need you, too. All of them."

"I'm not sure Brooke will forgive me."

"Your sister loves you, too. She'll be there for you when you're ready. She wants to help you."

"If it wasn't for her showing up, I still might not know the truth."

"Her showin' up had its good points and bad. But don't you think she struggled after findin' out what Pierce did to her own mother? Yeah, she had Dex but she needed you, too. Still does, darlin'."

"I'm going to try to be a better sister," she murmured, her hand sliding over his now bearded face. He'd forgotten to tell her to pick up a new razor that last trip into town and she was using his for her legs. He had convinced her to stop shaving her pussy bare, at least. He liked it better with a little blonde tuft at the top.

"You are gonna *be* a better sister. Not try. Just be." He studied her face for a moment. "It's amazin' how much you two look alike."

"Brooke is hot and classy."

"Yeah."

She arched an eyebrow at him.

He grinned, then laughed. "You waitin' for another response?"

"Not if it's going to be a lie, I'm not!"

"Gimme some sugar. That might convince me to come up with a better response."

She straddled him and moved until her lips were right above his and their gazes locked. "Got one now?"

"Nope."

She brushed her lips over his and, *fuck*, did she taste good.

"Now?"

"Not yet," he murmured against her lips.

She kissed him again, pressing her tongue to his. When he tried to deepen the kiss, she pulled slightly away. "How about now?"

"Yeah, darlin', I'll agree you're hot."

"And classy?"

"Might have to work on that a bit."

"You'd rather have classy?"

"I prefer down-to-earth." She wasn't there yet, either. But this week and a half had brought her closer. And right now he couldn't complain about the woman in his arms. Except that their time there was coming to an end.

Much sooner than he wanted it to.

Why did he feel like a momma bird shoving her fledgling out of the nest and hoping for the best?

No doubt he worried about her and would continue to. He knew how difficult it could be to stay on the straight and narrow. Some days could be good, some days not so much. It took a lot of dedication and determination to stay the course.

If he hadn't had that brawl with Steel all those years ago, he might have hit rock bottom and never resurfaced. If she slipped up and went back to her old destructive ways, he might not be able to be the one to pull her back out.

His chest ached just thinking about that.

But he was done saving her ass. He'd told her that. He told Diesel that.

He'd told himself that, too.

He needed to stick to that.

He showed her the path, now she needed to follow it. She was the one who needed to take those steps forward.

It was important that she do it on her own, so she can realize how strong she really was.

He saw it. He believed it.

Now it was all on her.

Chapter Sixteen

KELSEA STARED at her big galoot of a cousin who was sitting behind his desk in the warehouse that housed In the Shadows Security. Ryder stood at her back, not saying a word.

Diesel's gaze was currently pinned on her after staring at Ryder for a few uncomfortable moments.

She was waiting for D to explode in his Diesel-like fashion, but so far, so good. But he needed to say something instead of simply glaring.

"You're movin' out of that shit hole of an apartment."

That wasn't what she expected. "I have roommates, D, I just can't leave them in the lurch."

"Not sure why you think anythin' I'm 'bout to say's fuckin' negotiable. Got me?"

Kelsea's jaw tightened and every muscle in her body tensed. "You sit in that chair like you're the fucking King of England."

"In this warehouse I am the fuckin' king."

She lifted one shoulder. She wasn't one of his subjects nor should she have to answer to him. "Then I'm leaving."

As she turned to do just that, she not only faced Ryder

blocking her way but a wall of muscle named Mercy. When the fuck had he snuck in? The man was almost as big as D but moved like a ghost.

"Cost me a lot of fuckin' scratch, Kels, havin' Ryder come save your ass time after time. You owe me."

She turned her head and glanced back at her cousin, who was now sitting back in his chair, his thick, tattooed arms crossed over his broad chest.

Yep, the King of fucking England with a crooked crown, a whole lot of tats and a grumpy attitude.

She turned to face him. "What do I owe you? Tell me. I'll pay you back."

"First off, you couldn't fuckin' afford it. Second, not lookin' for money, woman, lookin' for you to get your shit together."

"It's together."

He cocked an eyebrow.

"It is. Ask Ryder."

Still Ryder said nothing behind her. What the hell was wrong with him? Why wasn't he coming to her defense?

"Gonna be some rules."

Oh, for fuck's sake, what was it with these men and their fucking rules? "I'm an adult, D. I don't need you to give me rules."

"These rules are what you're gonna follow to pay me back. Like I fuckin' said, you're movin' out of that skanks nest."

She didn't have to listen to him, but just out of curiosity... "And where am I moving to?"

"For now, back with your mother."

She frowned. The last place she wanted to live was with her mother. She'd rather live in a tent in the middle of a desert. She wasn't ready to "make nice" with Annie and wasn't sure when she would be. "Did you miss the part where I'm an adult?"

"Ignorin' it 'cause ain't seen you act like one in a long time. Maybe never. Ryder's gonna deliver your ass to Annie's. You're gonna stay there 'til you make enough money to get your own place."

He must have gotten her confused with his ol' lady. Since when did he get to boss her around like that? "Ace will probably let me live above the pawn shop if I ask." That was a good idea. She was going to call her uncle and ask as soon as she left the warehouse and got a new phone.

"Not without bein' able to pay 'im rent."

Wait. Hold up. "He never charged anyone else in the club rent!" she exclaimed.

"Right. You move in there, gonna pay 'im rent. No exceptions."

She sighed. She'd deal with that later. She was sure she could sweet talk her uncle in to letting her live there rent-free. "What else?"

"Gonna show up every fuckin' day at Brooke's inside shop."

Inside shop? "You mean her interior design business?"

He waved a massive hand around. "Whatever the fuck it is. Ain't gonna be late, ain't gonna cut out early. Gonna work your ass off an' help your sister out. Dex's gonna report back to me every fuckin' day. Got me?"

From one babysitter to the next.

Unfortunately, he wasn't done. "No booze. No drugs. No fuckin' Slit."

Ryder snorted behind her. "Slash."

"What-fuckin'-ever," Diesel barked and jabbed a meaty finger in her direction. "I find out you're down in Demons territory, I'm personally gonna go down there an' kill that motherfucker an' maybe you, too."

She wasn't worried about that, since that "rule" wouldn't be hard to follow. She wasn't planning on searching Slash out, not after that last time. And especially not after having sex with Ryder. Putting steak sauce on a hot dog did not make it Filet Mignon. Especially after getting a taste of that quality steak. Who happened to be still standing behind her way too quiet for her liking.

"This club don't need another war, woman, so don't be the reason to start one. Got me?"

Blah. Blah. Blah. Just agree so you can get the fuck out of there. "Yeah, got you. That it?"

He shook his dark head. "No. Gonna start seein' Rissa on the regular. This one ain't negotiable, either. She's gonna determine how often an' when. Better show up to every one of those fuckin' appointments. Every fuckin' one. Mercy's gonna be reportin' back to me, too, since she'll be reportin' to him. Gonna sic his ass on you if you skip out. He ain't gonna be as accomodatin' as Ryder here if he has to find your ass. Fuckin' promise you that. He's got a woman, he ain't gonna be swayed with pussy."

Kelsea's mouth dropped open, but she decided it was safer to keep her thoughts to herself on that particular point. She sensed Ryder moving restlessly behind her.

D's dark gaze lifted over her shoulder to him. "Got a fuckin' problem with what I just said?"

"No." Finally another word managed to escape the man behind her.

"Lucky you got a fuckin' job after pullin' that bullshit. It's one thing to be straightenin' that ass out, another to be tappin' it. Crossed the line, brother. You know it, I know it." Ryder must have started to say something because D raised his palm. "That discussion ends here. All that shit also ends here. Got me?" D pushed to his feet, planted his knuckles on his desk and leaned forward to roar, "Got me?"

"That was the plan," Ryder said behind her, his voice tight.

It was? She glanced over her shoulder at Ryder, but he

was making eye contact with D and his jaw looked as hard as concrete.

Well, at least now she knew where she stood with him. They were simply a distraction to each other. Something to pass the time in a place where there wasn't much to do. Except each other.

If that's all it was for him, then she was fine with that.

Wasn't she?

She turned back to D. "You can't dictate who I—"

"Not one more fuckin' word, woman. You've fuckin' proven time an' time again that you've made shitty motherfuckin' choices. That ends here today." He jammed his index finger a couple of times into his desk. "Today. Got me? You never had a father an' Ace is too fuckin' old to be dealin' with your ass. Wants to be enjoyin' his grandbabies, not teachin' a lesson to a child who should be an adult. So that puts it on my shoulders an' these fuckin' shoulders have enough weight on 'em. You ain't gonna be one of those anymore. Today all that shit stops. Gonna follow my rules an' do it with a fuckin' smile. You ain't just DAMC, but you're blood. You're a Dougherty, so act like it an' treat our family name like it means somethin' to you."

Kelsea waited for the "or else" but that didn't come. She lifted her chin. "And if I don't?"

"Don't wanna test me, woman," was all he growled before landing heavily back in his chair. "Now get the fuck outta my office. Mercy stay. Ryder take her ass to her mother's. No stoppin' for a quick fuck on the way, either. Got me?"

"Yeah, boss," Ryder grumbled as he snagged her elbow and began to steer her around.

They stopped short when Jewel opened the office door, carrying Indie and holding Violet's hand as the little girl toddled next to her. She shot Kelsea a look of relief and shoved the baby at her. "Can you hold her for a sec? I need to run to the bathroom."

"You don't look so great," Kelsea said as Indie was shoved into her arms and Jewel picked up Vi, handing her quickly to Mercy.

"You look green," Mercy agreed, the tall man taking Violet without a complaint.

Jewel's whole body heaved as she covered her mouth with her hand.

"Don't think she's gonna make it to the bathroom," Ryder warned, dropping Kelsea's elbow and grabbing a nearby trash can, just in time for Jewel to hurl into it.

Kelsea wrinkled her nose and covered it with her hand, trying not to gag at both the smell and the sound. She swallowed down the saliva pooling in her mouth.

"What the fuck, woman?" Diesel bellowed, coming around the desk and snagging Indie from Kelsea's arms. His dark brown eyes swung from the trash can Jewel held in a death grip to her face, which was now pale with a slightly green tint.

Mercy pinned his lips flat, but his gray eyes held amusement as he stared at Jewel. He shot Ryder a look, who shook his head and quickly wiped away his grin with his hand.

Jewel waved a hand around, after wiping her mouth. "Honey..."

"Better have the fuckin' flu," Diesel barked.

"I..."

"Jewelee," D groaned. "For fuck's sake..."

"Fuck, there's no more room in this office for another kid," Ryder stated.

"Don't need more room, she just needs medicine or somethin'," Diesel insisted, suddenly wearing an expression of panic, which the man probably only wore twice before in his life. Every time Jewel announced she was pregnant.

"Or something," Mercy said with a smirk.

"What she needs is for you to stop sticking your dick in her," Kelsea exclaimed. "Jesus. You got her pregnant again?"

"Ain't pregnant," Diesel answered with a scowl. "Ain't pregnant," he repeated, pinning his gaze on his ol' lady. "Better not be fuckin' knocked up again, woman." When Jewel didn't answer, he blew out a loud breath and scrubbed a hand over his short hair. "Better tell me you ate somethin' bad."

"Maybe she should be swallowing—" Kelsea started but Ryder grabbed her elbow tightly and dragged her from the office.

"You're not helpin' things," he muttered as he guided her down the hallway.

"But if she's pregnant again—"

"Not your business."

She jerked at her arm but he didn't let go. "But it's okay that he's in mine?"

"He's lookin' out for you, darlin'. That's what family does."

"How would you know since you don't have any?"

Ryder came to an abrupt halt and spun her to face him, his face tight. "Family ain't always blood, Kelsea. I told you that you need to start appreciatin' the people around you. I thought you got that. Apparently, I'm wrong."

The last part sounded like disappointment and that made her heart squeeze painfully. He was the last person she wanted to disappoint. Kelsea sucked in a lungful of air, then slowly released it. "You're not wrong," she murmured. She squeezed her eyes shut and shook her head to clear it. "I'm not ready to come back here."

"Yeah, you are. Just do what you gotta do and you'll be fine."

She tilted her head and met his green eyes. "How do you know?"

"Because I've lived it, darlin'." He softened his grip on her elbow. "You got that fire in you, you just need to let it light the way."

"It's that easy," she whispered.

"No, darlin', it's gonna be hard, but I know you can do it. D's right. The first step is to separate yourself from the people who were pullin' you down. Your roommates weren't helpin'. Slash and every other dick you were ridin' weren't, either. You also need to fix things with your mother. You need a purpose to get up every morning, which will be your job with Brooke. And you need to talk to someone who's gonna help you understand the turmoil that will bubble up from time to time. That's gonna be Rissa. And I'm tellin' you that shit will never completely go away but you'll learn to deal with it." He gently brushed a lock of hair out of her face. "You might think D's rules suck. You might think he has no right to dictate your life. But, darlin', he loves you and is only tryin' to help."

"Just like you tried to help."

"Hope I was successful somewhat."

"And now your job is done," she said flatly.

"Yeah, darlin', my job is done."

As she stared at him, his eyes slid to the side. He wouldn't look at her directly. Why?

"You're done with me," she said more firmly, hoping he'd meet her eyes again.

"Yeah. My job is done," he repeated.

"You're going to collect your paycheck and move on to the next job."

His eyes slid back. "You're beatin' a dead horse there, darlin'."

She nodded. "Then I guess there's nothing left to say." She tried to swallow the lump lodged in her throat.

She was disappointed when he didn't argue that fact.

Instead, he pushed the door open to the back parking lot and waited for her to step out.

She did and when the door slammed shut behind them, she realized how final that sounded.

He'd said nothing on the four-plus hour trip back to Shadow Valley in regard to where they would go from here. And she hadn't asked.

Now, she figured that last little conversation back at the warehouse had said it all. She knew from the beginning she was his "job," so she shouldn't let it affect her.

But it did. And as he pulled the Scout up to her mother's cabin that was situated on her Uncle Ace's farm, she felt the deep pull of dread in the pit of her stomach.

She wasn't ready for this. She wasn't ready to face the woman who she had loved and trusted, but turned out had lied to her her whole life.

"I can't do this," she murmured under her breath as she stared out of the windshield at the small cabin she grew up in. It was nothing like Ryder's cabin in the mountains. This one had been built as a rental unit along with other cabins that sat in a line behind the main farmhouse where her uncle and aunt lived. Most of them had tenants, but her mother lived in one and her Aunt Allie another. Their family had always been close. Until recently.

"You can, darlin'," he responded softly, shutting off the Scout but not moving to get out. "It's time you two made peace."

"Peace was up on that mountain, on that rock watching the sunrise."

"Can't stay up there forever."

She turned in her seat to study his profile. "Why not?"

"Because unless you're independently wealthy, you need

a job for food, propane, electricity. Shit like that. You're not wealthy and neither am I."

As she opened her mouth to ask him if they could afford it, would he stay up there on that mountain with her. Would he want that? To be with her if things were different?

But before the first word could escape, he pushed open the driver's door and got out, going around to the back of the truck to grab the few things she brought back with her from Kentucky.

She continued to stare at the cabin and wondered if her mother was inside also dreading the conversation both of them needed to have.

Ryder opened the passenger door, leaned his forearm against the top of the door frame and leaned in.

Kelsea fought the urge to shove her face into his chest and inhale his now familiar scent for probably the last time.

Life was so not fair.

But she knew that, she had told herself she would do better, be better, so now she had to deal with the shit that had been splattered on her. She needed to wipe it off, lift her head and be strong.

She had no choice unless she wanted to go back to floundering and being a huge let-down to everyone she knew.

She suddenly missed the club sisterhood and hoped she could reconnect with them again. They were family. True family.

And one thing she knew from growing up in the DAMC was that not all family was blood. Ryder was right, but she didn't need him to tell her that. She knew that since she was born.

Ryder waited patiently, his forehead pressed against his forearm, his green eyes intense as he studied her. Was this really it for them?

His low voice, the one that had sang so many songs in

the past ten days, swept through her, but instead of creating the warmth it normally did, it gave her a chill. "You gonna tell your mom?"

"Tell her what?"

She turned her head to see his lifted brow. Their faces were only inches apart. The mouth he'd used to skillfully kiss, suck and lick every inch of her body right there. Within reach.

She turned away before she lowered herself to the point of begging and stared back out of the windshield to avoid his searching gaze. She cleared her throat, hoping to reduce the tightness there. "I don't think so."

She expected him to disagree with that decision, but he didn't. "Talk to Rissa 'bout it first. See what she recommends. You tellin' your mom might just make her feel guiltier and that might not help either of you. But I'm not the expert."

No, he wasn't, but the man had some good instincts. "Rissa is a sex therapist."

"She's still a licensed therapist, darlin', and she's family. She's gonna care 'bout you more than any stranger would."

How did he know that? She'd never even met the woman. "I don't even know her."

From the corner of her eye, she could see his soft smile. "She was inducted into the club sisterhood without them even askin' her. So you're gonna get to know her one way or another."

"Not sure I'll want to hang out with someone socially who will know all my secrets."

"She's a good woman, Kelsea. She's not gonna judge you. Hell, she's with Mercy. With all the shit that man's done in his life, she doesn't judge him."

"She loves him?"

"Assume so. Why else would she put up with his fuckin' ass?"

He chuckled but that died quickly when she turned to face him and asked, "Why'd you put up with mine?"

A muscle in his jaw flexed, but he didn't answer her.

"I'm sorry," she whispered.

She caught his slight flinch.

"I'm sorry for everything you had to do for me. I'm sorry that you were the one who had to step in time and time again. I'm sorry that you were so tired of saving my ass that you had to resort to something desperate by taking me up to your personal haven. I'm sorry I fought you in the beginning and I was unappreciative. I promise you will never have to do that again."

He closed his eyes for a long moment and when he opened them, they were darker than normal. "Just you apologizin', darlin', made it all worthwhile."

She doubted that.

"But you're right, I'll never have to do it again. Because you'll never be in those situations again."

He was so confident. If he could be, so could she.

He stepped back, unblocking the passenger door. "Now, time for you to go settle things with your mother. Remember, she's the only one you got. If shit gets outta hand between you two, go take a walk to cool off. Call Brooke. Call Rissa. Call somebody..."

Just not you.

"Then lift your head up and try again. Yeah?"

She nodded.

He picked her stuff up off the ground at his feet. "I'll walk you to the door. Then it's all on you."

She climbed out of the Scout and followed him to the front door of the cabin. He set the stuff down and turned to her. She held her breath when he reached out and swept his thumb down her cheek. "You've got this."

I just don't have you.

She lifted her face when he pressed a kiss to her forehead and then turned. Kelsea watched his broad back and his narrow hips as his long stride made quick work of returning to his truck.

And every step he took farther away from her made her skin start to itch and her anxiety begin to rise.

"Dwight!"

He hesitated as he reached for his driver's side door, and he looked back over his shoulder. "Yeah?"

It hit her then why he was leaving, why this wouldn't work between them. At least not now, maybe not ever.

She had transferred her crutch of drugs, alcohol and random sex to the man who stood waiting patiently for her to respond.

She hadn't seen it. But he did.

He had said she needed to do this on her own and by him sticking around, she'd end up leaning on him too much.

She needed to stand on her own two feet.

Maybe once she accomplished that...

She shook her head and swallowed. "Thank you."

He dropped his gaze to the ground at his feet for what seemed like forever. Then he lifted his head, nodded and got in his Scout.

Before he was even out of sight, she inhaled a deep breath and opened the door to the cabin, stepping inside.

Chapter Seventeen

"How did dinner go with your mother the other night?" Rissa asked before taking a sip of her iced coffee.

Kelsea sighed and leaned back on the couch. The office Mercy's woman had rented for her new counseling services was pretty sparse at this point. She had explained that between going back and forth to Vegas and tying up loose ends with her house and patients there, she didn't have time to finish decorating.

But since Kelsea was now back working for Brooke, she had offered to help design it. Rissa jumped on that, so after their regular session today, they would sit down after analyzing Kelsea and analyze Rissa's office space instead.

Rissa also agreed for Kelsea to decorate their new house in the DAMC compound that Mercy and she were having built. She would do it in exchange for all the time Kelsea had spent bending her ear.

She had grown really fond of the woman. Ryder was right, Rissa hadn't judged once. But instead, had been teaching Kelsea techniques how to deal with things when they became overwhelming and was tempted to bolt to the nearest liquor store, club or bar. Or find someone to party with until her memories were once again wiped out.

One thing she didn't have a desire to do was go find Slash or some random fuck.

But she did struggle not to hunt down Ryder. She swore she had stopped herself from calling him over a thousand times in the last few weeks. Even to simply give him an update on her progress.

But that would only be an excuse to hear his deep voice because she missed that and his damn country music. But only when he was singing it.

"The whole thing was tense," Kelsea finally answered about her dinner with her mother.

"Why?"

"Because sometimes I want to tell her what Pierce did to me, and other times I don't want her to ever know. Depends on how pissed I get at her."

"Why pissed?" Rissa had a pad and pen on the small wooden folding table next to her, but not once had she picked it up in all the sessions they'd had together. Maybe the woman had a mind like a trap and made notes afterward.

"Because she sat across from me eating chicken fucking marsala clueless to what I've been through. What situation she put me in. What her lies cost me."

Rissa lifted a shoulder. "So tell her. Be open about it with her."

"I can't," Kelsea whispered, her heartburn suddenly flaring up. She rubbed at her chest.

"Do you want her to apologize for what she did?"

"She did."

"Yes, she apologized for never telling you who your father was. But what about the rest?"

Yes.

No.

"I don't know. It won't change anything."

"It won't change the past, but maybe it'll settle some things between you two to get it all out in the open. And you'll have let go of the blame that you're holding bottled up inside you."

"Maybe."

Rissa stared at her for a few seconds. When she did that Kelsea swore the woman could see right into her soul. She had a spooky knack.

"Only when you're ready, Kelsea. Don't force it. Tell her when the time is right for you, but be prepared for her reactions."

"That's what I'm afraid of." Kelsea met Rissa's gentle gaze. "I'm afraid her reaction will spur," she squeezed her eyes shut and shook her head, "things inside me and I'll end up on a bender."

"You can call me anytime."

"I know." The woman was more than generous with her time and patience.

"I was hoping that moving into your own apartment and then spending only short amounts of time with her would help ease the rift. Doesn't seem to be."

"I thought it might, too. Even so, I'm glad I'm out on my own. I'm starting to feel like a responsible adult again. Though some might argue and say I never was. But having my own place, a good job and a relationship with my sister..."

"You've reconnected with the DAMC ladies, too."

Kelsea smirked at the term "ladies." "Yes."

"That has to feel good."

"It does." And that was true. She didn't realize how much she missed them until she started joining in on their "meetings of the sisterhood" again.

"Have you told any of them yet?"

"No."

"You don't have to. No one needs to know."

She thought about talking to Diamond, but she was currently happy with her ol' man and their young son. Di had her own family now and a successful business. Kelsea didn't want to dredge up any of that shit with her, causing that happiness to dampen.

Diamond's secret had come out into the open unexpectedly when Pierce boasted about taking her virginity. After that night, no one ever saw him again.

They all knew the man had been dealt with, they just didn't know the details.

"Last time you were here, you said Coop asked you out. Did you accept yet?"

"I can't. He's a prospect."

Rissa sighed and shook her head. "What does that matter?"

She didn't know much about the club life besides what Kelsea told her. Mercy wasn't a part of the MC, so the woman didn't live the life like the rest of the club sisterhood.

"It would threaten his chances on becoming patched. Once he's patched over in the next couple months, it would be different."

"Will you say yes then?"

"I don't know."

"You said he's sweet."

Kelsea smothered her snort. "He's a biker. You don't ever call a biker sweet."

Rissa laughed. "So, he isn't?"

"He is. But you just don't point it out."

"Then there's potential there," she insinuated.

No, there wasn't. As hot as Coop was, as "sweet" as the club prospect had been with Kelsea, she had no interest in him. She didn't blow him off when she ran into him, but she also didn't encourage him.

She had another man still too fresh on her mind.

"Have you heard from him?"

Her attention went back to Rissa. "Who? Coop?"

"Ryder."

It took her a few moments to answer because she had to fight back the sharp sting in her eyes the pain of hearing his name caused. "No."

"They're stubborn," was all she said. There was no doubt that Rissa was talking about her own man, too. "I get it. Sometimes it's like beating your head against a wall."

"But you deal with it."

One corner of Rissa's lip curved up. "I do. But every day is certainly a challenge. These men aren't easy."

"I'm not, either," Kelsea admitted.

"No, and though I don't know Ryder's background, I can assume he's dealt with some of the same issues as Ryan and probably the rest of the Shadows have."

"Who?"

Rissa shook her head and her half smile turned into a full smile. "Mercy." Then a second later her smile dropped. "You and Ryder may not be the best choice for each other. I don't know if he has his own demons to fight and if he does, what they entail. These guys can have triggers, especially if they're struggling with PTSD. I know you may think differently, but being with you might not be the best thing for him since—and we've talked about this already—you're dealing with it, too."

"For different reasons," Kelsea reminded her.

"That doesn't matter. He probably knows what's best for his mental health."

"And I'm a threat to that."

"Could be."

Though that wasn't what she wanted to hear, she had no choice but to accept it. She didn't want to hurt Ryder in any way, even unintentionally.

It was time for her to move on. She couldn't be stuck waiting for a man who may never show up.

One thing Rissa had taught her was that for years, Kelsea allowed her life and her actions to be affected by a man. It was time for her not to allow anyone that power any more. Whether that man was Pierce or even Ryder. It was time for her to be happy and the only person who could ensure that happiness was herself.

That power was now in her own two hands.

If she failed, it was no one's fault but her own.

And she wasn't about to fail.

RYDER SLAPPED his cards face down and let his gaze circle the table. He hadn't missed poker night since he no longer chased Kelsea's ass down in the seediest of places.

He grabbed his lit cigar out of the ashtray near his elbow and puffed on it, letting the smoke encircle him. If he had to allow himself a vice, he guessed chomping on a stogie while playing poker wasn't a bad one.

And safer than the other one he'd considered. A blonde-haired, blue-eyed vixen who could be a tempting, but dangerous addiction.

The house they were sitting in was just a shell. The framing of the walls exposed because the plumbers and electricians had recently finished installing the pipes and wiring.

"When you movin' in?" he asked Mercy, who sat on a green plastic chair that bowed under his weight at the end of a cheap plastic table.

"When the fucking house is finished," Mercy said around his cigar, a swirl of smoke rising above his head.

"Ain't she gonna be pissed we're smoking cigars in here?" Brick asked at the other end of the table. He lifted a glass to his lips and downed the remainder of his whiskey in one swallow.

Ryder could imagine how smooth that whiskey tasted going down. His gaze landed on the bottle sitting like a beacon in the middle of the table.

"Who's gonna tell her?" Mercy asked Brick with his scarred brow cocked.

"The stink's gonna tell her," Steel answered, clipping the tip off his own stogie and lighting it.

"Look at you getting all domestic and shit," Hunter ribbed Mercy. "Got a woman who can deal with your black heart, building a house and now living together. Part-time now, full-time soon. Next, you'll be sliding a ring on that finger."

All eyes turned to Mercy and he pulled the cigar from his lips. "Fucking jealous you don't have a piece like mine."

Hunter's jaw got tight. "Right, instead of getting laid by some classy piece of ass, I'm chasing down a biker's brother who may not even fucking exist." He picked up his bottle of Iron City beer and guzzled half of it.

"Haven't come up with any leads yet?" Ryder asked him, surprised since Hunter was one of D's best trackers.

Hunter shook his head. "Not fucking one. And if he truly exists, then I would've come across something by now. I think this has all been a wild goose chase and a waste of my fucking time and skills."

"You're getting paid for it, so stop your fucking bitching," Walker told him, sorting his cards with one eye open and one squeezed shut like it helped him see better or some such shit.

"Shut up, asshole, and ante up," Hunter said, jamming his cigar back between his lips.

"Why does Slade even care about finding a long-lost sibling?" Brick asked.

"'Cause maybe he never had a real family and wants

one?" Ryder suggested, finding himself a little more annoyed with that question than he normally would be.

"He's got Diamond and Hudson now. He's got a family," Brick stated, telling them something they already knew.

Mercy slammed his hand on the plastic table and everything on it jumped an inch off the thin plastic surface. The Jack bottle toppled over, drawing Ryder's eyes back to it. He gritted his teeth at the sudden urge to feel that smooth whiskey sliding down his throat to dull some of his unwanted urges he'd been fighting.

Mercy barked, "'Cause it's what the man wants. Who fucking gives a shit? He's paying the bill. Are we here to play poker or chit-chat like a bunch of pussies?"

"What's up your ass?" Steel asked him.

"He's feelin' that noose tightenin' up around his fuckin' neck, that's what," Ryder said, just like he was feeling that call of booze tightening around his own throat, too. Normally it didn't bother him to be around his teammates when they drank. Tonight, for some reason, it was getting to him.

He needed to dig deep for his willpower and ignore that siren's call.

Mercy slammed his cards down on the table making it wobble again. "The whole point of poker night is to let off steam in a safe place, not to talk fucking shop. But you assholes wanna talk shop, then let's talk shop." He jabbed a long finger toward Hunter. "D'you even go talk to Rocky at Greene? He's the fucker who started this whole goddamn thing."

Hunter snorted. "Yeah. But he wouldn't talk to me since he didn't know me and I'm not DAMC. Said to bring Jewel and his grandbabies back next time and *maybe* he'd tell me what he knows."

"Fucking bikers are stubborn as fuck," Steel grumbled.

"Well, there you go," Mercy said to Hunter. "Get Diesel to bring Jewel and the girls."

"She doesn't want her girls at a max security prison to go visit their grandfather who's a fucking murderer. Would you?"

No one could argue that fact.

"What did D say about Rocky's demand?" Ryder asked Hunter.

"He grunted and scowled."

"Well, that could mean just about anything with him," Brick said, squinting as he puffed on his cigar and sorted his hand of cards.

"No shit. But I need to hear everything Buzz said before Rocky and Doc gutted the man. I need *something* to go on. Besides some random rambling of a man doing life without parole."

"Buzz is Slade's pop, right?" Steel asked.

"Was," Hunter corrected him.

"How fucked up is that shit? Diamond marrying and having a baby with the son of the man her own father butchered," Brick said with a shake of his head.

"And his father murdered Crow's parents," Ryder reminded them.

"Never ending pile of twisted shit," Mercy mumbled, grabbing the Jack Daniels from the center of the table and refilling his glass.

Ryder's eyes were glued to Mercy as he lifted that glass to his lips and swallowed the Jack down.

Fuck, his urge was strong tonight and his willpower weak.

This was not good.

He turned his head and saw Steel watching him intently. Steel lifted his chin slightly toward the sliders that lead to the back deck. The man's plastic chair squealed when he pushed it away from the table. "Gotta take a piss."

As he opened the sliders, Ryder also stood, saying, "Me, too."

"You two gonna hold each other's dicks or something?" Brick yelled. "I mean, only females go to the bathroom together. Unless you two need to tell us something."

"Fuck you, asshole," Ryder grumbled, flipping him the bird. "You only wish you could hold my massive cock."

Ryder slid the glass door closed and carefully made his way over to the edge of the partially finished deck where Steel really was taking a piss.

After Steel shook it off and tucked it away, he turned to face Ryder. Even in the dark, he could see the other man's concerned but angry expression. "I gotta beat your fucking ass again? Are you needing a reminder of how that shit was fucking up your life?"

"Got it under control."

"When you're staring at a bottle of whiskey like it's the best pussy you ever had, I don't think you do." Steel shook his head. "Brother, you haven't been the same since you got back from Kentucky. You let that DC get under your skin?"

Ryder sucked in a sharp breath, his fingers curling into fists by his side.

Steel spread his feet and rolled his neck. "I see you gearing up, brother. I see it even in the dark. So you let her worm her way in, didn't you?"

"I didn't let her do shit."

"The fuck you didn't. You never responded like that to her nickname before."

"Never said I liked it."

"Never said it bothered you, either." Steel tilted his head, his eyes narrowed. "Can I stand down?"

"Yeah," Ryder answered, forcing his fingers flat against his thighs.

"Telling you, you swing at me, it's on. And you'll end up like you did last time."

He'd be a fool to take on Steel, someone who trained constantly in a mix of martial arts and boxing. He spent more time at Shadow Valley Fitness, the business that Slade and Di ran, than he did at his own place or even at the warehouse. The man was a machine and he could break a man's neck with a single twist. "She ain't just a job, is she?"

"She was a job."

"Was," Steel repeated.

"Job's over."

"Not sure that's what you meant."

"You heard what I said," Ryder grumbled.

Steel shook his head, planted his hands on his hips and turned to stare out into the dark woods behind the house. "You got it bad."

"No."

"Then you're fooling yourself. Is it because you want her or because you're denying that you want her that's tempting you to pick up the bottle again?"

"I haven't drank."

"Yet." Steel turned back toward Ryder. "Dude, I get it. Shit gets lonely sometimes. Those cravings get strong, start tugging at you. Especially at night in the dark in your bed by yourself. But that one, she ain't good for you. She's a fucking mess. Go find some other pussy to relieve the tension. Eventually you'll find one who will grab your attention long enough to forget her."

Problem was, he didn't want any other pussy. Right now, he had one woman on his brain. Even though he knew she wasn't good for him, he couldn't wipe her from his mind.

But the last thing he wanted was to find himself back in the bottom of a hole trying to claw his way back out.

They heard the back door slide open, pulling their attention. It wasn't hard to recognize who it was because Mercy was taller than all of them.

"You two done whacking each other off?" Mercy jerked

his chin at Steel and, without a word, Steel went back inside, closing the door behind him.

Mercy rounded on Ryder. "What's going on?"

"Nothing. Just had to piss."

"Bullshit."

Both of them said nothing for a few seconds. The only sound in the night was an owl hooting and what could be some frogs chirping in the distance.

"She's still seeing Rissa twice a week, right?" Ryder asked.

"Who?"

Now Mercy was just being a dick on purpose. "You know who."

"Why do you care?"

"Because I worry about her." He worried about her every fucking minute of every fucking day.

"She's fine."

That didn't make him feel much better. "Rissa tell you that?"

"She can't give me specifics, but I do know she moved out of her mother's a few days after you brought her home."

Ryder pretended not to know that, though he already did. It didn't even take three days before she moved into the vacant apartment above her uncle's pawn shop.

A few times, from a distance, he'd watched her come home to make sure she got into her apartment at night safely. And he'd stick around just long enough to see she hadn't headed back out after she did so.

A few times he'd hopped on his Harley and followed her up to her sister's interior design shop right outside of Pittsburgh. From what he'd seen, she'd been doing what she said she would and also what Diesel told her she needed to do.

Staying sober, staying away from certain people, continuing to see Rissa and taking her job with Brooke seriously.

He was relieved that Kelsea was getting her life under control.

Helping her had taken a bit of a toll on him. But it was nothing he couldn't deal with. Steel was right, he just needed to find a distraction until he forgot all about her.

"She's doing good," Mercy said.

"Good."

"But you know that already. Just like you also fucking know where she's living."

Ryder's gaze landed on Mercy, whose eyes were shadowed from the lack of light on the deck.

He continued before Ryder could deny it. "Brother, I fought it, too. Thought I could beat it. That fucking addiction that pulls at you. Takes everything you've worked hard to keep tight and spins that shit out of control, making you scramble for your sanity. Hell, making it question your sanity."

"Just told Steel I haven't had a fuckin' drink."

"Wasn't talking about booze."

"Not sure you should be givin' relationship advice."

"I'm not giving you fucking advice, I leave that shit to Rissa. Just telling you that I know what you're struggling with."

"Rissa had her shit together."

"Yeah."

"Kelsea doesn't," Ryder reminded him.

"She's getting there."

Ryder's brows shot up to his head. "What are you sayin', Mercy?"

"Saying I almost fucked up and let a good thing go. Woulda been stupid on my part." He headed back toward the house, throwing over his shoulder, "Don't be stupid."

Chapter Eighteen

"We need to plan a baby shower," Jayde announced, then shoved what was left of her cupcake into her mouth.

"I swear every time we have a meeting of the sisterhood my hips get a little wider," Kiki complained after taking her own bite of one of Bella's luscious stuffed tiramisu cupcakes. Her eyes rolled as she moaned. "We need to stop meeting here."

A bunch of loud "no's" rose up.

"Bite your tongue. I need my fix. It's better than sex, I swear," Kelsea said, licking chocolate ganache from her finger.

"*You* bite your tongue. It is not!" Jazz yelled.

"Well, yeah, you have Crow, so of course not. And the rest of you get it on the regular. I'm the only one not getting any," Kelsea grumbled.

"Why not?" Emma asked.

She met Rissa's eyes for a moment before her attention was pulled back to the rest of the DAMC women around their "meeting" room above Sophie's Sweet Treats. "Can we get back to talking about planning a baby shower?" Kelsea asked, wanting to change the subject.

"Whose shower are we planning now?" Sophie, the club president's ol' lady, asked, glancing around the table.

Sophie had it right to be confused, it could be any of the women sitting there. Well, except for Kelsea. There would definitely be no baby shower in her near future. Nor bridal shower. Not even an engagement party.

Nothing. Because the one man who she wanted all of that with didn't want her.

"Mine," Jewel announced, biting into a second cupcake.

"You've already had two. How many more do you need? Seriously, what baby stuff don't you have already? You're like a baby factory," Diamond complained.

"After this one, this factory is going out of business. I'm going to talk to the doctor about tying my tubes."

Ivy shrugged. "Tell D to get snipped."

Jewel's eyes widened and then she burst out laughing. A second later, so did everyone else.

"You know that man's not going to let anyone near his nuts with a knife," Jewel stated.

"Zak and I have discussed it," Sophie said. "Two's enough for us. He may be willing to get it done since I can't get my tubes tied, in case I end up being Axel and Bella's surrogate."

"Is that going to happen?" Kelsea asked, surprised. She'd been so out of the loop for the past year or so. But she had to admit, she'd missed this. She'd missed the connection with her DAMC sisters. Why had she been so stupid to alienate them all?

They were the most supportive group of women she knew.

"I hope so," Sophie murmured.

Kelsea glanced at Bella. "Cuz?"

Her cousin gave her a small smile. "We're leaning that way. Sophie and I have already decided we're fine with it. Now we just need the boys to agree. And Ivy."

"Why Ivy?"

"Because my eggs carry the same—or the closest—DNA as Bella's since we're sisters. So take my eggs, add Axel's baby makers and voilà!" Ivy exclaimed. "A kid as close to their DNA as they're going to get."

"A joint effort," Sophie said with a smile.

"I don't get it. Why doesn't Ivy just be the surrogate?" Kelsea asked.

"Jag wasn't a hundred percent on board with this whole thing, so we negotiated," Ivy told her.

Bella leaned forward and stage whispered, "Because Jag was a bit freaked out over Ivy carrying another man's baby, even if it's his cousin's."

"That, and he's been bugging me for number two," Ivy added. "He said I can't bake his kid if I'm baking someone else's. His words, not mine. *Aaaand* I think if I had to carry the baby for Bella with it being my own egg, I might feel too much of a connection to the baby once he or she was born. More than an aunt, if you get my meaning. This way I won't have any maternal bond, I'll just enjoy being an auntie."

Kelsea pressed her palm against her forehead. "This all hurts my head. It's way too complicated."

"Well, it's what family does for one another," Brooke said, giving her a look.

"Right. But just don't expect me to carry your and Dex's baby."

Brooke laughed, then blushed. "I think you're safe from that."

Kelsea wasn't sure she ever saw her sister blush. Her eyes narrowed. "Why?"

All eyes turned to Brooke, who simply shrugged.

"Oh fuck," Diamond shouted, throwing her hands up. "We might as well pick a date on the calendar each month for a fucking baby shower. Is the fifteenth good for everyone?"

"Dex hasn't said a word to me. He's probably freaking the fuck out!" Ivy exclaimed, clapping her hands in excitement.

"About as excited as you," Brooke said, giving her sister-in-law a dry look, then continued with a smile. "But he's ecstatic, that's for sure. He didn't even blink when I told him that he would be designated as Mr. Mom since I'm not putting the business on hold. And he agreed."

"Well, at least you have Kelsea to help out now with the business. That will make things so much easier during the pregnancy and once the baby is born. I can't imagine having kids and running this bakery without Bella," Sophie said. "Congrats, by the way."

Congratulations circled the long table.

"Thank you. But you've reminded me that I need to take a dozen cupcakes over to Ryder," Brooke said.

Kelsea's ears perked up. "For what?"

"As a thank you," Brooke answered.

"A thank you for what?" Kelsea asked when her sister didn't explain what she was thanking Ryder for.

Though she had a feeling she knew why, which was confirmed when Bella said to Brooke, "I'll give you two dozen," then turned to Kelsea. "You had us all worried, Kels. He was the only one who got through to you. To be honest, we thought we were going to lose you." She swallowed hard and dropped her head, hiding her face.

Kelsea fought the sting in her own eyes when she heard her cousin sniffle.

"Hawk was out of his freaking mind," Kiki added. "He almost went down to West Virginia to get you that last time, but Diesel said that if any of the DAMC members went it might start a war with the Demons, so that's why he kept sending Ryder instead. I had to beg and argue with Hawk not to go, but it was a fight."

"I'm sorry."

"And you should be," Diamond snapped, pushing her hardly touched cupcake away. "Pierce was only... He didn't... If..." She shook her head, blinking quickly, her brow furrowed. "If anyone had the right to go crazy over that motherfucking asshole, it was me, Kels, *me!*"

Kelsea opened her mouth, then snapped it shut. No one at that table knew what Pierce did to her besides Rissa, who spoke up in a calm, soothing voice next. "We all process things differently. There's no right or wrong way to deal with trauma."

"What trauma did she have, besides her mother not telling her that motherfucker was her sperm donor? That's it. And that should be a fucking gift, which apparently she doesn't appreciate," Diamond pushed away from the table, her chair scraping along the wooden floor, a sob escaping her lips before she could stop it. "I need to pick up Hudson from my mother."

"Di!" Kelsea yelled as Diamond rushed toward the stairs.

Di lifted her hand over her shoulder and disappeared.

"Fuck!" Kelsea muffled her scream into her hands as she covered her face. She lifted her head. "I need to go talk to her."

The table had gotten way too quiet for Kelsea. Everyone seemed visibly upset and it was all her fault.

But unless she told them, they wouldn't understand her turmoil. And she couldn't tell them. Not now, maybe not ever.

Rissa stood. "I can talk to her. Things are a little raw with her right now since we started meeting."

Kelsea had no idea Diamond was meeting with Rissa,

too. She stood. "I'll go after her. I'm sorry to fuck up our meeting."

She hurried toward the stairs hoping to catch Diamond before she drove away. As she jogged down the steps, she came face to face with Zak, the DAMC president and Sophie's ol' man. He was carrying his youngest son, Zane, and was holding his older son Zeke's hand as they slowly made their way up the steps.

"Meetin' over yet?"

"No. Did you see Diamond?"

"She took off, spinnin' the tires. D'you all get into some sorta cat fight or somethin'?"

"No," she said as she pushed past him carefully, trying not to bowl them all over. "She say where she was going?"

"Fuck no. Why would I care?" he continued up the steps.

"Ugh! Z!"

"What?"

"Nothing!" she yelled over her shoulder and continued to the bottom and out of the back door to where she was parked. She yanked her cell phone out of her bag and quickly texted Diamond.

Plz meet me somewhere. We need 2 talk.

She got into her car and turned her air conditioning on full blast so she wouldn't melt as she waited for an answer.

Can't, was the answer she finally got after a few minutes.

Plz. It's important.

She almost gave up waiting when another text came through. *Picking up Hudson. The gym in fifteen.*

Kelsea started her car and pointed it in that direction.

———

Kelsea watched Steel and Slade spar with each other in the boxing ring set up to one side of the Shadow Valley

Fitness. Slade, Diamond's ol' man, was now the bulkiest she'd ever seen him. But then, he owned and ran a gym, so he probably worked out for hours each day. But Steel was also...

Impressive.

He wore no shirt and his bare skin was slick with sweat. But the man was quick on his feet. Maybe even a little quicker than Slade, even though he was a bigger man.

But no matter what, the power behind each punch was scary, even though both wore head gear and mouth guards.

As the two circled around, Steel's broad muscular back faced her and she studied the large tattoo that adorned it. At first, she thought it was similar to the colors all of the DAMC members had inked onto their backs. Slade himself had the rockers and patches tattooed into his skin after being patched in.

But this was a little different. All done in black and grey, it had an eagle with its wings spread, holding some sort of knife that included five stars in a half circle and a ribbon above all that read, "Spiritus Invictus." The large tattoo rippled as he moved.

Good thing both men were too busy concentrating on each other for them to notice a dribble of drool at the corner of her mouth. She quickly wiped it away.

"Yeah, I get to see that often," Diamond said behind her.

Kelsea turned to see the dark-haired beauty holding her son, Hudson. "Lucky you," she murmured.

Funny, now that she thought about it, looking at both Slade and Steel's tattoos, she realized Ryder was tattoo-free. Even though he wasn't a biker, he *was* former military and she thought he might be in the minority when it came to not having even one drop of ink.

Diamond stepped up to the ring and Slade shouted something around his mouth guard. A second later, both men stopped their dancing around the ring. Slade, a former Marine himself, came over, greeted his ol' lady with a "Hey, Princess" as he ducked his head through the ropes, giving Diamond a kiss, then bopped Hud gently on the noggin with his thick boxing glove. That, of course, made his ten-month old son scream with laughter.

The back of Kelsea's neck prickled, and she lifted her gaze from Diamond and her ol' man to Steel, who leaned back into the corner ropes, staring at her across the ring. His eyes held a bit of contempt as he chewed on his mouth guard and contemplated her.

What the fuck was up his ass?

Her attention was drawn back to Di when she told Slade that she was heading into the back office to do some paperwork.

Di then turned to her and jerked her head toward the back of the gym where her and Slade's office was. Kelsea followed on her heels, murmuring, "Fuck, girl. Your ol' man's getting to be a beast. How many women who work out here throw themselves at him?"

"A few. But I cancel their membership if they get too inappropriate. So, the warning's gotten around."

Her eyes slid back to Steel. "Do all of D's crew work out here?"

"Yeah. And often."

"You can get pregnant just walking in here, I swear."

"Bite your tongue. The DAMC sisters are populating Shadow Valley all on our own."

"Do you think Kiki will have a second one?"

"If it's up to Hawk, then yes, they'll probably have one more. Jag and Ivy will, too. Now Brooke and Dex are having their first of who knows how many. Sophie and Z have two. And then if Sophie ends up being a surrogate for Bella, Bella and Axel will have at least one. Emma and Dawg already have three. Oh, Diesel and Jewel with *three*! Which I never would have ever expected. My little man, Hudson. Then I'm sure Jazz and Jayde eventually. Fuck. We might have to start our own school district." Diamond pushed open her office door and once they stepped inside, closed it behind them.

She plopped Hudson down in a playpen near the desk before leaning back against it to face Kelsea. "Then there's you."

"What about me?"

"Eventually you may want to settle down and add to our growing numbers. Right?"

"Well, if I'm anything like our mothers, no settling down is needed. Your mother had three kids."

"My father married my mother," Di reminded her.

"And then went to prison for murder when you all were still babies. She had no one to help."

"Ace and Janice. And your mom helped, too. Hell, the club helped raise us all."

"And that's why I'm here."

Diamond's brows furrowed. "If this is about Pierce..."

"It is."

Diamond dropped her head and shook it. "I don't want to talk about it. I've been talking to Rissa. It's been really difficult."

"Was that your choice?"

"I was strongly encouraged by both Slade and Crow."

Kelsea's eyebrows rose. "And you listened?"

Diamond lifted her head and gave her a crooked smile. "I know, right? Crow suggested Jazz start seeing Rissa. She did and even in a short amount of time, Jazz has showed an improvement. So, he talked to Slade and then they both approached me."

"Damn," Kelsea whispered. "They ganged up on you."

"Not really. They left the decision up to me, but I could see the concern in both of their faces, so I told them I'd try it. But it's been difficult. Very difficult. I had a lot of repressed memories."

"I completely understand how difficult. I've been seeing her, too."

Diamond's mouth dropped open, after a second, she snapped it shut. "For what?"

Kelsea swallowed the lump that was attempting to rise in her throat. "For the same thing."

"What do you mean, same thing?"

Kelsea hesitated and took a deep breath. "Because..." She squeezed her eyes shut.

"No!" Diamond screamed so loudly, Kelsea jumped and Hudson began to cry. "No! That motherfucker!" She dropped to her ass onto the floor, hiding her face in her hands. "No," she moaned. "*Fuck.*"

Hudson began to cry louder, so Kelsea, unsure what to do, went over and picked him up, bouncing him up and down to try to settle him. "It's okay, Hudsy boy. It's okay."

When Diamond finally lifted her head, tears were slipping down her cheek. The woman was tough. Strong. She was not a crier. "This was my fault."

"How?"

"I should have come forward. I should have!"

"No, Di, it wasn't your fault. It was his. It's all on him."

"If I had come forward, maybe..."

"But you didn't remember everything anyway, right?" That's what Kelsea had been told. Was that not true?

"I remembered some of it. Not everything. But still... Fuck, Kels. Fuck!" Di shook her head, and then swiped at the tears on her cheek with the back of her hand. "Death was too good for him. I'm sorry."

"Nothing for you to be sorry about. No one knew about you. No one knew about me. I didn't come forward, either. I should have. Maybe I would have saved the next person."

Diamond's red-rimmed eyes met hers, her face getting hard. "Was there a next person?"

"I don't know. I can't imagine there wasn't. He was opportunist scum."

"How the hell did he get away with it if there were more? We know of Brooke's mom, you and me. We were young. But any adults..."

"Because who wants to be treated like they're the one to blame when they're really the victim? Who wants to relive it over and over? It would've been our word against his and you know how manipulative he was. It was why he got away with the shit he did for so long. And then there would have been medical exams, and interrogations, a possible trial."

Diamond pulled herself to her feet using the desk, rubbing away the remainder of her tears. "No, Diesel or one of the brothers would've taken him out. He never would've made it to trial."

Di took Hudson from Kelsea and now that he'd calmed down, she put him back in the playpen. Once she straightened, she surprised Kelsea by grabbing her and squeezing her tightly against her. "I'm sorry I was a bitch earlier. I had no idea."

"No one does," Kelsea murmured. "Well, Ryder and Rissa do. Now you. That's it."

Di released her and stepped back. "Poor Rissa. She's probably already regretting the idea of moving here permanently. Between me and you. Jazz..."

"And she has to deal with Mercy. Hell, she doesn't even have to build a new clientele, it was already here just waiting for her. She's probably wondering what the fuck she stepped into."

Diamond did a combination sniffle-laugh. "Maybe we need to get the club colors tattooed onto her back, so if she escapes, we can easily find her."

"Yep. She's stuck with us now. So anyway... That's what I

wanted to tell you. You got upset earlier and I felt bad. But I knew if anyone would understand, it would be you."

"But he wasn't even my blood. He was your..." Diamond squeezed her eyes shut, her hands clenching into fists.

"Yeah," Kelsea whispered.

"So glad that motherfucker is gone."

"Yeah," Kelsea repeated softly.

Diamond lifted her head. "You said Ryder knows?"

"Yes."

"Did things happen in Kentucky?"

"Things?" Kelsea pretended to be clueless.

"Between the two of you. You guys were gone for over a week." Di rose her brows. "Alone in a cabin."

This was her fellow "sister." Diamond and she grew up next door to each other on Ace's farm. They grew up in the club together. Kelsea could be open and honest with her, so she nodded. "Things happened."

Diamond kept her expression neutral. "And?"

"And we came back."

"And?"

"And nothing. He found me in West Virginia, dragged me against my will to Kentucky, forced me to open my eyes, even after I fought him to the point he should've just washed his hands of me and walked away, and then we came home."

"So, that's it?"

"That's it."

"Are you okay with that?"

"Do I have a choice?"

"Of course you have a choice. Us biker chicks get what we go after. If you want him, then you go get him." Diamond tilted her head and studied Kelsea. "Do you want him?"

That wasn't even a question. She never wanted anyone more.

"Fuck, Kels, if you could see your face... You don't even need to answer. It's as clear as day."

"Is it?"

"You've got it bad."

"Truth? I'm starting to wonder if I kept doing the shit I did because I knew he'd come get me."

"You mean subconsciously?"

Kelsea nodded. "Did I see him as some kind of hero or something? That he'd come and save me from myself?"

"Isn't that what he did?"

Kelsea combed her fingers through her hair and then stared at the floor for a few seconds. "He may have helped, but it wasn't all him."

"No, you had to help yourself, too. You needed the resolve, he just needed to smack you upside the head to recognize it. With a big bat."

Kelsea laughed.

"But whatever he did, whatever you two discovered down in Kentucky, we're thankful he did. Like a snow globe, he took you, shook you and gave you back all pretty-like."

What Diamond said surprised her. "What the hell is wrong with you?"

Diamond laughed. "Motherhood, I guess."

"And having a good man at your back."

"Yes, that helps, too. I've always stood on my own two feet, but sometimes when I'm mentally exhausted or overwhelmed, it's nice to have someone to lean on."

She wanted that, too. She didn't want someone she needed to rely on, but who would still be there if and when she needed him. And vice versa.

Fuck. She didn't want someone. She wanted Ryder.

But he didn't want her.

He had made that pretty clear. She was his job. The job was over. They were over.

She should just appreciate what they had in that short amount of time.

But that didn't mean now that she had a taste of that, she didn't want more.

None of the Shadows were tied down, besides Mercy. And she couldn't imagine that Rissa and Mercy had any sort of normal relationship. But whatever it was seemed to work for them. So far. But as for the rest of D's crew, none seemed to be searching for their soulmates, spouses, or even long-term lovers.

They all liked their independence. And unlike the Dirty Angels members who all lived and worked in the Valley, the Shadows needed to be able to pack a bag and head out to the next job on just a phone call.

They needed their freedom to do just that.

She sighed.

"What?' Diamond asked.

Kelsea shook her head. "Nothing. I'm going to head out."

Chapter Nineteen

Ryder grunted as he slammed the punching bag with his fist. Slade was behind it, holding it steady, while Steel stood to the side, observing, occasionally giving him a pointer or heckling him, calling him a pussy and telling him to hit harder.

Ryder put all his effort into the next cross punch, stepped back and then struck the bag with a side kick.

"Now you've only pissed that motherfucker off," Steel yelled at him. "He's still standing and ready to kick your fucking ass."

Ryder wiped the sweat off his brow with his forearm, planted his bare feet into a wide stance and...

Froze.

His racing heart was suddenly no longer from the exertion he'd been putting into training. Instead it came from the voice he heard and recognized, even over the gym equipment usage by other members, their talking and the music coming through the wall speakers.

He sucked in a breath and forced himself to remain facing the heavy bag. But it didn't matter, he felt her presence behind him. She was hard to ignore.

"I told Diamond."

He lowered his shoulders when he realized he had hiked them almost to his ears. Steel wore a steel-like expression as his gaze slid from Ryder to the woman behind him.

As Ryder began to turn, Slade asked, "Told her what?"

When Ryder finally faced her, her blue eyes were focused on him and she was holding Hudson. Seeing that made his heart skip a few beats before continuing to thump heavily in his chest.

While the baby looked a lot like Diamond, Kelsea and Diamond's features were similar except for the fact that Di had dark brown hair and Kels was blonde. They both even had blue eyes, though a slightly different shade.

Hudson looked close enough to what Kelsea's child might look like.

A child with another man. Because it shouldn't be his.

Fuck. His thoughts were going in a direction they should *not* be going.

Slade stepped between them, breaking their locked gaze and took the baby from Kelsea, pressing a kiss to his forehead. "What did she tell you?" Slade asked again but this time to his ol' lady.

Diamond's darker blue eyes landed on Kelsea. "Only if you're okay with it."

Kelsea nodded, breaking their connection. "But not here and no one else."

"Got you," Diamond murmured, her brows furrowed as she studied both Ryder and Kelsea standing so close, but not saying a word to each other. "Baby, can you come with me into the office? I need to show you something."

"What?"

Diamond made a noise and grabbed his elbow. "Something in the office. *Now*." She tilted her head slightly toward Ryder and Kelsea.

Slade frowned at his ol' lady, then picked up what she was putting down. "Yeah. Got you."

Steel still stood behind Ryder, not saying a word.

"Give us a minute, brother?" Ryder asked, not bothering to look over his shoulder at him.

"Sure that's a good idea?"

Instead of answering him, Ryder wrapped his fingers around the back of Kelsea's neck and steered her toward the rear of the gym. She didn't resist and he didn't stop until he had her in the small room where the gym's lone tanning bed was set up.

As soon as the door was closed and locked behind them, he had her up against it, his hands buried within her hair and his mouth on hers. He swallowed her gasp of surprise and swept his tongue through her mouth, realizing how much he'd missed her.

Why? Why did he miss her so much?

He shouldn't. She had always been a pain in his ass. A problem to deal with. How could spending less than two weeks at his cabin with her have changed that?

He'd had sex with plenty of other women in his life and never experienced the same pull as he did with the blonde who now kissed him as desperately as he did her.

Fuck. Fuck. Fuck.

He tucked a knee between her thighs, which were bare and tempting since she was wearing shorts that should be much longer. *Much* longer. Long enough to hang to her knees, not tempting men with the curve of her thighs.

He groaned and tilted his head just enough to deepen the kiss, relearning her taste, her reactions.

With a whimper, she ground against his thigh, the heat of her pussy unmistakable through the thin, silky fabric of his gym shorts. Her hands slipped from his waist where she had been clutching tightly to his still sweat-covered lower back and then down under his shorts until she cupped his ass and squeezed.

Fuck. He was as hard as a rock and his wallet was in his gym locker. There was no way to sneak into the locker room and back without revealing what they were about to do.

Or what he wanted to do.

He only assumed she wanted the same.

He broke the kiss and pressed his cheek against hers. "Darlin', there's nothing I want more than to fuck you up against this door right now. But I don't have a wrap."

Without saying anything, she slid her hands from under his shorts, grabbing his sleeveless T-shirt and yanking it up. He let her pull it over his head and he just about dropped to his knees when her teeth skimmed across his nipples.

"I don't care," she murmured against his damp skin.

"But I do. You're gettin' your life back in order, you don't need any complications."

"I'm on birth control."

It wasn't just about birth control. "When's the last time you've been tested?"

Her long hesitation was telling.

"Right. Not without a wrap. It's been a couple years since I've been tested, too. So don't think this is just on you, darlin'. I'm tryin' to be responsible." He pinned his forehead to hers. His aching cock was throbbing, and he was close to throwing caution to the wind. And it didn't help when her hot, little hand slid along his shorts and over his erection.

Nope. That didn't help at all.

He needed to keep his head together. "That's not why I brought you in here."

"No?" Her voice sounded husky and needy.

He couldn't resist taking her soft lips once more. Those were his lips. That was his pussy still being ground into his thigh.

She was all his.

"No, I wanted to make sure you're okay after telling Diamond." That was his excuse, but he also wanted to spend a moment alone with her. To feel her skin against his.

To see if missing her was simply all in his head.

"I'm okay."

I'm not okay. I haven't been okay since leaving Kentucky. "Good, darlin'. And you're still seein' Rissa?" He asked the question even though he already knew the answer.

"Yes."

"And everything's good with you and Brooke?"

"Yes."

"Your mom?"

When she didn't answer, he lifted his head and stared down into those blue eyes of hers that could swallow him up and drown him.

"It'll come. It'll take time," he reassured her. He hoped it would eventually happen for her. Family was so important. She just needed to be open to forgiving her mother.

"We'll see," she murmured. Her fingers spread wide over his chest and she whispered, "I haven't been with anyone, since..."

For fuck's sake, he knew that. He shouldn't. It should be none of his goddamn business. She should be able to fuck anyone she wants to without allowing it to bother him.

Except for that fuckwad Slash.

Not Slash. Anyone but Slash.

No. Fuck that! Not anyone.

No one should have her but him. For once in his life, he wanted to be selfish.

He ground his teeth and dug deep to say, "Nothin' wrong with takin' a break, darlin'. Wait to find the right man who'll respect you and treat you right."

"Know where I can find one of those?"

His nostrils flared at the thought of her finding "one of those." Again, how selfish was he that he'd wanted her to stay away from the losers she'd been hanging out with and now that she stopped, he didn't want her to find anyone better?

Fuck, and it killed him to say, "I'm sure there are plenty of good guys out there."

"I guess I'll have to find one," she said softly, avoiding his eyes.

He pressed his forehead to hers again and with eyes squeezed shut said, "But not tonight. Tonight. Me. You. Your place."

Damn. He had stepped over that edge and now was sliding down that slippery ravine.

"I'm not at my mother's."

He knew that, too. "I know."

"You know where I live?"

"I know a lot of things." He brushed his lips across hers. They were soft and pliable and a little swollen from their kiss. "So, tonight?"

Her chest rose and fell once. Twice. Her eyes became heated. "Yes. Please."

He swallowed a groan. "That word on your lips..."

"Kiss me again, *please*."

He could hear the amusement in her voice, but he didn't care. He took her mouth again. She wrapped her arms around his neck, digging her fingers into his hair, holding him to her.

He made quick work of the button on her shorts and unzipped them. He knew he was moving into dangerous territory by doing so, but he wanted to give her a preview of what would happen later.

Something to hopefully hold them both over.

Once her shorts were open, he shoved one hand down the back to cup her ass and the other down the front, pleased to find she wasn't shaved bare. She'd kept the strip he preferred. His thumb separated her folds, grinding the pad against her clit.

She groaned into his mouth and her hips moved against him. When he slipped his middle finger inside her, she was wet and hot, and his brain began to spin.

No condom, no condom, no fuckin' condom, he chanted in his mind.

His cock was not only throbbing but leaking in anticipation.

But he needed to wait. This would only be for her. Later he'd take what he really wanted.

He slipped a second finger into her slick heat and curled them, pressing more roughly against her hard, swollen nub. He swallowed her cry.

She jerked her head, breaking their kiss, her nails digging into his bare back hard enough, she might be drawing blood.

"Gotta keep quiet, darlin'," he panted. *Fuck*, when she came, he might come right along with her.

She didn't answer, but instead dropped her head until her face was pressed into his chest. He increased his pace and could hear her struggle to keep quiet. He could also feel her clenching and unclenching around his fingers.

"You close, darlin'?"

Fuck. She needed to be close, otherwise, he might rip her shorts down and fuck her unwrapped.

She let out a long, low moan.

"Gotta keep quiet, darlin'," he reminded her again with his lips to her ear. "Muffle your cries against me, if you have to."

He did not want the whole gym hearing her orgasm. Hell, *he* didn't want to hear her orgasm, he was already struggling for control as it was. He didn't want to be sinking his fingers inside her over and over, he wanted it to be his dick.

And he wanted her to be as noisy as fuck. Not to have to restrain her response.

He winced as she sucked on his skin right above his nipple so hard, he knew it would leave a bruise. There was no doubt a mark would be left behind when she sank her teeth in and bit down.

"Fuck," he grunted in pain as she came, her body jerking against his.

He pinned her tighter against the door, holding her up, until she went limp and released his flesh from between her teeth.

He was panting as hard as she was.

And his dick was screaming for relief. His balls, too.

Tonight couldn't come soon enough for him.

Kelsea wanted to yank his shorts off, shove him to the floor and ride him like a mechanical horse in front of the grocery store. Just like she had done so many times during their days in Kentucky. Ryder was strong—a hero, for fuck's sake—and her being on top gave her a sense of power that she never had felt before.

Most men she'd been with had never wanted to finish with her on top. Before they came, they always flipped her over and had taken control back. That never happened with Ryder. He would let her stay on top until he came, unless she decided otherwise. But he always left the choice to her.

Suddenly she understood why that might be. It was one subtle way of handing control of her life back to her.

Whether he did it deliberately or not, she didn't know. But it wouldn't surprise her if he did.

He was smart. And more caring than she ever expected any of D's Shadows to be.

His life had been full of selflessness. Whether during his time in the military by putting his life on the line while serving his country, or by saving a fellow Army Ranger from death, or by taking part in some of Diesel's missions. Yes, for the most part he'd been paid for being part of D's crew. But not all of the things he, and the other Shadows, had done they'd been compensated for. Like going after Jazz and Kiki's kidnappers.

And from what she discovered after returning to Shadow Valley, he hadn't been paid for his time in Kentucky. He took that all on himself.

Selfless.

Caring.

Unlike her.

But she had changed—"seen the light" as one might say—all because of him.

She owed him a lot.

But what she wanted from him was more than to repay her debt of gratitude.

Wait to find the right man who'll respect you and treat you right.

She had.

That man was now pulling his T-shirt with the torn-off sleeves over his head, after he'd gently pulled her shorts back up and fastened them.

He was the right man.

He may want to deny it. But it was clear...

He belonged to her.

Now she just needed to prove it to him. Prove to him that she wasn't the "old Kelsea" anymore. The irresponsible one. But was back to being the "old, *old* Kelsea" the one where she loved and felt a part of her family, be it her DAMC family or blood. When she felt a sense of belonging.

Before Pierce took what wasn't his to take.

Before she found out that man was her father.

Before she found out that man created her sister from an act of rape.

Before all of that. All which fucked with her head.

She once again saw with a clear vision that the people around her loved her and would do anything for her. All she had to do was simply ask.

And she loved them and would do the same for them, too.

Since returning from Ryder's mountain in Kentucky, that peace she found in that cabin in the woods remained within her. It was now deeply rooted.

Things weren't perfect. But life never was. And during those rough times, she could lean on any of her club sisters or talk it out with Rissa.

So, life was pretty good right now. It was finally on the right track after being derailed for a while.

But only one thing was still missing.

It was the man who stared at her with his expressive green eyes, probably wondering what the hell was wrong with her.

"You okay, darlin'?"

She nodded, then cleared the thick from her throat. "Yes."

She *was* okay. And telling Diamond her secret hadn't sent her into a tailspin. It actually had been a bit freeing. Rissa was right, she didn't *need* to tell anyone. But she *wanted* to tell Diamond. At least she understood and would be there for her since they both bore similar scars from the same man.

No, not a man. He had been a motherfucking sick bastard.

A "man" stood in front of her with a concerned expression. "You sure?"

"Yes." She pushed away from the door.

He reached for the knob. "You go out first. I'll follow in a bit."

As he began to open the door, she whispered, "Dwight..."

He hesitated. "Yeah, darlin'?"

She should tell him that she only wanted him. No one else. Drop to her knees and beg him to give them a chance. To promise that she'd never slip again.

She didn't say or do any of those things, because she wasn't sure she could keep that promise, even though she planned on doing her damnedest. Instead, she shook her head. "Nothing. See you tonight."

He nodded, an unfamiliar look crossing his face. "Once the pawn shop is closed and the lot is empty, I'll be over."

Of course. Because he wouldn't want anyone to know he was there. He would sneak into her apartment tonight after dark and she was sure he'd leave before dawn.

Disappointment landed heavily in her chest. She reached for the edge of the door to finish pulling it open, but he stopped her with a hand on her wrist. "Hey," he murmured, pressing a soft kiss to her temple. "Tonight."

As soon as he let her go, she slipped out of the room and made her way across the gym. She felt like all eyes were on her.

Maybe they were.

Maybe they were wondering why a badass and military hero like Ryder would be interested in a woman like her.

Because she was an easy lay?

Certainly not because he was interested in her for anything other than sex.

That was probably what they thought.

And that could be true.

She pushed through the glass front doors of the gym and out into the hot late summer sun. She paused long enough to dig out her keys from her bag and slip her sunglasses over her eyes before striding across the full parking lot to her Toyota.

As she weaved through the cars, she noticed something out of place which caused her to stumble in surprise. Her heart did a little loopty loop as she caught her balance and stared at what, or *who*, that was.

Steel leaned against her car, his bulky arms crossed over his well-defined chest, which was now covered in a white, skin-tight Under Armor tee and his powerful legs were now encased in camo-patterned cargo pants. He also wore a pair of sunglasses so dark, she couldn't see his eyes.

She didn't need to. She could tell this conversation wasn't going to be good by the way his muscles appeared. As tense as his jaw.

She cursed under her breath, set her own jaw, then approached him. She couldn't simply get in her car and drive away, because he had planted his ass over the driver's door handle.

"You've got a problem with me," she said, stopping a couple feet in front of him, hitching the strap of her purse higher over her shoulder, then planting her hands on her hips.

She wasn't backing down from whatever this was.

No, she would face him head-on because she was fucking DAMC, goddamn it. And nothing was scarier than a badass biker bitch.

Uh-huh.

Except for badass bikers and badass former special forces operators.

But even so...

She lifted her chin and they stared at each other, dark sunglass lenses to sunglass lenses. Who would blink first? No one would be able to tell.

"I got a problem with you," he confirmed. "Wanna know why?"

Kelsea shrugged. "Nope. My life will go on the same whether I know or not. And, honestly, Steel, I just don't give a flying fuck why."

He pursed his lips and planted the heels of his palms on the door behind him, crossing his ankles.

Shit. He was settling in, so she was going to hear why.

"Being who you are and where you come from, you should understand the bond of brotherhoods."

"You're wasting your time—"

"Brotherhoods aren't necessarily blood but they're family all the same."

She ground her teeth. "Jesus, Steel, tell me something I don't know."

"That means when one needs help, we step in and help."

"And you feel the need to step in." She tipped her head to the side. "Why?"

"You're not good for him."

That answer didn't surprise her. But since when did Steel appoint himself as Ryder's protector? Ryder was perfectly capable of taking care of himself. "Well, then... Once again, this conversation is a waste of time since I'm not with him."

"Maybe. Maybe not. But you were."

"Only because I was forced to live in a cabin in Kentucky for a couple weeks. Wasn't my choice."

"No, your *choices* were utter shit, that's why you ended up there. He's got a soft spot for strays."

"Ouch." The audacity of this motherfucker...

"And you've proven time and time again you'd do anyone, so it doesn't surprise me you'd spread your legs for him to get your way."

Oxygen fled her lungs. She wasn't sure if that was an insult to Ryder or to her. Either way, it shot a sharp shard of pain through her deflated chest. She had to suck in air to ask, "Is that what he told you?"

He hesitated for the slightest moment, but to her that was telling. Ryder hadn't told him shit.

"Gonna deny it?"

"No. We fucked. Happy now? Or are you jealous and just want some of this for yourself." She forced herself to smile, which she was sure looked more like a sneer, as she grabbed her crotch over her shorts and squeezed. If she wasn't wearing shades, she also would've winked at him. But she was, so she didn't.

And fuck him, anyway.

"I wouldn't touch you with someone else's dick, even if you had a tetanus shot, a penicillin shot, and a sterilization shot."

Kelsea struggled to breathe once again because he might as well have kicked her directly in the gut. She blinked away the tears that threatened. She would not let his words affect her. She. Would. Not.

Or at least she wouldn't give him the satisfaction of seeing how they affected her.

That's what he wanted. He wanted to pull a reaction from her. Possibly to prove she hadn't changed. And she would not play this game of his. For whatever reason he was playing it.

She unclenched her jaw. "Never realized you were such an asshole, Steel. Good to know."

"Don't you know? We're all assholes, Kelsea. And the king is your cousin. Unfortunately, Ryder just forgot who he was and how far he's come for a hot minute. Easy slit will do that to some men. Now he needs to get back on track."

Easy slit will do that to some men.

She let that insult roll off her back since she became focused on something else he said. "On track?" What did that mean? It was her who had needed to get back on track, not Ryder.

Kelsea didn't miss the slight flare of Steel's nostrils. She hated that she couldn't see his eyes.

"Straightening your ass out made him wobble."

Did he have mental issues he was dealing with that she'd been unaware of? "How so?"

"If he didn't tell you, then he didn't want you to know."

PTSD could mess a person up, *if* he was struggling with it. But if he was, he'd kept that to himself. "So, you're just going to leave it like that?"

"His business, not yours."

Oh no. He wasn't leaving it like that. "But you're making it your business."

"I did for him what he did for you, so, yeah, I'm making it my business."

Kelsea tilted her head, frowning, suddenly giving this conversation a lot more weight. Her heart began to pound, and her throat became dry. Had Ryder been self-destructive like her? Had he used drugs and alcohol to drown out bad memories? If so, was it Steel who stepped in to help him? "What did you do for him?"

Steel finally pushed off the car, stepped toe to toe with her and leaned down until his face was just inches from hers. "Just stay the fuck away from him," he growled. "Especially if you care even one fucking iota about him. But truth is, I don't think you care about anyone but yourself. You've proven that time and time again."

Her heart was about to beat out of her chest. He was in her personal space and she fought the instinct to step back. Instead, she powered deep and leaned in even closer. He was trying to keep her away from Ryder and that wasn't Steel's decision to make. "Shouldn't Ryder be telling me that and not you? Or are you his self-appointed Daddy? Do you have a crush on him, Steel? Is that what it is? You're jealous? You want his dick in your ass instead of in mine?"

When he sneered and his hands came up, she knew she was playing with fire. But she didn't care if she got burned. She didn't care if her fucking skin melted off. This man had no right to say the things he said to her. None.

Out of nowhere, a large hand landed on Steel's chest, pushing him back a half-step. Kelsea looked up in surprise, thinking it was Diesel, but her massive cousin couldn't sneak up on a deaf and blind mole. No one that big could, except for one person.

Mercy.

His deep voice rumbled through her. "There was a time, not long ago, when I put my hands on a female and you stepped in. Now it's my turn. Stand down, brother. Go the fuck inside and cool off. That's an order."

Mercy left his palm on Steel's chest until the other man nodded and his muscles loosened slightly.

Before Steel could respond, Mercy continued, "Be thankful the boss didn't witness this and I did, since D's on his way over here to lift. You should also be thankful that the man just about to come out of those fucking double doors didn't witness this, either. If he had, D might not be your biggest problem."

She was tempted to glance over her shoulder, but she didn't. Instead, she kept her eyes on Steel. And she wasn't done with him yet. "I get that you care about him, Steel. But whether you believe it or not—and right now, I don't give a shit if you do—I care about him, too. I also understand the bond between all of you is strong, so I forgive you for pulling this bullshit." She jabbed her finger toward him, letting her blood boil another degree hotter. "But don't you ever, *ever* insult me like that again. I admit I did some reckless things. I was stupid. I lost my head. But that man helped me find it. I owe him my life and would never do anything to hurt him. Because of that, I heard you loud and clear and will take your concern that I made him 'wobble' seriously. I would never want to be the reason he falls. Now, get the fuck out of my way so I can leave."

"Too late," Mercy mumbled under his breath, glancing over her shoulder. He twisted his head back to Steel. "Got one of two choices, brother. Head inside or leave. I'm not in the fucking mood to break up a fight between two of my teammates. Especially over a female."

"Headin' home," Steel grumbled.

"Good choice," Mercy said as he stepped back, letting Steel slip by him and head toward the other side of the parking lot.

When Ryder stepped up to them, his gaze slid from Steel who was now three rows away to Kelsea, then Mercy. "What's goin' on here?"

Mercy scratched his chin, his expression as blank as a brick wall. "Nothing. They were just chit-chatting like women do."

Ryder's green eyes narrowed on the taller man. "'Bout what?"

"Whatever fucking women chit-chat about. Periods. Men. The Real Housewives of Allegheny County. How the fuck should I know, do I look like a fucking woman?"

Kelsea swore Diesel was Mercy's spirit animal.

"I need to go inside and punch something," he growled, then headed toward the gym entrance.

Ryder watched Mercy walk away for a few seconds before swinging his gaze back to Kelsea. "What the fuck is goin' on? And don't tell me nothin' 'cause it looked too intense to be nothin'."

Well, there went the answer she was going to give him. *Fuck.*

She took a deep breath and asked what she really wanted to know instead. "Why am I bad for you?"

His brow furrowed. "What?"

She lifted her chin and stared Ryder down just like she had Steel. She asked more slowly and distinctly, so he couldn't possibly misunderstand her, "Why am I bad for you?"

"What the fuck are you talkin' about?" His lips flattened

out and his green eyes avoided hers long enough that an ache began to build at her center.

"You know what I'm talking about. As you saw, I had a little conversation with Steel. Or I should say, Steel had a little conversation with me."

"What did he say?"

"He warned me to stay away from you."

Ryder's face got hard and he glanced in the direction Steel had disappeared, but the man was long gone. When he turned back to her and his mouth opened, she lifted a hand to stop him.

"There's something you're hiding. But the truth is, you have every right not to tell me what that is. I was only your job. You sacrificed yourself and your time while in Kentucky to make sure that your job was done properly so you would never have to do it again. You were successful. You're good at what you do. So, I once again thank you for that. But here is where this ends. You made it clear that you were done with me when you dropped me off at my mother's, whether you meant saving my ass or otherwise. I don't blame you, I wouldn't have had the patience or skill to deal with someone like me. But I'm not going to fool myself thinking that there was anything more. There wasn't. The sex was great, but it's over."

"Darlin'..."

She didn't stop, she kept right on going, not giving him a chance to deny or lie. She talked slowly, careful not to let her words shake or her lips quiver. "You made me see that I had value. That was all because of you. Until today. I'm done being an easy lay and letting myself be used because I didn't care what happened to me. You wanted me to care about myself and now I do. Because of that, I don't want to be with someone who feels the need to sneak into my apartment after dark because he's afraid someone might see him. I will not accept a man in my bed until I find one who will walk up those steps to my place in the light of day when the parking lot is full of customers. I want him to be proud I'm in his life, not embarrassed. I realize I still have a ways to go before I find that right man... One who will love me for who I am, not judge me for who I was. You said, 'Wait to find the right man who'll respect you and treat you right.' I'm going to do that. It might not be today or tomorrow, or even anytime soon, but I'm going to find that man, whoever he is."

"Darlin'," he started, lifting his arm.

She shook her head and stepped back out of his reach. "No, please don't make this harder than it already is. I caused you nothing but problems in the past. I don't want to cause you any in the future. That's my true thanks to you for everything you have done for me." Her throat was closing, and she needed to get out of there before she broke down. "Now, I need to go." She pushed past him, pressing her car remote button to unlock her door.

"Darlin'," his voice sounded raw as she stepped around him and got into her car. "I'll see you tonight."

She slid into her driver's seat avoiding his touch and not meeting his gaze. "No, if you heard anything I just said, you'd realize that invitation is no longer valid. Have a good life, Ryder." She slammed the door shut and hit the locks, starting her car quickly. As he reached for the door handle, she shoved the shifter in drive and gunned the gas, hoping his toes weren't in the way.

She never looked in the rearview mirror to make sure, because even if she had, she wouldn't have been able to see much. Not with the tears blurring her vision.

Chapter Twenty

THE BLONDE he was watching wasn't the blonde he wanted to be watching.

She was just one part of a job he had taken—in truth, volunteered for—because it took him away from Shadow Valley and had greatly reduced the chance of him doing something stupid.

However, he'd been gone for weeks now. On a job that was complex because there were multiple moving pieces. Could he use extra eyes? Fuck yeah. But he told D he could and *would* handle this job himself. The reason being, a multi-faceted case should keep his mind busy. It was also supposed to keep his thoughts off another blonde, a whole lot curvier than the one he was currently stalking.

However, that was a complete fucking failure since he couldn't shake thoughts of Kelsea no matter what he did.

The client he was working for was being double-crossed by his wife of less than two years and his long-time business partner, so Ryder had been tailing them, doing some digging, and gathering the evidence of not only their embezzlement scheme but of their cheating on their spouses. With each other. These kinds of jobs weren't ones he normally enjoyed. In fact, he hated them. Walker was the one who enjoyed solving complex puzzles and putting two and two together.

Ryder hated puzzles and sucked at math.

He preferred jobs where he had a semi-automatic .45 in his hand, a tactical knife on his hip and was slamming his heavy combat boot into a door while taking out any threats with either a well-aimed bullet, a sharp serrated edge or his fists. Or all of the above.

That shit got his blood pumping. *This* shit made him want to run out into traffic on a busy highway.

And, not to mention, it pissed him off.

The bitch who was currently sitting in a Starbucks on a corner in downtown Chicago, drinking a triple, venti, half-sweet, non-fat, caramel macchiato with exactly four pumps of vanilla syrup and heated to a perfect one-hundred and twenty degrees, pissed him the fuck off.

Her two plastic Barbie doll-like friends who sat at the same table as her, sipping equally obnoxious drinks as they gossiped and laughed like rabid hyenas also pissed him the fuck off.

He hoped they all choked on their over-priced caffeine and spit it all over their obviously fake tits.

He hated fake tits. He hated fake bitches. He hated fancy fucking coffee.

Black. Coffee was supposed to be enjoyed black, like the good Lord intended.

He knew a woman whose blonde hair was natural, whose eyes weren't blue because of colored contacts, whose squeezable, suckable tits were one hundred percent real, who didn't melt down when she broke a fucking nail and could curse like a fucking tattooed biker. She could also ride his cock until his balls were nothing but empty sacs, while blinking those pretty blue eyes at him, talking to and touching him sweetly one minute, cursing him out and biting him the next, all while squeezing those real tits or digging those nails into his flesh. Preferably both.

That woman had also learned to appreciate black coffee.

But then, he hadn't given her a choice.

He also hadn't given her a choice to spend two weeks with him in a cabin in Kentucky.

Nor did he give her a choice when he dropped her off at her mother's.

But he *had* given her a choice when he let her get into her fucking Toyota in the parking lot at Shadow Valley Fitness and drive away.

He shouldn't have. But he, stupid fucking dumb fuck that he was, did.

And now, as he sat in a city that made his skin crawl, he realized he maybe should've done things differently.

He'd confronted Steel later that day—once he found the man—and they'd had words. Lots of words. Some words both of them regretted later. But they were said, they were heard, and unfortunately a lot of them were the hard truth. So, afterward they both moved on.

When any of D's crew had issues with each other, they hashed it out, either bare-knuckled, wearing boxing gloves, or simply with words, and then they moved past it. They did not hold onto that shit, because clinging to that would rot their team from the inside out.

He didn't like what Steel said to Kelsea, but he understood why he did it. While he appreciated Steel's concern, it wasn't his place to step in. Steel apologized to him, they clasped hands and bumped shoulders, but the damage was already done.

That day, Kelsea had driven away from him hurt, which had been plain to see.

And worse, he stood there like a dumb ass because he wasn't sure he was ready to reveal some of his own past struggles, even though he knew all of hers.

Unfair? No doubt. But when was life ever fair?

However, she was right about one thing. Any man walking up those steps to her apartment and her bed should be able to do it in the light of day.

Any man who wanted to do it only in the dark didn't deserve her.

So, he let her go even though every cell in his body screamed for him to stop her. Every instinct he had to chase her down, spill his secret and deal with the possible fallout, was extinguished like a lit cigarette butt crushed on the pavement under his boot heel.

He hated the fact that Steel was right, that he had been unsteady since Kentucky and every day had been a struggle to remain grounded. And until he had no fear of faltering, he wasn't ready to rip himself open and possibly undo all his hard work.

It wasn't a horrendous secret. He had plenty of those, too. Missions he could never talk about. But this secret was his and his alone, and he wasn't proud of that time in his life when he had been weak.

Kelsea needed someone who was strong, unfaltering, someone who could be her solid rock when needed. She didn't need an unstable rock that could topple over when she leaned on it and possibly take her with it.

He wasn't sure he could be that solid rock. Until he was...

Well, that was one reason why he'd taken this suck-ass job in Chicago.

The other reason was because every blonde he saw in Shadow Valley made his heart skip a beat until he realized it wasn't her. And that's why he convinced D to send him to the windy city instead of Walker.

Not that D needed a lot of convincing. Maybe the big man knew it was what Ryder needed.

The man could be surprisingly intuitive.

Now, weeks later, Chicago was leaving an acrid taste in his mouth. He wanted to strangle every one of those bitches sitting at that table in an effort to make the world a better place. And he wanted to cut off his male target's hands for not only stealing from a partner who trusted him but touching that partner's wife.

You do not fuck with another man's woman. Ever.

It should be an unspoken rule for men.

But his male target was just as much trash as his female target who was currently cackling with her friends, showing off her capped teeth and blood red lipstick.

Lipstick. Yeah, he hated that, too. If he wanted a ring left around his cock, he'd prefer it to be a cock ring, not something that came from a tube.

He yanked his baseball cap lower and clenched his teeth when all he could think about was that he never remembered Kelsea wearing lipstick in all the times he'd come in contact with her. Not once.

Whether she had started her evening wearing some, he didn't know, but she didn't seem the type to spend hundreds of dollars to cake shit on her face since she was naturally beautiful without it.

Her eyes, her lips, her cheekbones didn't need anything to enhance them. They were perfect the way they were. Like black coffee, the way the good Lord intended them to be.

He took a sip of his own coffee which he'd picked up at a gas station for a buck. Since he had a feeling those bitches were going to cackle for another damn hour while they picked at their lemon poppy muffins because, for fuck's sake, to take a real bite might make them take an extra Zumba class in a high-class, overpriced gym.

He would love to feed them a whistle pig sandwich without them knowing what they were eating. They'd probably shove two fingers down their throat to rid themselves of a meat that didn't come from the grocery store on a Styrofoam tray, wrapped in fucking plastic.

Kelsea hadn't even flinched when he told her she was eating groundhog. She'd gone for seconds.

The only gagging a woman should do should be when he fucked her face too hard.

Ryder shifted in the seat of his non-descript rental car when his dick became suddenly interested in the direction of his thoughts.

This trip had not helped rid him of thoughts of Kelsea one fucking bit.

In fact, during the rare opportunities he found a moment to lay his head down, he used memories of her sucking him off, riding him like the mechanical pony in front of the grocery store, or him taking her tight ass, so he could relieve the neglected load in his balls.

Unfortunately, he needed to break up with his palm soon. That relationship just wasn't working out for him.

And the occasional women who had approached him while in Chicago hadn't worked out, either. Some were pretty damn determined to get him out of his pants, especially if they got a whiff of his southern accent, no matter how hard he tried to hide it.

Not once had he been tempted. Not. Fucking. Once.

In the past he would have fucked one one night, another the next, then on the third night convinced both of them into a threesome. He would have laid it on thick, not only his southern accent, but his southern charm. It had never failed him.

But he couldn't.

For some fucked up reason, he didn't want to be like the male target he'd been investigating. A cheater.

Ryder was not a cheater.

Why would fucking another woman make him feel like he was cheating? It shouldn't.

And that's what pissed him off the most. He shouldn't feel obligated to keep his dick in his pants because of a woman who wasn't his.

But something happened in that cabin, something he never expected. And he was having a hard time convincing his brain otherwise.

He only wanted one woman.

One.

He couldn't shake the feeling that fucking any other woman would be wrong.

And, *fuck him*, no matter how much that scared him, no matter how much that made his psyche stumble and sway dangerously, he couldn't break the spell that blonde, blue-eyed woman with the fucked up past put on him.

He didn't blame her. He doubted she was even aware she had done it.

But she did.

He was done.

He was toast that came out of a toaster which had been set to the number ten.

In truth, he shouldn't be surprised. If it could happen to Mercy, who had a black heart and eyes that could freeze radiator coolant, it could damn well happen to any of them.

None of them were immune.

Mercy proved it.

The only difference was, Rissa was good for Mercy's scarred and damaged soul. Kelsea was not good for Ryder's.

Did he want her to be? Fuck yes. Could she eventually be? Possibly.

She was headed in that direction, but he wasn't sure when she'd get there. And until then, he couldn't risk it.

Mercy checked in with him every few days. And without Ryder asking, he'd mentioned that Kelsea was continuing to do well. She hadn't slipped once.

She had taken on even more responsibility with Brooke's

interior design business, including working overtime and weekends to bank funds so she could eventually build her own place in the DAMC gated compound.

That news surprised him. The apartment above her uncle's pawn shop was easy to deal with and most likely rent-free. A house was a lot of responsibility. Especially for one person.

Mortgage, utilities, taxes, upkeep. Shit like that could become overwhelming. She needed to be standing on solid ground before she took on that burden. Or she needed to find someone to help shoulder that burden first.

Someone like him.

Or...

Someone who was him.

For fuck's sake.

He should be paying attention to that bitch inside the coffee shop, not staring at his cell phone, fighting the temptation to call Kelsea.

He was slipping. Maybe it was time to call Diesel instead, get Walker out here to finish up what Ryder started. While Hunter was good at finding people who didn't want to be found, Walker was an expert at tailing people and observing. Steel and Mercy were intimidating and good muscle to have at your back. Brick was just cunning in general, as well as one of the best snipers Ryder ever met.

What was Ryder good for?

Maybe it wasn't Kelsea who had made his resolve waver. Maybe he had lost sight on what his purpose was. For a while it seemed as though his job was rescuing a woman who didn't want to be rescued. But now he didn't even have that.

He had done his job well enough that she no longer needed him.

Only now he needed her.

He needed her.

He.

Needed.

Her.

Fuck.

He grabbed his phone, hit the power button, punched in his passcode then scrolled through his contacts.

When he got to the one he was searching for, he pushed the round green phone icon. He needed to make some decisions.

It was time to go home or time to move on.

Head back to Shadow Valley or start again elsewhere.

Stay with In the Shadows Security or go lone wolf.

And if he headed back to the life he actually liked to work with a team he trusted, he needed to decide about Kelsea.

He was either going to claim Kelsea or he wasn't.

His only fear was, if she slipped, he might, too.

And that wouldn't be good for either of them.

Epilogue

Kelsea glanced down at the text message that popped up on her screen. It was from her sister, Brooke.

When UR done there, head 2 new house 2 doors down. Wants an estimate.

Who? she texted back. Who wanted an estimate? She knew it had to be one of the DAMC members, but which one?

As she waited for an answer, Rissa and Mercy walked back into the living room, distracting her. "Is everything as you wanted it?"

Rissa's smile was huge as she first glanced at Mercy, then at Kelsea. "It's perfect. I always hated decorating and, honestly, I'm awful at it. You have a natural gift, Kelsea. First my office, now our new home."

Kelsea eyed the tall man with the scar running across his handsome but fierce face. Unlike Rissa, he didn't crack a smile. Not even a small one.

"Well?" she asked him.

"Well, what?"

Kelsea sighed. Men! So fucking clueless. "Do you like it?"

"I don't give a fuck about decorations and furniture. All I need's a roof, a bed, running water and..." He let the rest trail off.

Kelsea had no problem filling in the blank, because the man's normally cold silver eyes suddenly flickered with heat as he stared at his woman.

Well, at least someone was getting some. Hell, all the DAMC sisterhood was getting some except for her. But she'd been working her ass off helping Brooke grow her interior design business, and had even taken some online design classes, with the hope she'd eventually get to be a partner instead of just an employee. While that kept her mind off her loneliness during the day when she was busy, after climbing into her bed at night alone, it hit her hard.

It had been three months since her time in Kentucky and she could never remember going that long without sex.

Then again, this was a "new and improved" Kelsea.

Yeah, whatever. The new and improved Kelsea's vagina still wanted some action once in a while. Something besides her own fingers or her vast collection of vibrators.

While they took the edge off, they didn't satisfy her like...

A certain someone.

But that someone took off, heading to Chicago instead, right after their "talk" in the gym's parking lot.

He left instead of fighting for the two of them and proving Steel wrong.

So that meant he didn't want to.

Apparently, he had been fine with how things turned out in the end. Which meant she needed to stop obsessing over a man who *she knew* didn't want her, but stupidly kept wishing that he did.

That was getting her nowhere fast.

However, whenever another man showed any interest in her, she just couldn't drum up any interest in him. Case in point, Coop. He chatted her up the couple of times she'd attended the pig roasts after the club's Sunday runs. He even invited her to be his backpack on the next one.

Even though she planned to turn him down, she never got a chance because Diesel had stepped in and made it very clear that Coop needed to "get gone." Coop was smart enough to do just that. And not even a half hour later, Kelsea witnessed the newly patched member getting a head job under the pavilion from a new sweet butt named Mini. Why Mini was named Mini, Kelsea didn't know or care.

But apparently Coop wasn't too torn up about Kelsea not sitting on the back of his sled. But then, neither was she.

There was only one Harley she wanted to sit on the back of, and it didn't belong to anyone in the DAMC.

A grumbled, "You done?" brought her back to the present.

"As long as you are satisfied," she answered Mercy.

"Gonna be satisfied once your ass is out of our house. Can't get satisfied while you're still standing in it."

"Ryan!" Rissa exclaimed.

Mercy shrugged.

"Sorry I'm cock-blocking you. I'll just take that as your seal of approval."

"It's beautiful. I love it and that's all that matters. Thank you for all of your hard work," Rissa said quickly, putting a hand on Kelsea's shoulder and guiding her toward the front door of their expansive, open-floor plan, ranch home with expensive tile and wood flooring and arched doorways, along with top-of-the-line furniture and appliances, thanks to Kelsea.

The home fit Rissa perfectly. On the other hand, Mercy would be perfectly fine in a drab olive tent. In the jungle. Surrounded by machine guns and enemy guerilla forces.

Kelsea wondered how total opposites worked. But they did. And the proof of that was ready to go knock boots in their newly decorated home.

Maybe that's why Ryder was currently in Chicago and Kelsea was in Shadow Valley. It turned out they were too much alike.

She should have left it alone, but, of course, she didn't. DAMC women were stubborn and demanding and didn't give up until they got what they wanted. And she wanted to know the truth.

Even though, in reality, it wasn't any of her business. But Steel's words had eaten at her. And she believed that if she knew what Steel had done for Ryder, knew why Ryder had "wobbled" because of her, then maybe she could finally have some closure and move on.

Though now she knew, that hadn't worked. But even so, she had given it a shot.

In her pursuit of the truth, she poked and prodded Diesel until he snapped—or what Jewel would say went into his "beast mode"—and in his irritation, let it fly that Ryder had been abusing alcohol after being discharged from the Army. He had spiraled out of control, spending his days and his nights drunk, whether in bars or otherwise, getting into fights and living recklessly.

In more words than he normally grunted, D said Ryder was an alcoholic and that she needed to leave him the fuck alone because he was not going to lose one of his crew due to her being a needy bitch. His words, not hers.

She needed to find dick elsewhere.

Also, his words, not hers.

But she still didn't know how Steel came into play. Kelsea found an "excuse" to talk to Jewel one day at the warehouse and just so happened to "accidentally" run into Steel. He ignored her, but she didn't let that stop her. She had cornered him in the room that Jewel had dubbed "Badass Central" where they kept their computers and electronic equipment.

He wasn't happy about it, but she didn't give a shit. After

that awkward conversation spurred by the information D had spilled, they kissed and made up.

Okay, not really, but at least they no longer wanted to slice each other's throats. She was grateful Steel had stepped in and helped Ryder when he needed it the most.

Just like Ryder had done for her.

She also now understood why Steel said the words he did that day in the parking lot, and why he didn't want to reveal Ryder's secret.

It wasn't his to tell.

It wasn't Diesel's, either, but D was the kind of man who just didn't give a fuck. If Ryder had a problem with him telling Kelsea, he could take it up with D. Again, Diesel's words, not hers.

Ryder wasn't a stupid man. Most people didn't want to take up anything with D if they didn't have to.

In reflecting back on all of that, she missed the part where she said goodbye to Rissa and left their house. Because somehow she ended up outside.

Leaving her car at the curb where she had parked it earlier, she wandered past an empty lot between two houses. The ranch home two doors down was new construction of a similar style to Mercy and Rissa's. Only it was even bigger. Like someone planned to raise a family in it. A large family.

Kelsea went through her mental Rolodex of club members who had kids. However, all of them currently lived in the DAMC compound since their houses had already been built. Unless one of them was planning on upgrading?

She doubted that. The lots were generous enough that anyone who currently lived there could easily expand their current home without running out of space.

So, it had to be one of the brothers who didn't have an ol' lady yet. Or maybe he did and was keeping it on the DL.

Hmm.

Interesting.

She went down her list of the single club members.

Nash was a confirmed bachelor, but his house had been built already, even though it still sat empty. His band, Dirty Deeds, had hired a manager and had been touring the east coast more often now, so he'd hardly been in town.

Crash and Rig hadn't built anything yet and neither were in a rush to do so.

And seriously... Why would Crash or Rig want someone to decorate their house if they did build one? They'd make a table out of truck rims and plywood. A pickup bench seat would be a couch. Either would be happy with a mattress on the floor, this way when they were trashed and rolled out of bed, they wouldn't have far to go to hit the ground.

Moose, Coop, Rooster, and Jester weren't moving out of their free rooms above church any time soon since they had access to free booze, food and pussy twenty-four-seven. And the prospects... Well, they were advised to go live with their mommies until they were patched in. "If they're gonna suck on anyone's tit for free, it should be their mommies an' not the club's until they prove themselves," said Zak. And since he was the prez, anything he said went.

Which brought her back to the house she now stood in front of, and a Harley she didn't recognize parked in the driveway.

The sled was badass and appeared to be a Jag Jamison custom. Just looking at it made Kelsea a little wet, proving that shit was in her blood and always would be.

She walked up to the bike, searching for any identifying info. Nothing. It was just fucking hot and she wouldn't mind planting her ass on the back of that for a four-hour run.

She glanced up at the house. But whoever built this place most likely already had an ol' lady, and she wasn't going to stir up trouble.

She was the "new and improved" Kelsea.

Right.

With a sigh, she approached the front double doors, admiring the narrow, etched glass windows that framed both sides. Very pretty. Something she would pick if she was building her own house. Which was the plan once she got enough money saved to do so.

Which was most likely no time soon. Her bank account was still pretty anemic.

But the truth was, she was okay with that. She was fine in the apartment over the pawn shop for now. She didn't need a big house or even a little one just for her. But it did give her a goal. And Rissa had said that having goals and working toward them could help keep her focused and on the right track.

The "new and improved" Kelsea.

She rolled her eyes and jabbed the doorbell. She pressed it again, listening to make sure it was even hooked up. It was, but she heard nothing.

Wait. No. She heard something. But not footsteps.

After waiting a few minutes, she muttered, "Fuck this shit," and tried the handle, finding it unlocked. She swung the door open and popped her head inside. "Hello? Anybody here?"

Her question echoed through the empty foyer. From what she could see, the house was completely void of furniture and still had evidence of recent construction on the floors and walls. Which meant a total clean slate for her to work with. Which also made her giddy for this project.

Who would have thought interior design would be her calling?

If it wasn't for Brooke, she never would have discovered that.

She hated the man who sired her and her sister. But Pierce was the reason Brooke came to Shadow Valley. Pierce was the reason she now had a sister in her life.

They had made treasure out of one man's trash.

She stepped into the foyer and froze because whatever sound she had heard muffled through the doors began again.

And the acoustics in that empty house were *fucking amazing*.

RYDER TOOK a deep breath and began again. His heart was thumping wildly because some of the words he was about to sing had meaning. Real meaning. Words he wasn't sure he'd ever utter to anyone.

Especially not to someone who had been a pain in his ass for so long.

One he had wanted to strangle.

But in the last three months, he'd done a lot of soul searching. And before he made any major decision, he'd also made sure he was standing on solid ground.

Not a wobble, not even a shake.

And he had to admit to himself why, when he dragged Kelsea off that mattress in West Virginia, he took her to the only place he himself found peace.

His sanctuary.

A place he never took any woman before.

And now, he'd never bring another woman there again.

Only one.

If she'd have him.

She wasn't the kind of woman who needed mushy shit. And he wasn't the kind of man who would give it to her anyway.

But what he could give her was solid and true.

And the words he needed to express to her came from someone better equipped to say them than him.

So, he started at the top and began to sing John Legend's *All of Me*, which first asks what he would do without Kelsea's smart mouth.

Way too fucking fitting.

And he hoped she didn't knee him in the balls when he sang the part about how she was crazy, but so was he, because he loved her.

Fucking crazy but it was true.

He loved her curves. Her edges. Every imperfection.

And he was willing to risk it all. For her.

He was ready to give all that he had. To her.

He was willing to walk up those steps in the middle of the day when the sun was bright, and the parking lot was full.

She had proven to herself how strong she was when she put her mind to something.

Keeping sober. Excelling in her job. Working harder than ever to sock away any extra money she had so she could buy her own place.

Someplace she could call home. Something that would belong to *her*.

And when the world threatened to come tumbling down around her, he wanted to be there. To steady her. To encourage her to continue. To clear away the rubble.

He also wanted her to be there for him. To remind him why he fought so hard to become sober and stay that way.

They needed to remind each other why life could be good.

Not just good. Fucking *great*.

When he finished the song, he turned around to see if she had stayed or left.

Muscles that had been tense released, and as he took her in, standing there in the doorway, he was blown away by how beautiful she truly was.

"You could've told me," she whispered.

He knew she had talked to Steel. And Diesel. She was now aware of some of his past. Not everything, but the part that might affect her.

He shook his head. "I couldn't. I wasn't ready. It was a time in my life where I let weakness rule it. I wasn't one of those good drunks who cracked jokes and was everyone's buddy. I was a bad one. I drank until I blacked out. I got into fights. Because the truth was—and it took me too long to figure it out—I wanted to die. I figured if alcohol couldn't rid me of some of my nightmares, then death would."

Surprise filled her blue eyes. "Like me."

"Like you." He blew out a breath and turned to face her. "So, I understood what you were doing. I understood what you were going through. I just didn't know the reason why."

"And what were your reasons?"

"Shit I can't talk about even to this day. Mostly because I'm not allowed to. And even if I was, I wouldn't want to give you those nightmares. They're things best left forgotten and buried."

"Like Pierce."

"In some fucked up way, some good came out of all of his evil. You. Brooke. Your new career. You and me."

She tilted her head, the blonde hair he wanted to run his fingers through falling over her shoulder. "Is that called looking on the bright side of things?"

"Yeah, darlin', it is." They were quiet for a moment as they took each other in. *Fuck*, he missed her. And standing so far away from her right now made his chest ache. "Did you listen to the words of that song?"

"Oh, was that song for me?" she teased, a slight smile pulling at the corners of her lips. Lips he wanted to kiss, suck and bite.

He made a show of glancing around the room. "See any other pain in the ass in this room with us?"

Her smile grew as she shrugged. "No, just me." As she moved closer, the ache in his chest became more intense. But she didn't stop until they stood toe to toe and she was forced to tilt her head back slightly to meet his eyes.

Again, he was blown away by her natural beauty. Especially now that the memories that had haunted her no longer clouded her eyes or made her appear troubled.

"You're not worried I'll pull you down?"

She asked a good question. A valid question. One he had thought long and hard about once he considered their future together.

He cupped her cheek and brushed his thumb over it. "Honestly, darlin', I'm afraid I'll fall without you."

He could see her confidence waver. "That's a lot of pressure."

"Pressure I'm confident you can handle." Because he was.

"You could've told me," she whispered again. Only she was no longer talking about his alcoholism.

"I couldn't. I wasn't ready."

She tilted her head slightly and asked, "But you're ready now?"

"Only way you're gonna find out is if you put that quarter in the slot and take a chance."

She patted her pant's pockets and then pouted. "I don't have a quarter."

"I might be willin' to barter."

He ran the pad of his thumb over her bottom lip.

"With a kiss?" Her breath tickled his fingers.

"No... Well, yeah. But no, that's not what I was thinkin' of but I'm not gonna turn a kiss down."

"Can I hear it in your own words instead of Legend's?"

He raised his brows. "I'm not a legend?"

"Maybe in your own mind."

He laughed and slapped a hand over his heart. "Damn, darlin', that hurt." He sobered and leaned forward, capturing her face in his hands. He waited until his lips were almost touching hers before saying, "You really need to hear it?"

"Yes," she whispered back, her warm breath now meshing with his.

"You sure?"

"Uh huh."

"Do you feel the same way?"

"Only way you're gonna find out is if you put that quarter in the slot and take a chance," she echoed, dropping her tone an octave.

She was such a fucking smart ass, but he wouldn't have her any other way. It was part of who she was.

His lips curled slightly before he dropped them for a brief kiss. He forced himself to keep from deepening it. Then gave up and did so anyway, finding her tongue with his and tasting every corner of her mouth.

He dropped one hand to wrap it around the front of her throat and when she groaned, he felt the vibration against his palm.

She pressed a hand against his chest and pushed just enough to break the kiss. "I've missed kissing you," she whispered.

"Then why'd you stop me?"

"Because it's hard for you to say anything when your lips are busy."

"What do you want me to say?"

"Anything that you mean."

"Like how much I love you?'

She grinned. "That's a start."

He waited.

And waited as she just stared back up at him.

He shifted his feet. "Darlin'," he began.

"Yeah?" She pinned her lips together and her eyes crinkled at the corners.

"You forgettin' somethin'?"

She pursed her lips and rolled her eyes to the ceiling as if she was in deep thought. "Nothing I can think of."

"You sure?"

She placed a finger to her lips and again thought hard. "I'm *preeeeetty* sure," she smiled big, "that I love you, too."

Thank fuck.

Her smile dropped and her eyes got serious. "I've had no one since you. And I want no one else but you, Dwight. You're in my dreams every night, you're in my thoughts every day. And that short time we spent in Kentucky has given me some good memories to replace some of the bad ones."

"Good memories," he arched a brow, "of eating whistle pig sandwiches."

"Yes, that and more. Like... oh, I don't know... a few spankings I admit I deserved, but still enjoyed."

"Liked that, huh?" he teased.

"Is there any doubt?"

"There might be. Guess I'll have to take you over my knee and make sure."

Her nipples pebbled hard enough that he could see them through the silky blue blouse she wore. A blouse and dress pants a professional woman would wear. One who had her shit together.

He was so fucking proud of her.

But he'd take her however he could get her. Wearing a business suit. Or wearing a leather DAMC cut, holey jeans and scuffed biker boots.

And most of all, wearing nothing.

Both of them needed to be naked soon. But since the house was empty of any furniture and the kitchen counters hadn't been selected yet, the only option they had was the floor or a wall.

And after they just declared what they did, he preferred to take his time and appreciate everything about her in a bed, where he could do everything he wanted to do to her.

And maybe she would even reciprocate.

He grinned, then adjusted his dick which was giving its approval with that plan.

Kelsea's thoughts must have run along the same lines, since she asked, "I assume you didn't break into this house simply to lure me here and it's yours?"

He took a deep breath, then said, "No, darlin', it's yours."

Her smile slipped and she blinked. At first, he thought she just blinked in surprise. Until she blinked quickly again. For fuck's sake, if she started crying, he was done for. He watched her face as she struggled to keep her shit together. She bit her bottom lip, then her throat undulated as she swallowed hard.

She even did a little sniffle.

His nostrils flared and he pinned his lips together.

She needed to say something.

Anything.

She loved it. She hated it. She was surprised. She was disappointed.

Something, damn it.

"Does my house have a bed?"

His lips twitched. Well, that response seemed about right for her. "Not yet."

"I know a place that not only has a bed, but a mirror above it. The only problem is, you'd have to walk up a set of stairs in the middle of the day, in the middle of a busy parking lot."

That didn't sound like a problem to him. "Darlin', I'm gonna jog up those steps, carrying my woman, and then I'm gonna fuck her so long and so hard that everyone in that parkin' lot and in that pawn shop hears her."

"I'm not sure Ace will appreciate that."

"Will you?"

"Fuck yes," she whispered, her hand fisted in his shirt, holding onto him tightly.

He hoped she'd never let go. And he hoped to always be there for her to hold on to.

"Well then, darlin', that's what I'm gonna do because you're the only one that matters to me."

"For now?"

"For forever."

Turn the page to read the 1st chapter in book 3 of the In the Shadows Security series:
Guts & Glory: Hunter

Guts & Glory: Hunter

**Turn the page for a sneak peek of
Guts & Glory: Hunter
(In the Shadows Security, Book 3)**

Sneak peak of Guts & Glory: Hunter (Unedited)

Chapter One

HUNTER STARED at the older man on the other side of the thick, shatter-proof glass.

Orange wasn't his color.

He had deep lines on his face, especially around his greyish-blue eyes, and the bottom half was covered in a long salt-and-pepper beard that matched his shaggy hair.

Rocky.

Jewel, Diamond and Jag's father.

Diesel's and Slade's "father-in-law."

Doing life without parole in SCI Greene for a couple counts of murder. One of those "victims" being Slade's father, Buzz.

And Buzz was the reason Hunter was here sitting on the other side of that fucking glass.

Because Slade asked Diesel to track down a possible sibling.

One no one knew about, but Rocky might have info on.

Maybe.

But probably not.

The man giving him the eyeball might not know shit. All this could've been a play to get to see his grandchildren. Because that was what the "payment" was to get Rocky to talk. He wanted Diamond and Slade to bring their son, Hudson, and Diesel and a currently pregnant Jewel to bring their girls, Violet and Indigo, to a max security prison to meet their granddaddy.

They all agreed to it reluctantly since a state correctional institution wasn't any place young children should be.

Now, Rocky sat back in his bolted down metal chair, his heavily tattooed arms crossed over his chest, looking like the cat who ate the goddamn canary.

And still, Hunter had shit to go on.

Good thing there was a thick glass partition and a cinder block wall separating them. Because, at this very moment, Hunter felt like gutting Rocky from dick to throat just like the man did to Buzz.

Not that Buzz hadn't deserved it. He most certainly fucking did. No doubt about it.

But Hunter was weary of this wild goose chase that began because of a few words Rocky had uttered to Crow many months ago. And then Crow had mentioned it to his Dirty Angels MC brother, Slade.

Who let that info fester.

Now the DAMC member wanted to see if what Buzz had uttered in his last few moments of life was true. That Slade had another brother out there somewhere, another product from Buzz's sperm.

And if he existed, Slade wanted to find him.

Why? Hunter couldn't care less. He was getting paid to find this long-lost brother, so that's what he would do.

If it didn't kill him first.

He was good at what he did, which was find people. But this case, this job, was enough for him to throw in the towel and go get a fucking job cleaning toilets.

And he hated cleaning toilets.

That's why he hired a cleaning lady to come in once a month to do just that.

But here he sat—*again*—trying to get Rocky to shake some memory loose that might help him with this "case."

Because what he had to go on was basically bullshit.

No fucking name.

No fucking birthdate.

Fucking nothing.

All Rocky said was that Buzz mentioned a son during his last moments of breathing and he didn't think that son was Slade. Why Rocky thought that, Hunter didn't fucking know.

But one thing Hunter wasn't, was a quitter.

He was going to do his fucking best to find this possible second offspring that Buzz put on the earth.

The only thing Hunter had was Buzz's real name and the fact that Buzz knew that he had a son. Buzz didn't know Slade existed. At least, Slade didn't think so.

Hunter scrubbed a hand over his hair, surprised he had any left to do so. Which really pissed him off, because he wanted to keep it. Especially since there was nothing better than a woman pulling on his hair when he was eating her pussy and making her come.

Something Rocky hadn't gotten to do in decades.

Poor bastard.

That was one good reason Hunter needed to stay on this side of the glass instead of being on Rocky's side. The other was, he hated tight spaces. And prison was full of them.

"Let me just say, I'm fucking glad I'm on this side instead of that one."

"An' let me just say, with the shit you probably done in your life, you should be sittin' on this fuckin' side. You probably done more than I ever fuckin' did. Just got fuckin' lucky, boy."

True fucking that.

But that's where he and Rocky were different. While, yes, he would have fucking trussed Buzz up like a freshly killed deer and gutted him, Hunter would've gotten rid of all the evidence and not gotten caught.

Rocky and Doc were out of their fucking minds when they wreaked havoc on the rival MC, the Shadow Warriors, so they weren't careful when they did it. They only sought retribution for the death of some of their own members of the Dirty Angels MC, including one of their founders and Rocky's pop, Bear.

"You talk to Doc?" Hunter asked him.

"Yep."

"And?"

"Doc's got old timer's. Doesn't remember shit."

Hunter knew that. Diesel had visited his grandfather hoping to get some details about Buzz from him. Unfortunately, D had no luck and said Doc had no memory of even what he ate for breakfast. Even so, Hunter was hoping that the old man would have an occasional sliver of clarity. Apparently not.

"Got nothing to go on," Hunter grumbled.

"An' why the fuck should I care?" Rocky asked, frowning. "Why the fuck do you want to dig up a spawn of a fuckin' animal who not only raped Crow's momma but slit her throat an' her ol' man's, too?"

"'Cause Slade wants to find this spawn."

"Bad enough that my baby's fuckin' the other one an' havin' his babies."

Hunter fought the roll of his eyes. "Your *baby* is happy."

"Yeah?"

"Yeah. And you ever think if you'd been smarter about what you did, you never would've been in here and you could've protected your *baby* from what that motherfucker Pierce did to her?"

Hunter's jaw flexed. *Fuck.* He hadn't meant for that last part to slip out. But his patience with this whole thing was down to nil. He needed to get his temper in check.

"What the fuck you talkin' 'bout?"

Damn. Rocky didn't know. That made his mistake even worse.

Now the man was leaning forward in his chair, both palms pressed to the glass, his jaw hard, and his gray-blue eyes intense. "What'd Pierce do to Diamond?"

Hunter pressed his lips flat. It wasn't his story to tell. And, fuck him, his slip of the tongue was pulling them off track.

"You would know if your ass wasn't in the joint."

Rocky slammed his hands against the glass and growled, "So, you're gonna tell me, asshole."

"I'll think about it if you answer some of my questions you've been avoiding."

"Shit I've been avoidin' 'cause there are fucking ears in here." His eyes flipped to the speaker and back.

"Yeah, so? It's not like you're ever gonna see the light of fucking day again, Rocky. That ship has sailed. You won't even get the chance with good behavior because since you've been in here, you've been in the hole more often than not."

Rocky sat back and shrugged. "I can meditate in the hole."

Hunter snorted. "Yeah, I bet."

Rocky studied him for a long moment. "You gonna tell me if I answer your fuckin' questions?"

"You were supposed to answer my questions because you got to see your fucking grandbabies."

Rocky shrugged again. "Payment terms have changed."

Fucking motherfucker.

"You don't answer my fucking questions, I will make sure you never see your fucking grandkids again. You got me? All I gotta do is tell Diesel how you're fucking over one of his club brothers by going back on your word. And don't forget, that brother you're fucking over is your *baby's* ol' man. Think Diamond's gonna be happy about that?"

Rocky scowled but Hunter could see his wheels turning.

And turning.

Finally, the older man gave a single sharp nod.

Right. Time to get to business. "Where'd you kill Buzz?"

"In a barn right outside of Shadow Valley."

"Where'd you find his ass?"

"Outside of Uniontown."

"That where he was living?"

"Yeah. Some dumpy trailer park."

"You know who he was living with?"

"Nope."

"He mentioned a son, you sure he didn't say a name?"

"That shit was like thirty years ago. You expect me to remember somethin' like that?"

"Yes."

Rocky tilted his head and scratched at his beard. "Well, I fuckin' don't."

"You kill him because he butchered Coyote and his ol' lady?"

"Yeah."

"He didn't kill Bear, though, right?"

"No. When those fuckin' Warriors killed Bear that's when the war started."

"So, you went back and forth killing each other like the wild fucking west."

"Sounds 'bout right."

Hunter blew out a breath. "As you know, Diesel tasked me with finding this possible son. You ain't making it easy, Rocky."

Even with Rocky's thick moustache covering his upper lip, Hunter could see the fucker smirk. "Life ain't easy, boy."

"Betcha doing life ain't easy, either. Hope it was worth it."

"Would do it again."

"I'm sure your fucking wife and kids appreciate that."

"Was doin' it for them."

Sure he was.

"You tell Diesel I cooperated an' to bring his girls back for a visit. And also Jag's little girl, too. Alexis didn't come last time."

That's because Rocky hadn't mentioned Jag or his baby girl, so Jag wasn't volunteering to bring Lexi to this hole.

"When's the last time you saw Jag?"

Something flashed across Rocky's face before he hid it. "When he was still livin' with Ruby."

So the man hadn't seen his only son since Jag was probably a teen. And once Rocky's kids got out on their own they probably never visited. Or rarely.

But then, Hunter had never visited his father, either. And his mother never forced him to. She wanted nothing to do with Danny Delgado, Sr. once he plowed the tractor trailer he was driving full speed into a crowd of people while drunk. And in doing so, killed six children and two teachers on an elementary school field trip. Not to mention, the many others who were injured.

After a couple years his father fucking hung himself in his cell because he was too much of a pussy to do his time like a man.

Hunter ground his teeth.

So, yeah, he wasn't going to judge Jag, or even Diamond and Jewel, for not wanting to visit their old man in prison.

A loud buzz filled the small room Rocky was in and the metal door swung open.

"Let's go, Jamison. Time's up," a guard yelled into the room.

Rocky stood and leaned to the speaker, saying, "You tell Diesel. Yeah?"

Hunter pushed to his feet, too. "Yeah. I'll tell him."

"An' I wanna know the truth about Diamond."

"I'll tell him that, too."

With a last nod, Rocky turned and headed toward the door and the waiting guard. Hunter waited until the heavy door slammed shut behind them before spinning on his heels and heading toward freedom.

Today was a good reminder that he always needed to be careful and cover his tracks. He did not want to end up like Rocky or his father.

It was time to head to Uniontown to do a little hunting.

**Get Hunter and Frankie's story here:
mybook.to/Shadows-Hunter**

If You Enjoyed This Book

Thank you for reading Guts & Glory: Ryder. If you enjoyed Ryder and Kelsea's story, please consider leaving a review at your favorite retailer and/or Goodreads to let other readers know. Reviews are always appreciated and just a few words can help an independent author like me tremendously!

Want to read a sample of my work? Download a sampler book here: BookHip.com/MTQQKK

Also by Jeanne St. James

* Available in Audiobook

Made Maleen: A Modern Twist on a Fairy Tale

Damaged *

Rip Cord: The Complete Trilogy *

Brothers in Blue Series:

(Can be read as standalones)

Brothers in Blue: Max *

Brothers in Blue: Marc *

Brothers in Blue: Matt *

Teddy: A Brothers in Blue Novelette *

The Dare Ménage Series:

(Can be read as standalones)

Double Dare *

Daring Proposal *

Dare to Be Three *

A Daring Desire *

Dare to Surrender *

A Daring Journey

The Obsessed Novellas:

(All the novellas in this series are standalones)

Forever Him *

Only Him

Needing Him

Loving Her

Temping Him

Down & Dirty: Dirty Angels MC™ Series:

(Can be read as standalones)

Down & Dirty: Zak *

Down & Dirty: Jag *

Down & Dirty: Hawk *

Down & Dirty: Diesel *

Down & Dirty: Axel *

Down & Dirty: Slade *

Down & Dirty: Dawg *

Down & Dirty: Dex *

Down & Dirty: Linc

Down & Dirty: Crow

Guts & Glory Series

(In the Shadows Security)

Guts & Glory: Mercy

Guts & Glory: Ryder

Guts & Glory: Hunter

Guts & Glory: Walker

Guts & Glory: Steel

Guts & Glory: Brick

About the Author

JEANNE ST. JAMES is a USA Today bestselling romance author who loves an alpha male (or two). She was only thirteen when she started writing and her first paid published piece was an erotic story in Playgirl magazine. Her first erotic romance novel, Banged Up, was published in 2009. She is happily owned by farting French bulldogs. She writes M/F, M/M, and M/M/F ménages.

Want to read a sample of her work? Download a sampler book here: BookHip.com/MTQQKK

To keep up with her busy release schedule check her website at www.jeannestjames.com or sign up for her newsletter: http://www.jeannestjames.com/newslettersignup

www.jeannestjames.com
jeanne@jeannestjames.com

Blog: http://jeannestjames.blogspot.com
Newsletter: http://www.jeannestjames.com/newslettersignup
Jeanne's Down & Dirty Book Crew: https://www.facebook.com/groups/JeannesReviewCrew/

- facebook.com/JeanneStJamesAuthor
- twitter.com/JeanneStJames
- amazon.com/author/jeannestjames
- instagram.com/JeanneStJames
- bookbub.com/authors/jeanne-st-james
- goodreads.com/JeanneStJames
- pinterest.com/JeanneStJames

Get a FREE Erotic Romance Sampler Book

This book contains the first chapter of a variety of my books. This will give you a taste of the type of books I write and if you enjoy the first chapter, I hope you'll be interested in reading the rest of the book.

Each book I list in the sampler will include the description of the book, the genre, and the first chapter, along with links to find out more. I hope you find a book you will enjoy curling up with!

>Get it here: BookHip.com/MTQQKK

Printed in Great Britain
by Amazon